A DEMON'S DESIRE
THE DEMONS OF YIDDERA BOOK TWO
LOUELLA RANES

PUBLISHED BY LOUELLA RANES

CONTENTS

DEDICATION

THIS BOOK IS DEDICATED once again to my mom, Carol, for always being there and encouraging me to be my best self.

This one is also dedicated to my husband, Joe.

I would unlock the gates of hell to be with you.

YEAR 825

"HAVE YOU EVER FELT as if everyone around you was moving forward but you?" Tayin asked in barely a whisper.

Neviah looked at him with sadness. "No." She said simply.

"I watched Kest falling for Diem more with every day they spent together. I watched all my friends as they eventually fell in love, and I felt left behind. My heart, my very soul, was filled with such a heavy darkness that I couldn't move forward with them. My mind was stuck in the day that Tam died." Tayin picked up a rock and tossed it across the barren wasteland.

"But you did move forward."

"Yes, and this is where I landed."

"This," Neviah waved her hand at the landscape in front of them. "was lifetimes in the making, created by

many people and much misunderstanding. You landed here because you are the only one that can fix it."

Tayin shrugged his shoulders. "How?"

"Continue your story, and let's figure that out together." She, too, picked up a rock and threw it out in front of her, smiling when it landed several feet shy of where his did. "What happened next?"

"What happened next was the beginning of what brought about our release. It led to the start of my revenge, the start of the Yidderian's hell, the pain of the Allurmonuhra." Tayin said in response to her question.

"And it was the start of your eventual healing," Neviah said.

"No, her birth was."

"Show me the next part of our history." Neviah watched as the landscape faded, and this time, she found herself somewhere she knew well, the grand ballroom of the monastery.

YEAR 375

Ava was at her wedding reception, having just married Finnick, and was already waiting for the celebration to be over with. She sat on a chair next to her husband and looked about the room, noticing that many of the people here tonight were unknown to her. Ava, the new Prophetess, had married a son of one of the most prevalent families on Kahlali. Their families had decided it would be a good match and introduced the pair a year ago, and soon after, the two became engaged.

Ava was the first to admit that while Finnick was handsome enough, he was dull. Nevertheless, she agreed to the engagement because her parents insisted that she did. Ava knew that although she found him boring, he would help her in her role as the Prophetess. She agreed because she was already 25 and had not yet met anyone else she was even remotely interested in. Ava knew that Finnick was good at making conversation with strangers, and he was great at social gatherings. Still, when it came to intelligent conversation, he had none. However, Ava also knew that he was a good choice for her mate as he was well-connected politically, and as the Prophetess, she must have someone by her side who could help her in that arena.

She smiled at the audience and made small talk with a few well-wishers that came her way. Her face hurt from smiling for so long, and all she could think about was getting home so she could take off her shoes and relax from the ordeal of her wedding. It struck her that maybe she shouldn't think of her wedding celebration as an ordeal, but it was. This nuptial gathering was more for the people than it was for her. Ava would have had a quick private ceremony instead, but her station insisted she put on a show for her followers.

A disturbance from the back of the room caught her eye, and she watched as a tall blond man picked up the chair he had just tripped over. Ava smiled at his awkwardness and continued watching as he made his way toward her and Finnick. The man stopped in front of their table and waited for Finnick to end another conversation before making himself known.

Finnick stood up, walked around the table, and hugged the man once he noticed who was standing before him.

"My friend, I didn't think that you would make it. It is so good to see you. How was your trip to Malseka? Did you map all the villages that you wished to?" Finnick sat back down and waved someone over to pull up another chair.

The man took the offered seat, "I did not. I will return in two months and be there for another year before I am done. After that, who knows, I might stay here on Alenar." He turned his attention to Ava. "Are you going to introduce me to your lovely wife?"

"Ava, this is my childhood friend, Ephraim. He is an explorer and has taken it upon himself to map out all the new villages and towns worldwide. Ephraim, this is my new bride, Ava, the reigning Prophetess."

"It is wonderful to meet you, Prophetess," Ephraim told her as he took a drink from his champagne flute.

"Please call me Ava." She replied back. "I would like to hear more of the work that you are doing if you have time to visit before you leave."

Ephraim smiled at the lovely, dark-eyed beauty and said, "Anytime. I love talking about my work, and though you will probably grow bored, I would love to tell you about it."

Finnick laughed and poured himself more of the fine Champagne from Kruger, "It will have to wait till after our honeymoon, old friend. We will be leaving tomorrow and be back in three weeks. Once we get back home, you and I will reminisce about the old days, and then you can regale my lady with your adventures."

Ephraim stood up, took Ava's hand, and brought it to his lips. "Until then, my lady." He nodded to Finnick and left to make his rounds among the other visiting guests.

Ava watched the man leave, still feeling the slight tingle in her hand that started when his lips touched it. There was something about him that made her wish she had not agreed to this arranged marriage, but then, if she hadn't, the chances were that she would never have met Ephraim. She turned her eyes away from his retreating back and once again paid attention to her husband and the conversation around them.

YEAR 376

"WHY IS THAT LITTLE village your favorite? What makes it special compared to all the others that you have seen?" Ava asked as she and Ephraim sat on a blanket underneath a giant weeping willow tree out by the fish pond. It gave them a semblance of privacy that was hard to find outside the main building. Sitting here, they could see the novitiates walking around, talking with the crafters and healers that lived among them. Occasionally, a 'Daughter of Allura' would walk by, though not often, as there were not very many of them. So far, 23 'daughters' had been brought to live at the Monastery. All of which had been born in the last six years. It was written into law that any child born with the blue marking must be brought to the Monastery before they were two years of age. This was to protect them and the people who lived in Yiddera. It had been prophesied by the original Prophetess that one of these children would free the demons from the Myst. So, the girls were brought here to be watched and to ensure this did not happen.

It was odd that no boys had been born with the marking. The prophecy had stated that it would be a girl who released the demons, but it did seem odd that only the girls showed the markings of the demons. Many miscarriages and stillbirths occurred when the world turned Alluran blue, and only girls seemed to survive birth while the Alluran moon was in the sky. Ava had often wondered why but, as of yet, still had no answer.

Ava brought her attention back to Ephraim as he told her about the little village in Malseka he enjoyed the most. He stated that it was the animal life there that attracted him.

"The animals are quite varied and unusual. There are the most beautiful birds, and their songs are melodic and peaceful. There is one that is so big it has over a sixteen-foot wingspan, and when its wings are fully spread, they are a bright yellow color, but held close to the body, they are a blue so dark as to look black." He stretched out on his side before continuing.

"The people are the same as anywhere but have a unique view on life. They believe that the demon that lives in the Myst that borders their town can communicate with the animals. So, while they believe in the Goddess, as we do, they also believe that the demon is an animal god. So, they set out fresh meats and vegetables once a month by the gates in honor of him."

Ava sat up straight, "This belief must be stopped. It is dangerous. The demons are not gods and will harm us if they are released. Do they honor the law and send their blue children to us, at least?"

"They do. The three blue girls born in Akteon are considered blessed by the gods, and they held a big ceremony for each girl before sending them to live here with you. They respect you highly and know the babes come to you for protection from those who might wish to hurt the little girls. Ava, you would like the people there. Someday, I will take you with me, and you can see for yourself how interesting they are."

"I would like that, but I do not know when Finnick and I can take that much time away from the Monastery," Ava replied.

"I didn't invite Finnick. I invited you." Ephraim told her and then took her hand in his. "Finnick can take care of things here, and you can travel with me. But, Ava, please tell me that you feel as I do?"

Ava hesitated and then made the decision to answer him honestly. "Ephraim, I do feel the same for you as you do for me, but I committed myself to Finnick and will keep that commitment.

However, I would love to travel to the places you talk about, and surely, as the Prophetess, I should meet my followers worldwide. I will plan a tour, and you can show me the wonders you have seen." She touched his cheek longingly.

"I will talk with Finnick about you coming with me to tour the world, and I will take that time to convince you that you married the wrong man." He leaned in closer to her and gave her a quick kiss, then got up and left the tree's privacy.

Ava sat on the ground under the tree and contemplated all that they had talked about. For over one month, they had met under this very tree and talked about his travels and her plans for the future. He had listened to her trials as the Prophetess and her triumphs. In the past month, they had talked more than she and Finnick ever had. Ephraim's conversation was intelligent, fun, and heartfelt. He was right. She had married the wrong man, but she had married Finnick and would honor their vows.

She got up from the grass, folded the blanket, and walked out from under the tree. She squinted her eyes in the bright sunlight and headed back to reality.

YEAR 378

"FINNICK, I WOULD LIKE to do some traveling. Now that No-valie is a year old, I think it would be okay for her to travel with me. I want to see the world and meet the people who look to me as their spiritual leader." Ava sat at her dressing table and brushed her hair.

Finnick finished buttoning his shirt and, leaning down, kissed Ava's head. "I think that would be a fine idea. I will go with you and meet with their political leaders and see what we can do to help their communities. You have a meeting with the world leaders next year, and It would be wise to get first-hand knowledge of the people you represent."

Looking at him through the mirror's reflection, she said, "I thought that maybe you should stay here and tend to things while I am away. I do not want to leave the Monastery in the hands of someone I do not trust to do my will. I know you will do what I would want, and I can trust you to make the decisions I would."

"Hmm, I do not want you to travel alone, but I understand your point and agree." He straightened his tie, "Let me see if I can contact Ephraim. He will ensure you stayed safe, and he is very knowledgeable about the world. He will make you a good travel companion. As for Novalie, I would like her to stay here with me. You can take her on another trip when she is four or five. I would like some time with my daughter before you start training her to be the next Prophetess."

Ava smiled. "I still do not know if the gift was passed to her. It skipped my mother, and it might skip her. But I do think she would enjoy the time alone with you, and it would be much easier to travel without a toddler to watch over. And if you think that I need a companion, Ephraim is a good choice. He is a dear friend to both of us, and you are right, he has the knowledge I need to stay safe and educated on the people I plan to meet."

"It is settled. I will send Ephraim a letter today to his last known location. We will see if he can help plan an itinerary and go with you on this trip. Now I have to get to a meeting." Finnick kissed her again, kissed little Novalie, playing quietly on the floor by the door, and then left the room.

Ava smiled to herself. She would finally get to see the world and have the travel companion she wanted with her. Ava frowned at that thought. Though she had hoped Finnick would suggest Ephraim go with her, she worried about being alone with him for several months. She knew she would be unable to keep the promise made in her wedding vows to be faithful. Ava sighed, knowing this was why she wanted to take the trip in the first place.

Ava took Ephraim's arm and stepped off the ship and onto the firm grounds of Kruger. Anchorage was a bustling city, the oldest Yidderian city. Ava watched as the many people scurried around, going about their busy day. She noticed the luggage was being taken off the ship and put in a pile on the dock. Ava saw a strangely dressed couple picking up her bags and placing them in the back of a carriage where a woman wearing a flamboyant hat sat.

Ephraim guided Ava to the carriage and introduced the woman as Nicollete. Nicollete bowed her head in deference to the Prophetess and invited her to join her in the vehicle. Ava was helped up into the seat by Ephraim, and they took off to their destination after settling in.

"Ephraim tells me that you are interested in getting to know the many different cultures and people on Yiddera," Nicollete said to break the silence.

"Yes, and he tells me that you are one of the leaders of the sect of the Calling that teaches silence to honor the Goddess. May I ask why the silence?"

"That is a good question. We practice silence to hear the Goddess speak with us and bring ourselves closer to the 'heartbeat,' if you will, of the planet. Too many talk and never listen. By remaining silent, we can listen to Y'ddra through nature and the many voices of those around us."

Ava nodded her head in understanding. "And the outfits that your followers wear? What is their purpose? And if you teach silence, why do you not follow it?" She waved a hand, indicating the dark robes and veils of the two followers that sat next to the luggage.

Nicollete laughed a light, happy laugh. "My, you are curious. The outfits are so that one does not judge another by their appearance. Accepting people for who they are and not what they look like is essential. This way, we can accept everyone for their actions, not their words. As for myself, a few of us have not taken the vow of silence, as talking is vital in spreading our word to others and getting the things we need from the townsfolk."

"I look forward to meeting your people and learning more about the town where you live," Ava said after thanking Nicollete for answering her questions.

The group of people pulled up in front of a beautiful sprawling house at the very edge of town. Ava could see the Myst quite distinctly from the front porch and was surprised to feel somewhat comforted by its presence. Not that she felt anything but on edge around it, but it made her a little less homesick to see a sight she was used to seeing daily.

They went into the house, and after being shown their rooms and freshening up, they met back downstairs for a light repast. Nicollete was a charming hostess and spoke of how they mimicked the Prophetess in making sure that the grounds they lived on were as self-sufficient as possible. Nicollete and Ava talked about the Calling and other religious matters well after the delicious fare was finished, when Ephraim let out a big yawn.

"Ladies, as much as I would love to continue this conversation, it has been a long day, and I need some sleep so that I can be refreshed for the adventures that tomorrow will bring." He scooted out of his chair and, standing up, offered his hand to Ava. "May I walk you to your room, Prophetess?"

Ava put down her napkin, excused herself, and accepted Ephraim's hand. "Thank you for a wonderful meal, and I look forward to talking with you again tomorrow, Nicollete."

Ava walked down the hall and up the stairs with Ephraim. They stopped at the door of her room, and opening it, Ava stepped inside. She walked a few steps into the room before turning back to Ephraim.

"Would you like to come in for a while?" She asked.

"Only if you are comfortable with it. I do not want you to do anything you might regret in the morning." He said while leaning against the door jamb.

"I would regret it tomorrow if you didn't join me this evening." Ava watched as Ephraim smiled and stepped into the room, shutting the door behind him.

Within the first two weeks that Ava was in Kruger, she learned that many of her followers did not honestly believe that demons were living in the Myst. They went to the meetings and listened to the sermons, but overall, it seemed that the general idea was that the demons in the Myst were a metaphor for the old Earth belief of the devil and hell. If you were not good and did something wrong, the demons would gather you up and take you into the Myst, hell, where you would suffer for eternity.

While this belief wasn't precisely wrong, Ava worried that it would cause the people to be less cautious and that if the opportunity presented itself, someone with much curiosity might want to open the gates to see if the demons were real. She knew that once she was back home, she would have to devise a way to impress upon the people that the gates must never be opened. Ava wondered if she could use the daughters of the Alluran moon to enforce her message. While she did not want them hurt, she could say that their coloring was caused by the demons choosing them to do their bidding. The girls had a faint aura about them that caused others to be uneasy, and this could work to her advantage.

Ava knew that she would have to come up with something as these people were not cautious enough around the Myst and did not hold faith in what the Calling taught as well as she would like them to. So, maybe she would begin by telling her followers that the children born during the blue moon phase were proof that there were demons in the Myst. And it was their lack of faith that had allowed the demons to steal these girls' souls, and if trust in the Calling was not restored, then someday, all children would be marked this way. While using the blue girls for this purpose went against her nature, Ava decided that maybe this would cause people to rethink their beliefs. She would start calling the daughters of Allura, Dimoni, so that people wouldn't forget the girls were cursed by the demons.

Within these first two weeks, Ava started to think about her role as the prophetess differently than she had before. It used to be something that she knew she was. Still, Ava had never realized how much power she had in influencing people worldwide. As she walked around the village and met the Yidderians living there, Ava learned they took her words far more seriously than she had imagined anyone would.

This new realization brought with it a new confidence, and though she did not want to admit it, it also brought out the darkness in her that she hadn't known she had. Ava would do anything she needed to make sure everyone believed in the Calling and her words. She was no longer just the young woman who could see visions of the future; she was the one person on Yiddera who could shape the future to her liking.

Ephraim and Ava explored Kruger together for three more weeks before boarding a ship to Kahlali. They stayed in several villages around Kahlali for almost three months. One village, again next to the Myst, was almost opulent in its architecture and layout. In the middle of the town square was a marble fountain with a basin that was used as a wishing well. The fountain was a miniature replica of the Rainbow Falls. The water poured from the top and fell over small basins that contained rocks of different colors. Surrounding it were plants and flowers of rainbow colors as well. It was impressive and elegant and made Ava dream of home.

The people of Yiddera would not follow her lead if she did not live what she taught. Ava made sure that everything she did publicly was above scrutiny, and no one could doubt her faith in the Calling. She wanted everyone to see her as the first Prophetess, since the original, to enforce the idea that the demons were real and dangerous. She wanted renewed fear in every person planet-wide so that no one would ever want to release those who lived in the Myst.

As Ava traveled with Ephraim, she enjoyed her nights with the man she loved, but she made sure that no hint of their relationship was shown during the day. The couple behaved with decorum in front of others and in private loved as only two people, who knew their time together was short, could. The ship they took from Kahlali back to Kruger was overbooked, so they shared a room, making sure that a cot was brought in to maintain their façade of respectability.

As the Prophetess, Ava was shown respect, and if anyone suspected that she and Ephraim were more than just friends, no one said anything. Ephraim lamented when they arrived once again on Kruger that the trip had not taken long enough. Ava had laughed at him but silently agreed. The next time they boarded a ship, it would be to return to Alenar, and they would have to go back to being just friends. Their affair would have to end.

They did not visit the village of Akteon during this trip, but she made plans to go there soon. Ava would ensure their belief that the demons were gods was put to rest. The only deity was Y'ddra, and as her voice, Ava planned to see that no one worshiped another.

A baby girl was given to Ava the day before they would be heading home. She was a beautiful little one but had blue locks mixed in with her black hair. Her startling blue eyes were the same color as her hair. This Alluran daughter was only two months old when she was given to the Prophetess. The parents had named her Sameen and asked that the name be kept. Ava stated that all the Dimoni kept their given names, and wrapping the infant up took her back to where she was staying. Ephraim and Ava gathered everything they would need to travel with an infant and, the next day, boarded the ship that would take them to Alenar.

It was a few months since Allura graced the sky when he found another of the Yidderian blue girls. Adym had not gone out while the world was blue. Instead, he had waited. It was easier to find the infants a few months after their birth since they had become the talk of their village by that time. He walked silently behind the parents and watched as they handed the child over to the woman he knew was the current Prophetess.

As the Prophetess took the child, she gave a small, almost imperceptible shudder, which piqued Adym's curiosity. Did she shudder because of coincidence or because the blue girl caused her a small jolt of fear? He continued watching the Prophetess until she entered her hotel, where he lost sight of her. Once back in his own body, he called out for Nicollete.

"I do not know the answer to the question that you seek." She answered his unspoken query.

"Will you find out for me, please?" He requested.

"I have business to finish up here, and as soon as I can, I will go to Alenar and find the answer that you seek."

"Thank you, my friend." Adym looked out of his window and watched the sunrise peak out from behind the high mountain range. "How are you doing, Nicollete, really? Are you happy out there?"

"I am doing fine. I miss my home and my brother, but yes, I am happy here. The Yidderians are interesting people and very similar to us in many ways. I find their differences intriguing.

Adym, do not worry about me. I am doing well, and I know that soon you will find who you are searching for."

Adym sighed deeply. "I hope for all our sakes that this search ends soon. Nicollete, I am tired."

"I can feel your exhaustion. Adym, why do you not let the Tarikans and I take over? We may search more slowly, but we can search for longer periods of time. Let us help you." Nicollete stepped up into her conveyance and headed back to her current house. She signaled the Tarikan to drive before she picked up her conversation with Adym again. "You cannot keep going like this. You need to stay healthy and strong for the day that you are required to fulfill your destiny and receive the key."

"I will continue my search, but all the help that you can give me will be greatly appreciated. I need to replenish my strength. Be safe, li uhra. I await your answer." Adym left Nicollete and went in search of the nearest Yidderian village.

It was around seven months later that Adym heard back from Nicollete. She ran her hand against the Myst gates close to the cabin he had given her, and try as he might, he could not get her to answer his question until he arrived at the gates across from where she stood. He placed a hand on the Myst and felt the energy pass through them once she placed her hand on his.

"It is good to see you again, Adym. It has been so long since I have seen any of you that I decided to deliver my news in person and not telepathically." She smiled at him and gazed at his face for a few moments. "Adym, all the girls release the istotymir. They all give off a faint aura of fear, not enough to cause harm or even enough to always notice. But they make those around them uncomfortable. Their caregivers get used to it after a while, but if they are not around the girls for long, they notice the feeling once again. It seems that prolonged contact with the blue girls lessens the feeling of, well, not quite fear, but unease that the children put off."

Adym sat on the ground in front of the Myst. "That is interesting. Unless a child becomes SeiOrhii, even Alluran young do not give off the istotymir. I wonder what this could mean. What do you think, Nicollete?"

Nicollete sat down and leaned against the gates, her shoulder touching where his did. "I wonder if this means that they are more like you than we thought they would be. Do you think that maybe, if introduced to the colored pools, they might be SeiOrhii?"

"An interesting theory, but I do not think so. How can a Yidderian become SeiOrhii? Diem touched the blue waters, and she felt nothing, and as far as I can tell, no one is afraid of her."

"But are you sure? She has lived among the Yidderians, who are exposed to the istotymir daily, all her life. What little she may be emitting may not be enough for the Yidderians in the Myst to feel. Those that are around her often may not notice, or they might be immune to her, but those who are not may not notice because it is something they are used to in much larger doses."

"Hmm, I never thought of that. Regardless of the fear that these girls produce, I still do not believe that they are SeiOrhii. We are not born often, and we are born already Alluran. Again, I repeat that I do not think it possible for a Yidderian born to become an immortal." Adym stood up. "Nicollete, you have given me much to think about."

"Adym, give Raighn hugs for me, please." She laughed at his frown. "Okay, maybe not a hug, but at least a shoulder squeeze. Really, the rivalry the two of you have is funny. If you would both admit how similar to each other you are, I think you would get along much better."

"We are nothing alike, Nicollete, but I will send him your regards." Adym walked away, leaving her laughing on the other side of the gates from him.

Ava walked off the ship and was met by a group of her followers, all of whom had looks of worry on their faces. They rushed over to her and quickly led her to a waiting wagon, not giving her time to gather her luggage or take the child she had brought back with her from Ephraim. As Ava sat on the cushioned seat, she looked back at Ephraim, still holding the infant, and waved at him to follow her. Then, she ordered one of her acolytes to get another transport for her companion.

Ava started listening to the excited group. All she could make out from their jumble was 'accident,' 'we hope he will recover,' and 'Finnick.' She held up her hand to silence the devotees and then, pointing at one of them, asked what she was trying to say.

"There was an accident, Prophetess. Finnick was with a group who decided to do some mountain climbing, and while climbing, he was attacked by a mountain lion. He was badly injured and has been barely hanging on to life for the past week. We have our best healers working on him, but they are not sure if Finnick will live." The girl spoke in a worried rush. "We have been coming to the docks daily to see if you had arrived back home yet. I am so glad you are back now. I know that you will want to see him before he dies."

"My husband is not going to die. He will recover and be as healthy as he was before the accident. Have some faith in Y'ddra, dear girl." Ava bit her lip in worry. Was her lack of faithfulness what caused this accident? Was Y'ddra punishing her? No, she mustn't think this way. Finnick's accident was in no way her fault. She willed the cart to go faster and sighed in relief when they reached the monastery grounds. Ava was helped out of the conveyance and taken to the healers. One of them then took her to see Finnick. He was lying on the bed with a lightweight sheet spread across him, looking as if he would take his last breath at any moment.

Finnick was usually so full of life that he drew the attention of everyone around him. It was hard to see him so pale and lifeless. Ava sat in the chair beside his bed and gently took his big hand in hers. She just sat and held his hand for what seemed like hours until she felt another one placed on her shoulder. Ava looked up and saw Ephraim standing above her. She smiled up at him and waved him over to the chair across the bed from her.

Ephraim sat down and watched his beloved softly cry over her husband. "Ava, he is going to be alright. He is too stubborn to die, and you know it."

"I know." She whispered.

One of the healers came by and checked Finnick's vital signs and his wound. Ava saw the ugly gashes across his stomach and upper legs and wondered if he would ever walk again. She looked closer and saw that the injuries did not even look like they were starting to heal. Ava grabbed the sheet from the healer and looked closer at the damage done to her husband's body. She gasped, dropped the blanket, and ran out of the building. She reached her room inside the Monastery and, opening a drawer, pulled out a very old and very treasured sketchbook. She flipped through the many pages until she found the one she sought.

Written in the book, next to a drawing of a rare purple flower, was a description of a wound made by an ageetah that would not heal. The author of the book noted that this plant, when crushed and mixed with pure distilled alcohol, would eradicate the poison released by the claws of the jungle cat and the mountain lion. Ava left the book open, went into her cabinet, and found the small bottle of alcohol she kept for sterilizing things. She then ran back to the healers' greenhouse, where she found the plant that she needed. Ava was in luck as the plant was blooming, and the fresh blossoms would work better than the dried ones she was expecting to find. She placed the blooms in a small bowl and then added the liquid. Using a pestle, she ground the flowers until their essence was released and then mixed more of the ethanol into the petals, she then strained this mixture into another bottle.

Ava returned to the healer's hall and gently poured the tincture onto Finnick's wounds. She was busy trying to make sure she covered every inch of the injury and did not notice that Finnick scrunched up his closed eyes at the sting that came with the healing liquid. Once satisfied that she had not missed a single gash, she sat the mixture down and then covered Finnick back up.

"What was that?" Ephraim asked her.

"I remembered something I had once read in an ancient book about wounds similar to this and so decided to see if we had the ingredients and if it would work." Ava signaled a healer over. She took a piece of paper out of the table drawer next to her and, after asking the healer if she could use his pen, wrote down the ingredients and recipe for the healing tonic.

"Take this recipe and use it on his wounds every six hours. It will clear out the poison which is keeping the wounds from healing. We will know within a few days if it will work." Ava stood up and, taking Ephraim's arm, walked out of the room. "I will be back tomorrow, but I must rest. It has been a very long day."

The two walked out of the healer's building and into the Monastery, heading toward Ava's apartment.

"What did you do with the child?"

"I gave her to one of your novitiates. I figured the young man would know what to do with her. She will be well taken care of here, but it is a shame they cannot stay with their natural parents. I would hate to have to give up my daughter solely because she had different colored hair and eyes."

Ava looked at him reproachfully, "You know that is not the only reason they are brought here. The Dimoni are dangerous to us. One of them is destined to free the demons from their cage, and many Yidderians would wish to do them harm because of this prophecy." She entered her room and waved him ahead of her. "Would you like to stay for dinner?"

"I would love to." Ephraim shut the door behind him and took her in his arms. Kissing her passionately, he helped her undress and then led her into the shower so that they both might clean away the dust from their travels. After a leisurely loving, they redressed and then called for dinner to be brought to them.

While they were eating, Novalie was brought in by her nanny. The little girl was now almost two, and not having seen her mother in five months, she was a bit shy around her. However, Ava got on the floor and opened her arms wide, and the little one went running to her after a bit of coaxing. Novalie was given big hugs and many little kisses before Ava scooped her up and tucked her in bed for the night.

Ava returned to the living room and sat on the couch next to Ephraim.

"I wish our nights together didn't have to end, but they do." She snuggled next to him and placed her head on his shoulder. "When will you head back out?"

"I will stay for a couple of weeks to ensure that you are okay and that Finnick will heal, and then I will go. I cannot stay here knowing you, and I cannot be together. But I will not stay away long. I will have you on another voyage with me as soon as possible." He kissed the top of her head, and then, sighing deeply, he stood up from the couch and left the room.

Within a week, it was evident that Finnick would live, but there was still a long road of recovery ahead of him. So, at the end of the second week, Ephraim left for another voyage after wishing his friend a speedy recovery. Ava was both sad and relieved that Ephraim had finally gone. Sad because if she had her way, he would always be able to stay with her, relieved because being around him and unable to touch him was unendurable.

By the end of the month, Finnick was up and walking and back to his good sense of humor despite learning that it was now impossible to have another child. Ava and Finnick were saddened by this, as they had wanted another. Grieving over the lost possibility yet rejoicing that Finnick was alive, the couple picked up their lives where they had left off a few months back.

Ava worked hard on reworking the Calling to teach her followers to fear the demons even more than was taught before, and she used the blue girls to help with this. She made it a law that no girl or boy born under the influence of the Alluran moon was to be hurt by anyone while they were on Monastery grounds. She passed another law that all children born at that time would be brought to her as soon as they were born. If it was found that a child was not, the punishment would be harsh.

Finnick was astonished at her new hellfire approach to the Calling and wondered what had caused the change. Ava explained all she had seen in her travels and how the people were falling away from the belief. She wanted to remind the people of Yiddera that the prophecy made by Alena, the first Prophetess, showed signs of coming to pass. It had been prophesied that the blue girls would start appearing with increasing frequency as the time neared, and Ava wanted to make the people remember what was going to be released if this prophecy was fulfilled.

While Ava wanted all the blue girls under her control, she still felt that giving them a decent life was proper. With this in mind, she educated the girls and found them exceptionally smart and very talented at whatever they chose to do. Several of the young ones were gifted artists, dancers, and singers. A girl of just six could play the violin with haunting poignancy and skill than many older and more experienced violinists could not replicate. A couple of daughters were brilliant as healers and herbalists, while a few were more talented with animal husbandry. It was amazing to watch them grow and bloom within their chosen path.

Ava allowed the Dimoni the freedom to go into the village but insisted they take someone with them for protection. Some of the older girls would soon be allowed to date, but Ava pressed upon them that they were not permitted to have children. So each daughter, when she became a woman, was required to eat the Op leaves that prevented pregnancy every night without fail. Finally, Ava explained that she did not want them to pass on the 'Demon' gene and that pregnancy would be punishable by death. While she did not look down on the daughters of Allura, she did not want to risk passing the demon markings to innocent children and taint the Yidderian bloodlines.

The Dimoni children accepted the new rules without complaint. The Yidderians belief in the Calling grew stronger and Ava was satisfied that everything was as it should be.

YEAR 382

AVA LAY NEXT TO Ephraim on a blanket spread out on the second floor of the old chapel. The dusty window allowed them a bit of light in the growing gloom of the wintry sunset. She had not seen him in over a year, and her love and desire for him had not waned in that time. She caressed his bare stomach and laughed low in her throat at his response.

"Do you have to leave so soon?" she whispered as she ran her fingertips over his chest.

Ephraim placed a hand on top of hers to still her movements. "You know that I do. I have to pick up supplies from Kruger and take them and Finnick to Kahlali. We must be there in time for the election of the new town council members if we want Rork and Konrad to be chosen. We cannot let any others take the two open seats. Finnick and I will ensure your choices are known to all." He rolled over onto her and kissed her. "Will you miss me?"

"I always do."

The couple made love once more and then, continuing their earlier conversation, got dressed to head back to the Monastery.

"Kahlali tends to choose the leaders that we encourage them to. They have always closely held the same views as Alenar. I think it may have something to do with the nightmares that so many of them are prone to. I have always wondered if the horrible dreams are linked to the Myst they live so close to." She turned around for Ephraim to do up the buttons of her dress. "It is Kruger that I worry about at times. They are more lenient in their views. I wonder if we might more effectively influence their elections if we knew more about what their young people want for their future. Listen to the people while you are there, and let me know if you hear anything useful, will you?"

"Of course. Now hurry and kiss me goodbye." Ava tilted her head up and kissed Ephraim before dashing out into the darkness. Ephraim stood by the window and watched her until she was out of sight. He sighed and ran a hand through his hair before he finished buttoning his own shirt. How he would handle a long voyage with his friend was beyond him. How would he not let slip that he was not only in love with Finnick's wife but was also sleeping with her? Ephraim knew things about Ava that even Finnick didn't know. Not having spent more than a few days alone with Finnick in ages made him worry that he would accidentally let the secret out. Ephraim shrugged his shoulders and decided to let fate happen. He waited a few more minutes and then left the little chapel and headed back to the Monastery via a different route than Ava had taken.

Ephraim and Finnick left for the docks the following day before Ava or her daughter had awakened from their night's slumber. It would take a few hours to make it down to the wharf, and then they would wait another couple of hours to board before the ship started on its journey.

Ava woke up to the sound of Novalie screaming loudly from the next room. At five years old, now almost six, her daughter had never had a bad dream, and Ava scared of what might be happening, rushed to her side. The girl had the wide-eyed, glazed look that Ava associated with prescient visions. She hugged her daughter to her and let the vision happen. Novalie started to cry and repeatedly said 'daddy' over and over again.

"Tell me what you saw, my sweet." Ava brushed the young girl's bangs out of her eyes and continued holding her tightly.

"Daddy is in the water, and he can't breathe." The little girl said, her voice full of fear.

Ava got off the bed and threw Novalie her robe. "Put this on and meet me in the living room. Ava went out and called for a servant. While she waited for a response, she pulled on her robe and a pair of shoes.

"I need a wagon brought here as quickly as you can. Make sure that the fastest horses are pulling it." Ava told the servant who answered her call. When the girl did not move fast enough, she shouted, "Go. Now." She watched as the young woman went running to do her bidding. Ava gathered Novalie up in her arms and headed to the garages. Once they were in the conveyance, they sped to the docks.

As they traveled, Ava asked her daughter to tell her everything she could remember from the dream.

"Daddy is in the water, and he is not moving. Daddy's friend is with him, so he is not alone."

Ava sucked in a breath, "Is daddy's friend moving?" She asked, afraid of the answer.

"No, his eyes are open, but he is more underwater than Daddy." Novalie stopped talking and curled her legs under her before falling asleep with her head in her mother's lap.

Ava jumped out of the moving vehicle, ran to the edge of the dock, and saw that she was too late. The ship carrying Ephraim and Finnick was already out of sight. She hoped that Novalie was wrong about what she saw. How was she going to live without ever seeing Ephraim again?

Nicollete stumbled through the forest, crying in relief when she finally fell against the Myst gates. She had traveled for two days to reach a point in the forest far away from her attackers and was now in a remote and rather dark part of the woods that surrounded Tayin's domain. Nicollete could hear Tayin coming to her and could also hear him calling for Raighn to join him.

Tayin sat on the pine needles and spring flowers that covered the ground. He touched the Myst and watched as it shimmered in response to Nicollete's answer. In silence, he waited for Raighn to appear. He knew that while he could comfort her, she needed her brother. He watched the memory playing over and over in her mind of the attack, and with each scene, he gritted his teeth in anger over what the Yidderians had done. He could see Nicollete's tears pour freely down her face once Raighn sat next to him, and he placed his hand on Raighn's shoulder to keep him calm as Raighn, too, watched the scenes flash in Nicollete's mind.

"Why?" Raighn asked through gritted teeth.

"I was in a pub with friends on the other side of Kahlali when the light caught my hair wrong, and a group of party-goers saw the color." She started through her tears. "I knew that they had noticed the blue by their faces, and so excusing myself, I decided to leave before they could cause a scene. They followed me, and I couldn't outrun them. The people are afraid now that blue girls have started appearing. They were afraid that I would release the demons, and so they decided to make sure that I did not." Nicollete dabbed at the blood running down the side of her face, even after two long days, with the edge of her skirt.

"They caught up with me and began to hit me and then kick me once I had fallen to the ground. It felt like hours, and I went numb with the pain and quit fighting. At some point, I must have passed out because I woke up, and dawn was beginning to break on the horizon. I could barely stand, my dress was torn, and my hat missing, but I knew that I had to get up and get away before they came back or I was found by others. It took me two days to get here, and I don't know what to do or where to go."

Nicollete broke out into fresh sobs and lay down on the forest floor in exhaustion and pain.

Raighn was barely controlling his anger, and Tayin was doing all he could to calm him down. Both of them could see that she was glossing over the brutality of the attack. Her memories, though broken, showed that a knife had been used on her, along with fists and feet. One of the men had urinated on her before the blackness overtook her mind, and she could remember no more. What had happened after she had lost consciousness was a mystery, but both men could speculate on what had occurred based on her injuries before the blackness took hold and those they could see now.

"My sweet little sister. I am so sorry I wasn't there to protect you." Raighn said with tears of sorrow running down his face and the sound of anger in his voice.

"There is a cave about a mile from here. It has a natural hot spring in it, which will help heal your wounds, and several pain-killing plants grow around the spring. Go there, rest, and recover." Tayin told her.

"After you have healed, go back to Alenar and hide in Adym's cabin. The Tarikan are still there and will help you. There are a few here living in the house that you set up for them, and they can bring you one of their robes. You will look like one of the silent sect of the Calling, and that should get you safely to your destination. Once there, call for me so that I know that you made it safely." Raighn told her and watched as she nodded her head in acknowledgment that she understood the plan.

"And cut your hair," Tayin told her. "It will be easier to hide the color if it is kept short. I will let Adym know to expect you in the next few weeks. He will let the Tarikan on Elynas know you are coming." Tayin said as he stood up and left the brother and sister alone so that they might grieve together without him there.

"It hurts so much that I do not know how I can make it to the cave," Nicollete whispered.

"Rest here for a while. I have called the Tarikan; they will be here soon and help you reach safety."

"Don't leave me." She cried.

"I promise that I will not leave you until it is time for you to leave for the cave. Even then, I will be in your thoughts. I will stay in your mind until you are safely hidden once more." Raighn assured her.

The two sat there together, in silence, until the five Tarikan arrived. Raighn watched as they gently lifted her and carried her through the forest. He stayed at the edge of the Myst until he saw that she had made it to the cave, where several other Tarikans waited after having made the place comfortable for her. He watched as they began their ministrations that would help her to heal. Raighn left and headed back to Lioleta, anger increasing within him with every step that he took.

By the time he returned home, his body was shaking with hatred and anger over what had been done to his sister just because her hair was blue. He went out onto his secluded beach and paced the ocean's edge, trying to calm down, but once he saw that a ship was just off the coast, he could no longer keep his anger in check. He gathered all the strength he had and unleashed a violent storm that penetrated the Myst. He brought lightning down on the vessel, causing it to catch fire as the giant swells broke the ship apart, sending its passengers into the darkness of the water. He heard the screams that came from the drowning Yidderians. He increased the power of the storm, watching the people struggle to stay above the death-bringing depths. He increased the wind, and the waves grew higher, making it impossible for the people to get enough breath before being pushed back down into the Stygian darkness.

The storm came to an abrupt stop as Raighn succumbed to the dark of nothingness. He had used all his strength reaching through the Myst to kill those on the ship without thinking of what it would mean to him. He had used all the energy he had until he was too weak to continue. His mind had shut down.

Kest ran to the rock that jutted out into the ocean and sat down by his friend. He could see that Raighn was still breathing but only just. He opened his mind to his friend, gave him some of his energy, and watched as Raighn's eyes opened once more.

"It does your sister no good for you to go and kill yourself," Kest said in the way of greeting.

"I know." Raighn sat up and looked out at the destruction that his storm had caused and felt a sense of satisfaction over the death of those on board the ship, now reduced to splinters. "I needed to unleash my anger somehow, and I didn't think of the consequences. I need to eat."

He stood up shakily and, with Kest's help, managed to walk to his room. He was unsurprised to find two Yidderians waiting for him. He looked into their eyes before releasing the istotymir. He could feel their fear entering his body, and his energy starting to come back. He fed on their fear until their last moment, where he breathed in their death. His body, still exhausted from his efforts, felt his strength start to return, and with Kest by his side, he walked down to the Yidderian village and fed until he was fully recovered. Never had he fed so extensively on those who lived within the Myst with the Allurans, but never had he needed their fear as much. For the first time, the Yidderians ran from him instead of accepting the feeding as part of normal life. For the first time, they saw him as not the benevolent angel they thought he was but as an angel of death coming for their very souls.

Adym was getting tired. He pulled his shadow back into the Myst, let out a frustrated yell, and then stood up to go find nourishment. It was becoming harder and harder even to shad-ow-walk the outside world, and he became tired more quickly with each time he tried. Adym stepped away from the window and reflected on what he had discovered during his "walk" today. This turn of the blue moon had brought forth three new still-born girls, and this time, he had found a living allurmonuhra, but once again, she was not the one he looked for. He was sure of it. While he could enter her mind, she did not even acknowledge that he was there. Granted, she was only a few weeks old, but Alluran babies could "mind talk" at birth, and this one had no coherent thoughts in her little head.

He wondered if the one they waited for had already arrived. Perhaps he had missed her. Perhaps she would not have the Alluran ability to share minds as they believed she would. He would keep watching. Patience was one of his many virtues, but it was starting to wear thin. Many Allurans had given up hope of ever being released. After all this time of searching and waiting, he was beginning to wonder if they were right to give up hope.

Maybe he would wait another year or two before looking again. This way, he could search only the monastery as the girls would be there, and he could save his strength by looking all in one place. He thought of the suggestion given to him by Nicollete and decided he needed her help. He sent out a thought to the Tarikan and to Nicollete and asked them to alert him if a blue child was born on the outside of the Myst. They replied back instantly that only the one he had found was new but they would listen and watch for him.

He paced the great room and looked out the large window onto the gardens and the Myst in the distance. And while he still found pleasure in looking at the shimmering barrier, it also caused his anger to well up inside as it served as a reminder of his captivity. He knew he was not the only one to feel this way. With each passing day, he felt Raighn's pain increase and also his usage of the numbing drug. Kest was restless with his limited hunting grounds, but Diem brought him solace. Adym smiled, happy that one of his friends had found some happiness in this dark time.

He frowned as he thought of Tayin. Tayin lost more of himself with each passing day. His friend, riddled with anger and the need for revenge, had stopped mending the dreams of the children. He had stopped the teaching dreams as well. Now, he only produced nightmares, and the villages surrounding his home struggled with the dark illusions that leaked out and encompassed the Myst of Kofira. Adym knew that Tayin kept himself, as much as possible, confined to his room of meditation. It helped block his thoughts and ease his pain, but just barely. Adym was afraid that if he did not find the girl they were looking for soon, he would lose his best friend, if not to death, to madness.

"Madness, yes. Death, no," Tayin spoke, and Adym laughed ruefully, not realizing he was thinking loud enough for others to hear.

"You weren't, but I hear everyone regardless of how quiet they try to be," Tayin replied.

"I am still looking, my friend."

"I know, and your health worries me. You are not as strong as you once were."

Adym left the beautiful room he was in and walked out into the garden, heading down the path to the Yidderian village. "I just came back from a walk and have yet to feed. I will be strong enough soon."

"Yes, but each walk causes you to need more and more fear."

"I will find her soon, and then it won't matter. We will be free to walk Yiddera without worrying about losing strength, and you will have your revenge. We all will." He thought briefly of Raighn. Once, Raighn had cared for the Yidderians, and now he used them as he pleased and couldn't care less about how he left them afterward. Adym knew that Raighn would make those who had hurt his sister pay for what they had done to her, and Adym hoped that he could release Raighn to do this in his enemy's lifetimes as he had been unable to do for Tayin.

"Ah, but there are so many more of them to hunt down now than there were at the beginning. It makes it, in some ways, more satisfying. The hunt will take longer, and there will be more of her offspring to kill."

Adym ignored the remark and continued on his way to the village. In two years, he would check again for the girl, and then every two years after that. He would let the Tarikan inform him in the in-between times. He wanted to preserve his strength for when it was needed. He wondered how old she would need to be before she was able to retrieve the key. The minute he deemed her capable, he would direct her in her destiny no matter what it took or what shape it left her in, after all this was what she was born to do, and nothing else mattered but her finding the key and releasing the Allurans from their gilded cage.

YEAR 383

Ava had managed to keep her pregnancy a secret owing to the fact that, at this point, she was still not very big with her child. She was due in another month, and she suspected that the next five weeks would not only increase her belly's size but make it harder for her to hide her condition. She knew that it was time to visit her cousin, who lived down the mountain and across the valley from the monastery. She packed her bags and, taking Novalie, now six, with her, left the monastery in charge of her very competent advisers.

They reached their destination a day and a half later and settled into the set of rooms that Syrah, Ava's cousin, had made up for her. Novalie enjoyed playing in the spacious garden and meeting the kids in the neighborhood. Ava smiled as she watched her oldest acting like the child she was instead of as the proper girl she thought she had to be due to her station in life. She enjoyed the peace and quiet of her surroundings, which was so different from the hectic bustle of the Monastery for two weeks, and then the blue moon made its appearance in the night sky. It was late summer, and the moon turned the world a magnificent blue when she felt her first pains begin.

Ava tried to ignore them as she was not due for three more weeks, and she knew that to have a child with Allura in the sky would result in one of two things. First, she would deliver a still-born, and she would be devastated to lose Ephraim's baby, but this would be the better option. The second would be that she would give birth to a blue girl, but she, as the Prophetess, could not have a blue girl. She had touted that a blue girl represented a lack of belief in the Calling, and it would undermine all her hard work and teachings if she was linked to a Dimoni. It was the next morning, on the third day of Sedemis, the 7th month, that she could no longer deny that she was in labor. She had her cousin call for the midwife and sent Novalie to play with one of the neighbor girls.

Ava took a deep breath in preparation for the ordeal ahead of her and gathered her bag to her side, making sure that the tinctures that she had so carefully packed inside, in case something went wrong, were still there. She placed the bag on the side of her bed and then, succumbing to a harsh contraction, sat down in the bed with her pillows fluffed up behind her. She could hear the midwife and grimaced when she saw who had come to attend her. This midwife, while more than competent, was a gossip, and Ava was glad of the tinctures that she kept beside her as the one would be needed to keep this woman from gossiping about this day.

Labor was hard but went rather quickly, and after both she and the baby were cleaned, she held out her arms to receive her daughter. She felt tears run down her cheeks as she knew by the little one's lusty cry that she had lived, and it was this same cry that told her she had given birth to a girl. Ava knew that she would not be able to keep this infant born during the phase of the Alluran moon. Still, she longed to look into her eyes and dream of what might have been had the child been born one week earlier or two more later.

She gasped in shock as a vision took hold of her the moment she touched her little girl. Ava's body shuddered with recognition of who this child, her child, truly was. Not only was she a daughter of the third moon, but Ava knew without a doubt that she had given birth to the one that was foretold to open the Myst gates once again.

Ava tried to harden her heart against this child but could not do it. This little girl had been conceived in love, and she was all Ava had left of that love. She gently caressed the soft, downy blond hair and fingered the streaks of cornflower blue hair that marked the child as a Dimoni born during the demon's moon. The infant made a soft mewling sound and opened her startling blue eyes. Eyes that glowed the same blue as her hair. Eyes that glowed more brightly than any other blue girl's.

Ava kissed her daughter on the forehead and then laid her child down on her lap. She knew what she had to do. It was the only thing that could be done to save the humans in this world from the evil that lurked within the Myst. She placed her hand over the baby's nose and mouth and pushed gently. The baby squirmed under her hand and gasped for breath. Ava sighed deeply, knowing that she could not bring herself to kill her own child, and so she removed her hand.

She told the midwife bustling around the room to run and bring Samuel and Syrah to her and not speak to anyone else on the way. Ava reached over to the bag that lay on the floor next to her birthing bed and took out the bottle of the balsama bark and rueberry tincture she had prepared for this occasion. No one could know that she had given birth to a child, any child, but definitely not one that was demon blue.

The midwife came back into the room, followed by the couple, and sat on the couch under the window. Once the couple was situated, Ava asked the midwife to prepare some water for tea as she felt in need of it and would like them to share a cup with her. While the midwife was busy, she looked at the couple who lost their newborn girl to the moon only two days before.

"As you know, I have given birth to a little girl." Ava saw the pity in the man's eyes and the shared pain in the woman's. "What you do not know is that she has, unfortunately, survived."

She took a deep breath and continued on. "According to the law, she is to be taken to the monastery to be kept from giving in to her evil nature, but I cannot do this for obvious reasons. I cannot have her there as it may one day become obvious who her mother is. I cannot let people know that I have given birth to one chosen by the demons." Ava looked around the room and observed the curious stares of those she talked to.

She asked the midwife to get the bag beside her bed and reached inside for the tea she had brought. The midwife steeped the tea and then poured it into four cups. Ava then added four drops of the tincture she had withdrawn earlier to the cup of the midwife. "You have had a long day, and this will help you relax and get some restful sleep," She lied. Ava knew that the poison would soon take hold, and the midwife would never wake. But she could not have it spread about that her child had lived, and this midwife would definitely tell everyone she came across that the Prophetess had given birth to a blue girl.

"Now, I want you to take my child and raise her in secret. I have a house in the forest outside of the village with a walled-in garden that is now yours. I will also supply you with an annual income. To keep others from wondering where you got your newfound wealth, I will give you, Samuel, a new job in which the house and the salary can then be explained." Ava looked intensely at the couple sitting before her, "As you might suspect, I want no one to know of this. I am trusting you with this secret. I have killed one today," Ava pointed at the now-dead midwife, "and I will not hesitate to kill again to keep this girl hidden and unknown to others. Raise her as you wish, but she cannot be taken into the village, and you cannot let her be seen by anyone other than yourselves. Is that clear?"

The couple nodded their heads in understanding.

"My lady, what should we name her?" Syrah asked.

"Name her after the moon, yourself, whatever, but not after me. She is yours. I do not want anything more to do with her." Ava waved her hand in dismissal and watched as the young woman took the baby into her arms and left the room. Once alone, she turned her head into the pillow and cried. She cried for her lost love, the baby girl she had just given birth to, and her own weakness for not killing the child.

YEAR 388

FIVE YEARS LATER, ADYM was reading when he felt a soft brush of thought against his mind. He put the book down and concentrated on the distant thought. There it was again. It was faint, feeling very far away. He followed it to the mind of the one it originated from and found it coming from a very young child. Adym knew it could not be an Alluran child as they were born with the ability to project their thoughts almost as well as any adult could. Therefore, this invasion into his mind must come from someone outside the Myst. He found the thought came from a young girl, one with the striking blue hair of a child born during the rising of the Alluran Moon. He realized that she had no idea that she was reaching out to him with her thoughts. He was fascinated by the realization that this child might be the one who was destined to set him free.

Adym placed his book on the side table and went over to the window to look out at the Myst. He whispered hello into her mind and watched as her head came up from her play and looked around for the voice that she had heard.

"What is your name, li uhra?" asked Adym.

The young child looked around again and whispered something unintelligible. Adym tried to make sense of the word but could not understand what she tried to say. It sounded like moon something, but he wasn't sure. So, he asked the child her name once again.

"Moon," was the reply. Adym was not familiar with human children and could not decide if the child was really named Moon or if she did not understand his question. He stayed quiet when he saw the girl's mother enter the room and ask the little one who she was talking to. Her answer surprised Adym and scared the child's mother.

"The man with blue hair who is standing in the yellow room looking out his window."

How could the child know where he was? How could she have found his memories without him noticing she was that far in his mind? He withdrew from her mind and looked around the yellow room he was indeed in. He was positive this was the Yidderian girl predicted to release his people from their imprisonment. He must let the council know that he had finally succeeded in his search.

Adym headed into the Hall of Myst and then hesitated. The child was too young to accomplish the task of setting them free. Maybe he should watch her for a while and make sure she was indeed who he suspected. He did not want to bring his people false hope. He turned back and went outside to enjoy the bright sunny day; he knew that it would not be long now before he once more hunted outside of the Myst.

"You found her, haven't you." Adym heard Tayin ask.

"What alerted you to my thoughts?" He questioned his friend.

"Your excitement. You have an unusual sense of anticipation running through your thoughts that I couldn't ignore." Tayin replied in answer.

Adym continued his stroll through the garden, enjoying the warmth of the afternoon. He came to the edge of the Myst and looked out, "It won't be long now, my friend. I do, indeed, think I have found her. She is very young and not able to do her task yet so I decided not to tell the others. I do not want to get their hopes up until I am positive she is the one the prophecy speaks of."

"I will keep your secret, but I expect to be notified the minute you are positive that she is the one we await." Tayin left Adym alone with his thoughts. His own excitement over the end of his long wait was hard to keep down. Soon. Soon, he would begin his hunt and fulfill the promise he made to Amalie.

YEAR 825

*"**What was it like** knowing that this girl was the one you waited for?" Neviah asked, curiosity seeping out through her words.*

"At this time, I still had doubts. Adym seemed to think she was the one, but then Kest had thought Diem was the awaited one. I held reservations until it could be proven who she was. Until the girl personally handed the key to Adym, I would not let myself believe. I wanted Adym to be right. I needed him to be." Tayin smiled a sad smile and looked at Neviah.

"I was eaten up inside with the desire to kill those of Amalie's blood but also to bring pain and fear to all the Yidderians. I was beginning to believe that Yiddera would be better off with all of the Yidderians gone. I was starting to believe that they were all responsible for Tam's death."

"But you know that they were not." Neviah was astonished at the amount of hate she felt coming from his words.

"You are correct. First and foremost in my mind was the need for revenge, for the need to excise all of Amalie's descendants from the world. However, the next conclusion in my hate-shrouded mind was to rid the world of all who were not Alluran."

"Did you feel anything good? Like hope or joy?"

"I lost the ability to feel hope or true joy with the death of Tam. It wasn't until my Lokiia was born that hope returned. And hope is cruel." Tayin, done with the conversation, continued with his story.

YEAR 389

"But Mom, why can't I have lunch with you? You promised that today we would have the whole day to ourselves and that you would take me to lunch at the teashop." Whined the 12-year-old Novalie.

"I am so sorry, my dear, really I am, but one of our biggest supporters stopped by, and I can't ignore her as we need her donation to add a wing to the healer's building." Ava looked up at her daughter and sighed with understanding. "As soon as I am done here with her, I will take you to dinner instead of lunch, and we can stop by the ribbon shop and get you some that match your new peach-colored dress."

Novalie frowned at her mother and stomped out of the room.

"Novalie, come back here, now," Ava said with a slightly raised but firm voice. She watched as her disappointed daughter reluctantly came back into the room.

"This is not the attitude I expect from you. As you are to be the reining Prophetess one day, I expect you to understand that sometimes work must come before pleasure."

"I do understand, but you are always working."

Ava frowned, knowing this was true. She had tried to stay busy with work since her life was turned upside down with the birth of her second child. She did not want to give herself time to think about what might have been and what terrible things were coming in her lifetime. Ava stood up and reached for Novalie's hand.

"You know what? You are right. If you will go and make sure that the guest quarters are ready for Nicollete, I will let her know that our business must wait until tomorrow as I have a prior engagement that I must attend to."

Novalie smiled and quickly raced out of the room and down to the wing that housed the guest rooms. She busied herself with making sure the room was tidy and fixed the pillow, which was crumbled. Novalie noticed that the vase on the bureau was empty and decided to go and gather a few stems so that the room looked more inviting. She went out into the extensive flower gardens, picked her favorite orange-colored lilies, and added a few sprigs of white baby's breath and yellow daisies.

Novalie carried the bouquet back into the monastery and stopped abruptly a few yards away from the room in which their guest was to stay. Inside was a beautiful young woman who looked to be around 25 or so. She was taking off her magnificent green hat, and Novalie could see the blue highlights in her thick, dark hair. Novalie crept a bit closer, and yes, the woman's hair was blue, not the black that it appeared to be at first glance.

Curious, Novalie wondered if she was a blue girl who had recently come to the monastery and had mistakenly been placed in the guest quarters but was instantly dispelled of this notion.

"Novalie, there you are," Ava said, and Novalie, still staring at the woman inside the room, saw that she had quickly replaced her hat upon hearing someone in the hallway.

"Sorry, Prophetess," Novalie said. "I was just bringing flowers to place in the vase so that our guest would feel welcome. Let me put them away, and then I will be ready to go." She skirted around the woman who was now standing by the door and opened it wide for her to enter. Novalie quickly arranged the flowers and then exited the room.

"Thank you. They are beautiful." The woman had a sweet voice that made Novalie smile at her.

"Nicollete, this is my daughter and prophetess-in-waiting, Novalie. Novalie, this is Nicollete, our esteemed guest."

Nicollete smiled at Novalie, "It is very nice to make your acquaintance."

"And yours as well," Novalie replied. She was a bit confused about how this woman with the blue hair could be the heir to the light stone fortune. Blue girls were brought to the monastery as children and were not considered part of their birth families once they arrived. They were never heirs to anything but stinking demon traits. She stared up at the woman and was nudged in the side by her mother for her rudeness.

"I am sorry to stare milady. Your hat is beautiful, but so is your hair. Why do you wear the hat inside and not let your hair show?" She asked, wondering what the blue girl would say.

Nicollete laughed softly. "Thank you for your kind words. It is the tradition in my family for women to wear a hat at all times while in company. I am sure you understand how hard it is to break from tradition."

Ava smiled at her guest, "Well, please make yourself comfortable. I will see you this evening for dinner, and tomorrow, we can talk about business. Come Novalie."

Novalie followed her mother down the hall and out into the cool morning air. The two walked down to the tea shop and sat down for lunch. Novalie decided to ask her mother about the woman.

"Is Nicollete a blue girl?" She asked

Ava looked shocked at the question. "Of course not. Why do you ask?"

Novalie was surprised that her mother had not noticed the color of the woman's hair. "Oh. I thought she had a blue tinge of color to her hair, and so I was curious. It must have been a trick of the light making it look so." Novalie thanked the waiter and picked up her fork to start on her salad.

"It must have been. I have met with her a few times over the past two years, and never have I noticed any demon marking on the young woman. As a matter-of-fact, she is the spitting image of her mother, though maybe a bit taller, but definitely not a Dimoni." Ava paused for a moment, "I think that tonight you might have dinner with us and then sit in our business meeting tomorrow. It is time that you began your training on the more tedious aspects of being the Prophetess. Hopefully, soon, you can help me with them." She began to eat.

"I would like that, Mom. I want to learn all that I can about what I need to do for when I am grown up." Novalie wiggled in her chair in excitement. While she was only twelve, Novalie was a serious child and looked forward to learning what was needed for her future. The few visions that she had seen so far indicated that she would become the Prophetess around the age her mother had, and she was very much looking forward to that day.

YEAR 395

Seven years had passed since Adym had first felt the thoughts of the young girl, and for seven years, he had tried to talk with her again. Somehow, the child had learned to block her mind. To keep him out completely. This was not something he expected a blue girl to be able to do. All Allurans had a place where they kept secret thoughts. A place in their mind that others could not enter, but to be able to keep a SeiOrhii out of your mind completely was unheard of. How could you possibly hope to communicate with others if your mind was as impenetrable as a rock wall? How could a human even begin to block their mind from him? Human minds were easy to enter and even easier to manipulate. He needed access to her mind, thoughts, and memories if he was going to convince her to do what was required. He pushed more forcefully and still could not break through her mental barrier.

Adym thought for a minute about what he should do next before he decided that there was not a way to get into her mind without force. So, instead of her mind, he found the mind of the girl's mother and entered. He pushed a thought into her head and, for several days, repeated the idea until the woman did as he wanted her to. Then, smiling, he left her and prepared to meet the daughter of the third moon at the sacred waters.

Moonsyrah helped her mother pack a few sandwiches and other food items in the basket and then watched as she placed a large cloth over the top and closed the lid. Moonsyrah picked up the other basket that contained a change of clothes for both her and her mother and then together, they walked out the door. Syrah, her mother, opened the gate that led to the outside world, and while excited to leave, she was hesitant. Moonsyrah had never left the gardens surrounding her home before. She paused by the gate and looked out at the road ahead of her, a bit scared to leave the safety of her home. She had always been told that the color of her hair and the glow of her eyes put her in danger and, therefore, she must never leave the gardens in order to stay safe, but today her mother was taking her out.

Moonsyrah adjusted her hair covering more securely around her face and then, taking a deep breath, stepped outside. She let the excitement of the coming adventure eclipse her fear of it and found enjoyment in the walk down the road. Her mother laughed every time she exclaimed in joy over the many new things she came across.

She came to a fork in the road, and unsure which way to go she went running back to her mother, who took her hand and led her up the right side of the fork. The road became rocky and more difficult to run on, so Moonsyrah walked carefully by her mother's side.

"Mom, why did you let me come with you today? Am I safe today?" Moonsyrah asked.

"Well, I thought it was time for you to see more of the world you live in, but this excursion must remain our little secret. If your father knew that you were off our property, he would be very mad at the both of us. Which is why I chose this weekend, as he is not here for the next few days. As for being safe, I think that if you keep your hair well covered until we get to the place we are going, you will be." Syrah replied and stopped to adjust her daughter's hair covering as one of the blue braids was peeking out.

"Where are we going?" Moonsyrah asked, her voice filled with excited curiosity.

"Actually, we are heading to a place that is forbidden by the Prophetess for anyone to visit. It is a beautiful waterfall that has hot springs in every color of the rainbow. I figured that if I was going to take you out, it should be somewhere special and beautiful and somewhere that no other Yidderian would be. Once there, I believe it will be safe for you to let your hair loose and enjoy the beauty of the water." Syrah explained and then continued their walk.

"Why is it forbidden?"

Syrah laughed at her daughter's inquisitive nature and looked at her with pride. Moonsyrah's curiosity over the world had led her to devour books on the geography of the planet and the cultures of the people who lived in other places, and she had taught herself some of the older dialects that were spoken when the people first made Yiddera their home.

"It is thought to be held sacred by the demons that live in the Myst. One of the stories that the Calling tells of is that the first

Prophetess came here with her husband to swim, and a demon appeared and threatened death to all that visit the falls and enter the sacred pools. He was said to have told the Prophetess that this place was of great importance to them and that the Yidderians did not belong there. The Prophetess then made it a punishable crime to visit the falls and bathe in their waters."

"Do you believe that there are demons in the Myst?" Moonsyrah asked with wide eyes.

"I believe in the Calling and the Prophetess, so I feel I must believe in this as well, but between you and me, I think it is just a story told to keep us in line. I will admit, though, that when you get close to the Myst barrier, it does have an eerie feeling to it, and a person's fears seem to come to the forefront of their mind. The falls that we will visit have the same quality, but I still think they are worth visiting."

"I don't believe that anyone lives in the Myst, and I am glad that we are going to visit Rainbow Falls. Since this may be my only chance to see the world outside of our garden, I am happy that we are going to see something that few other people get to see."

The walk to the falls had taken the full morning, and they arrived soon after the sun reached its highest point in the sky. The world had a blue cast to it that only occurred when Allura was in orbit, and the magic of the slightly blue tint and the beauty of the dazzling colors of the falls left Moonsyrah speechless. She stared in wide-eyed wonder at the beautiful sight in front of her and was surprised that more people did not come here despite the law that forbade it.

Moonsyrah walked along the lake full of crystal clear rocks and marveled at how they glittered in the sun, causing them to be almost too bright to look at. She let her gaze take in the magnificence of the falls. The waters fell over a high cliff, and halfway down, they fell over stones of every color of the rainbow. The highest point was pink, with bits of deep red running through it. Then, following the horseshoe shape of the mountain, she saw yellow and orange rocks followed by a large section of green stones in varying shades of green coloring. Next was an area of lavender and deep purples. She stared at this one for the longest amount of time. The water was more forceful around this outcropping, and it drew her eye to it. She closed her eyes and heard music faintly playing and somehow knew it was coming from the colored gems. The music from the purple stones was the loudest and seemed to beckon her to enter their pool.

Moonsyrah climbed up the rocky, winding path and found herself in a cave behind the falls. She heard her mother behind her and watched as she placed the baskets on the ground and sat down by the green pond. Moonsyrah walked slowly toward the purple pool, marveling at the peace of the lavender half. Across the hot spring was a purple stone bridge, and on the other side were stones of the deepest purple in which the water pounded with the violence of a fierce storm. Moonsyrah could swear that she saw flickers of lightning in the air above the water. She walked even closer and tripped over a stick in the path. She fell, and her arm, up to her elbow, came in contact with the very hot spring of water. The music she heard from the stones intensified, and a jolt of electricity ran up her arm and surged through her whole body. Moonsyrah quickly pulled her arm out of the water and, righting herself, walked over to sit beside her mother next to the green pool.

"The stories were right." Syrah began. "The air feels different here and leaves me a bit on edge. Maybe we shouldn't be here."

"I don't feel anything scary about this place, mom. Let's stay and swim for a bit." Moonsyrah replied, enthralled with all the music and the magic she felt from the place.

"Alright. I like the green waters. They seem more welcoming than the other pools do, and it looks big enough to swim in." Her mother slipped off her dress and entered the water, which was the temperature of a warm bath. Moonsyrah joined her, and for the first time, a sense of uneasiness entered her. The same energy she felt in the purple pool entered her body and made her think of blue fire. She swam around with her mother for a while, but the intense feeling of something waiting for her caused her to exit the pool and watch as her mother swam around for a while longer.

Once out of the pool, Syrah and Moonsyrah made their way back down to the crystal clear lake and, spreading out the large cloth, had a very enjoyable dinner. She watched as her mother made a small fire once the air became chilled and was surprised when her mother took a large slice of cake out of the basket. She had not seen Syrah place it in the container and smiled at the gesture. Syrah sang happy birthday to her, and together, they indulged in the sweet lemon taste. After the treat, they swam in the lake, which was slightly colder than they had expected it to be, and then finished making camp for the night.

Syrah pointed out the constellations in the night sky to Moonsyrah until she became tired and fell asleep. That night,

Moonsyrah dreamt of the strange Myst that she had seen in the distance above the falls and of a strange blue fire. She dreamt that the fire was coming from her hand. She woke up in the night to a voice that seemed faintly familiar to her. It seemed to be educating her on how to draw upon the energy she had felt from the waters and produce the fire she had dreamt about with her hand. She ignored the thoughts that she felt were not her own and finally fell back into a restless sleep.

The next morning, after a repast of the appleberries she was fond of and muffins that her mother had made, the two decided to take another swim in the green pool before leaving for home. Moonsyrah watched her mother frolic in the waters and joined her after watching the purple storm for a while first. She entered the green pool, and this time, when she felt the energy enter her body, she got right back out. She sat at the edge of the water and listened to the melody that echoed in the cave around her.

Moonsyrah listened to the quiet voice in her mind, still instructing her on how to bring the fire to life. She wondered why she was imagining the voice and why she thought about fire. Finally, her mother swam out of the pool and dried off. Moonsyrah took her mother's hand, and together, they left the cave and walked back down to the lake's edge.

"Did you enjoy your birthday outing?" Her mother asked.

"I did. It was wonderful. Thank you for bringing me here and showing me the Rainbow Falls. They are beautiful. I will never forget how wonderful these two days have been." Moonsyrah told her mother before becoming quiet once again, trying to concentrate on the words and pictures repeating in her mind.

Moonsyrah did not notice that they did not follow the same path back home. The much longer path they took caught her attention when the sky began to darken once more. Looking at her mother in inquiry, she was told that Syrah did not want the trip to end too soon, so she was taking a circuitous route that would allow them to camp out for one more night. Moonsyrah liked this idea and helped her mother decide on the perfect spot for their campsite. They found a large clearing next to the road that was hidden away from view by several tall trees and flowering bushes. They spread out their blanket, and Syrah once again started a small fire so they could remain warm throughout the night.

As Moonsyrah ate, her mind listened to the voice that was full of the same energy she had felt in the warm waters. She felt that she was on the edge of discovery, and being naturally curious, she wanted to know what that discovery was, so she continued to dwell on the voice and on the new and increasingly more intense feeling of fire coursing through her body. She absently stood up when her mother asked if she would like to go for a stroll before the sun fully set and together they walked out of the clearing.

She was brought out of her thoughts when a loud crack split the quietness of the sunset, and a large tree branch fell right in front of her. Instinctively, Moonsyrah held out her hands in front of her and was shocked as the blue fire that she had dreamt of flew out from her hands and scorched the ground in between her and her mother. She was frightened to see the line of fire crawl up her mother's dress, and she cried in despair as she saw her mother back away from her and fall over the edge of the cliff.

Moonsyrah jumped over the fallen branch, raced to the lip of the cliff, and saw her mother. On a ledge thirty feet or so below the path, her mother lay at an odd angle, lifeless. She found a way down to the ledge and held her mother in her arms. Tears streaming down her face as her mother's eyes fluttered open and looked up at her in horror. She cried as she heard her mother's last words: "Your mother was right. You are demon born." Moonsyrah held her mother's lifeless body all through the long, cold night, and she forcefully shut out the voice that tried to tell her that everything was going to be okay. The voice tried to sound comforting, but she could hear an excitement in it that belied the comfort it tried to give. She could feel the voice trying to push against her mind, to make her listen once more, but the barrier was back in place, and keeping it strong, the voice could no longer be heard or felt.

Dawn came, and Moonsyrah gently laid her mother's lifeless head back on the ground. Tucking the head scarf she wore around Syrah's cold body in an effort to keep her warm, she left to go find help. She made it to their house and found that her father had arrived home from his trip early, and so, in anguish and tears, she led him to Syrah's body. Her father looked at Moonsyrah in disgust and hate and pushed her away from his wife's body. He picked up his love and carried her home, where he laid her on the ground under her favorite tree and began digging her grave. He did not talk to Moonsyrah or offer her the comfort she so desperately needed. He sat next to the grave for hours before noticing the girl who sat quietly next to him.

Grabbing her arm, he led Moonsyrah back outside and down the path once more. Instead of taking the right fork, he turned down the left. They walked through the village, ignoring the people who came out to look at the blue girl that Samuel dragged behind him. Moonsyrah had to run to keep up with his long strides and quit trying to get him to answer her questions when she realized he would not answer her queries. They came to a large brick wall with an impressive stone gate in the middle of it, and Moonsyrah watched as her father pounded on it and yelled for entrance.

A young man let the pair in, and Samuel continued dragging Moonsyrah behind him until he came to the doors of the Monastery. They stood open, and as they entered the massive building, she held her tongue as Samuel yelled for the Prophetess. People scurried around, trying to get her father to quiet down and figure out why he was yelling with such disrespect for their great lady. Finally, someone did as he demanded and brought the Prophetess to him.

"Leave us." The Prophetess said as sounds of people hurrying to do her bidding echoed across the foyer could be heard.

Moonsyrah looked up for the first time and, pushing her hair out of her face, saw an imposing woman dressed in black standing at the bottom of the stairs a few feet in front of Samuel. She was pulled forward and then pushed to the ground at the feet of the woman who stood before her father. She sat there staring at the woman when she heard her father for the last time.

"She is your mistake, and I should never have let Syrah agree to keep her for you. This demon has killed my wife, and I will no longer have her in my house. She is your responsibility and your sin."

Moonsyrah turned and watched as her father left her there, never looking back or saying goodbye. She laid her head on the floor and cried great sobs over the loss of her parents, knowing that it was her fault they were gone. She was the demon he had called her, for what else could she be? Only a monster would have killed their own mother. She lay there in stunned grief until the Prophetess took her hand and bade her to stand and follow her. Moonsyrah did as she was asked and knew that her life was now changed forever.

A few months later, Moonsyrah was walking to her classes alone, when she thought she heard music. Her head came up, and she listened intently to the sound. It played a tune reminiscent of the ones that she had heard that day at the falls. She had tried so hard to block that memory from her mind, but the music pulled it up and replayed the memory. She was curious to find out why she heard the music of the falls within the monastery. She followed the sound until she came to the door that she knew belonged to the Prophetess's rooms. She hesitated for a moment and then quietly opened the door. Seeing no one around, she followed the sound until she came to a wall next to the windows. She pushed the curtains aside and found that the wall contained a well-hidden door. She found a secret latch that, when depressed, opened the door and led to a darkened set of stairs. Her breath coming quickly, she knew that this stairway would take her to the source of the music. She left the door slightly ajar behind her and descended the staircase. She found herself in a room lit softly by green light stones.

Moonsyrah looked at the works of art around her and slowly made her way to the back of the room where the music seemed to be coming from. She walked by an intricately carved box that emitted a soft pink light and touched it lightly. She smiled at the images that appeared and the delicate lullaby it played. Moonsyrah took her hand off the beautiful box and made her way to the farthest corner of the room, where she stood in front of a pedestal that held a dark blue stone. This stone was the source of the music she heard. It intensified, and all she could hear was the music singing loudly in her head. She reached out to touch it when a voice broke through the intriguing song.

"Moonsyrah, what are you doing?" The Prophetess asked softly but with a hint of worry in her voice.

"This round stone has music coming from it. Like the ones at the Rainbow Falls do. Its sweet song asks me to pick it up and take it back home."

The Prophetess went over to the girl and gently pulled her from the pedestal. "My child, surely you know that rocks do not play music."

"But can't you hear the slightly off-key tune? It is coming from this blue gem. It beckons me to touch it." Moonsyrah reached for it once more and felt the Prophetess place her hand on her arm to lower her reach.

"This particular stone is not safe to touch, especially for you. Forget that it is here and come away with me. The music you think you hear is surely coming from the music hall. The musicians there are rehearsing at this time of day, and I am positive this is what you are hearing."

Moonsyrah reluctantly followed the Prophetess out of the underground room and only looked back once at the stone still calling for her with its haunting melody. She sat at the table that the Prophetess directed her to and took a drink of the warm tea the lady brought to her.

"What is on your mind, child?"

"I went to the falls with my mother, and the crystals there played a similar melody to that of the stone that you keep hidden. It reminds me of that terrible day." Moonsyrah wiped a tear away and took another drink of the healing tea.

"Tell me about it." The Prophetess asked of her.

Moonsyrah told of the trip they had taken and of the horror of what she had done, and it was in this telling that she remembered her mother's last words and the words her father had said as he pushed her toward the Prophetess. Moonsyrah looked at the woman sitting across from her, and despite the difference in color, she knew that her eyes were the same as those of the Prophetess and her daughter, Novalie. Their delicate facial structure and mannerisms were the same as her own. She knew at that moment what the sin of the Prophetess was that her father had mentioned. She did not ask the Prophetess if her speculation was true because living here these past months had taught her why the Prophetess would not tell her the truth.

Moonsyrah finished her drink and became rather sleepy. The Prophetess guided her to the dormitory that held the younger blue girls and put her to bed. The Prophetess kissed her forehead telling her to sleep the sleep of forgetfulness. Moonsyrah smiled and then fell into a dreamless sleep.

Adym waited in shadow form for the girl to arrive at the falls, and when he saw her, his heart sped up in excitement. He knew that this girl was the one who would hand him the key to his release. Not sure exactly where the key was, he suspected somewhere within the Monastery walls. He needed to be sure this girl could hear the music and follow it to the key. Adym watched as she climbed the path to the sacred waters and raised his eyebrows in surprise when he felt her hesitate and then turn toward the purple hot spring. Was she interested in it because of the color, or was there more to her interest? He pushed a stick in her path and saw her trip over it. Her fall had exactly the effect he was hoping for. Her arm fell into the pool, and he could feel her mind open to him and the energy course threw her body.

He was surprised that an allurmonuhra could respond to the energy in the waters. Diem had not been able to, at least as far as he could tell, but then they had only had her try the blue waters. He would make sure to ask Kest if Diem was attracted to any of the colors. He turned his thoughts back to the young girl and felt her confusion about why she now thought of blue fire. He watched as the two females played in the green pool and watched as they left for the lake below.

He kept the idea of fire running through her mind, and as quietly and unobtrusively as he could, he instructed her on how to pull on the energy she was feeling to bring the fire out of her mind and into reality. He continued speaking to her even as she slept. She woke briefly and tried to push him away, but she was too preoccupied with her thoughts to accomplish this, and so he stayed within her mind.

After watching her all the next day, he knew that her mother would help her put the wall against him back up once the young girl told her of her thoughts of fire. He could see that her mother had been warned that it was important to keep the allurmonuhra safe and her mind strong in case a demon tried to speak with her. He delved into the girl's mother's thoughts and found the memory associated with this warning. He laughed to himself as he saw that the girl's real mother knew that she had given birth to the one to set him free. Adym thought for a while and knew that he had to get rid of the adoptive mother and somehow get the girl to be given to the monastery. He knew by the birth mother's look and words of warning that the key was indeed within the monastery.

It was late evening, and he could feel the allurmonuhra was ready. Adym knew that she would produce fire without thought, given the right circumstances, and lucky for him, fear would startle her enough to do this. He broke a large branch from the tree above her, and as expected, she jumped back, startled, and pushed the fire toward the branch and toward her mother sitting across from her. He smiled as he watched her mother respond by backing up from the girl. Adym then helped the woman fall from the cliff.

Adym tried to comfort the young girl as he could see that she loved the Yidderian woman, but the girl forcefully put the wall in her mind back up, and try as he might, he could not get back in. Still in his shadow form, he followed her to her home and saw that the man she called her father followed her back to her mother's body. He stoked the grief the man felt and his dislike of the young girl until the man, after laying his wife to rest, dragged the girl to the monastery. There, his suspicions were confirmed. This girl belonged in the monastery with her birth mother, and he knew by the look on the Prophetess's face that the key was indeed within these walls.

Adym left the outside world and entered his own body to find Tayin sitting quietly next to him with a couple of Yidderians, awaiting his return. Adym ate their fear and dismissed the last man when he felt replenished.

"How long have you been here?" He asked his friend.

"About a day and a half," Tayin replied. Then, he stood up and, stretching his stiff body, went to sit on the couch. He watched as Adym also stretched and sat in the chair that faced him.

"You found her, didn't you? The girl who you think might be the one? Did you send her after the key?' Tayin's questions stumbled over each other in his need to learn their answers.

"I did find her." He held up his hand to quiet Tayin, "But she is not yet ready to find the key. I have set the stage and sent her to where she needs to be, but still, we must be patient for the time being. She has, once again, blocked me from her mind, and it will take me a while to get her to lower them again. It will be soon, a few more rotations at the most, my friend." Adym waved away a Tarikan and frowned when Tayin waved him back.

"Adym, you need to eat and drink. Your body, as well as your mind, went without for several days. Eat, drink, feed, and rest. I will be back to check on you later." He stood up to go. "I agree with you that we should wait until you are sure she can find the key before we alert the others, but we may want to let them know that it is a possibility that she has been found so we can plan our next steps." Tayin walked out of the room and back to Kofira.

Adym did as Tayin suggested and replenished his body. Now that he knew where she was, he could keep an eye on her. She would once again open her mind to him. He would just have to wait a little while longer. Adym lay on his bed and fell asleep, his body tired from walking in shadow for so long, and he dreamt of the girl who would release him.

"What? Did I hear you correctly? You voted, again, to keep the Yidderians imprisoned in the Myst once the gates were opened?" Diem stood up in shock and disappointment. She angrily advanced on Kest and shook her finger at him. "Go back there now and tell them you are rescinding your vote. Tell them you have thought about it and you made a mistake. Tell them whatever you must, but do not tell me that you actually voted no once again."

Kest stood his ground. He had known that she would not understand but had hoped she would hear him out. Once again, she would not listen to his reason for voting the way he did. No matter how hard he tried to explain, she wouldn't listen.

"My pet, if the Myst's are ever opened and then closed unexpectedly, once more, we need to be sure that we have what we need to survive. I cannot in good conscience vote to get rid of our reserves." He told her and added silently so she could not hear his thoughts that this also ensured she could not leave. Diem had never once told him that she loved him, and after all this time, though he knew she did, he was worried that maybe she didn't love him enough to want to stay.

"Reserves? Reserves? Is that how you see us? Not as people with feelings, longings, and lives of our own but as reserves?" She asked him quietly, her anger loudly heard within her words.

"The Yidderians are just that. You are not." He knew she would not like his answer, but he wanted to be honest with her. He had no real like or dislike for the people who lived in the village, and until he met Diem, he had almost no contact with them outside of retrieving the fear he needed from them.

"Unbelievable." Diem walked out of the room, off the veranda, and into the stand of trees that led to her favorite spot along the river. Kest watched her go and did not follow. He would let her calm down for a while and then go after her. She would probably go find Jack and lament over his decision with the troublesome human. Kest did not like her friendship with the man, but there was nothing he could do about it. Since he gave Diem his promise not to hurt the man, he tried to accept her need to talk to him.

"Welcome, my friend," Kest said to Adym without turning around.

Adym had heard part of the argument that Kest and Diem had and wondered why Kest voted the way he did, knowing that it would make Diem mad.

"Because of the reasons I stated in the council meeting but also because I am afraid that if the Yidderians are released, she will go with them," Kest answered.

"She won't. She will stay with you, but you already know that, so why do you worry?"

Kest gazed out at the view before him and ignored Adym's question. "What brings you here today?" He asked instead.

"Do you remember when we first found Diem and took her to the blue waters? She wasn't in any way attracted to them, but

I am curious if she has ever shown an interest in any of the other colors."

Kest turned around and saw his friend leaning against the door jamb. He sat down in one of the chairs on the veranda and waited until Adym sat as well.

"She has never said it, but I have always wondered if she is attracted to the red waters. I have never asked her, but I have noticed that the few times we have sat around them while visiting Tayin she gazes at them with a look of longing. I have never thought about asking her to try getting in the waters."

"Why not?" Adym queried.

"I am not sure. I guess I figured that if she was, she would find herself unable to resist and enter on her own. She has never expressed interest in swimming in the red waters, so I assumed that the longing I have seen might be for something else entirely." Kest leaned forward, "Why do you ask?"

"I have often wondered if the one we search for may be more like us than we thought. I think it may be possible that she will be drawn to the waters and become as we are, at least in some ways. We thought that of Diem, and while she was not drawn to the blue waters, maybe she would be drawn to one of the others. The one we wait for, of course, could never be SeiOrhii as she is part Yidderian, but maybe the allurmonuhra can be as some of the LuZivot and have our gifts in a much more minor form."

Kest let a look of hope cross his face, he knew that Diem was not SeiOrhii, but he had never thought that she might have the lifespan of the LuZivot. This meant that his time with her would be far longer than he had hoped. He smiled, "I have never given that a thought. If she ever shows more than a passing interest or actually swims in the water and does receive SeiOrhii gifts, I will let you know."

"Thank you. Now I must be off. Say hi to Diem for me when she finally cools down enough to talk with you again."

Kest watched Adym leave and then went looking for Diem. He shifted into one of the smaller birds and flew through the trees until he found her, and sure enough, she was with Jack. He sat on a branch high above them and listened in to their conversation.

"There is no need to be angry Diem. We will find a way to escape once the time comes and the gates are opened. For all we know, they might not even be open in our lifetime. We will wait and plan once the monsters find the Yidderian girl they are waiting for." Jack said, his arm around Diem and her head resting on his shoulder.

"They are not monsters, Jack. They are SeiOrhii, and their need to feed on us is not something that they have a choice in. You know that. And it is not so bad; after a few hours of being scared, life returns to normal. They are actually quite kind and caring." Diem reprimanded her friend.

Kest smiled inwardly at her words. She did understand, and she did listen to why he had chosen to vote no. She just didn't like it. He continued listening to their conversation.

"Tell him you love him," Jack said after a few minutes of silence.

"I can't," Diem replied, sitting up and raising her head from Jack's shoulder.

"Why? I do not like the man, but he deserves to know you love him."

"You know why, and I won't discuss this topic again." Diem stood up and went to stand by the river's edge. The water moved slowly by the bank, but she could see the eddies created by its swiftness curling around the rocks and branches that protruded from the water. She smiled in memory of swimming this river with Kest. She loved watching him take animal form and enjoying the simple things of life as the animal he inhabited did. Diem turned back to Jack.

"Thank you for listening to my worries and troubles, Jack. I don't know what I would do without you. When the time comes I will help you in any way that I can. Someday, you and our daughter and grandchildren will leave the Myst and be free to explore the whole of Yiddera." Diem kissed Jack's cheek. "I must go, my friend. Kest will soon come looking for me, and I do not want him to find you here with me. He already doesn't like you and I spending time together and I do not want to give him an excuse to break his promise."

"What promise is that?" Jack asked her.

"The promise not to feed on you." She laughed at the scowl on Jack's face, gave him a big hug, and told him goodbye. Then, she walked back toward the house.

Kest followed leisurely, high in the sky, and smiled at the beauty of the day. Diem was intent on helping the Yidderians escape the Myst when possible. He would have to keep an eye on her and Jack. He could not let her know that he had overheard her words, but he also could not let her think that he would let her go once the gates were open. He let his mind wander to what Adym had said earlier and wondered if Diem might be attracted to the waters. While he had accepted the idea that his life would be short once they bonded, he did like the idea that if she was like the LuZivot, they would have much longer than he had ever hoped to have with her. And, if she was LuZivot, the Yidderians had no hope of his changing his vote. He would never risk her leaving him for the outside world.

Usually, Novalie didn't pay much attention to the blue girls, but this one was new, and she had come to them at the age of twelve. Odd as that was, since the law stated they must be brought to the monastery by age two, it was something about the way she looked that caught Novalie's attention. This girl reminded her of herself in many ways when she was that age. Her looks, movements, and even what she liked to eat were similar to her and her mother. Novalie watched as the girl walked down the hall with the other stinking blue girls around her age.

Novalie walked up to the line of girls and pointed at this new one. "You come with me."

Moonsyrah looked up at the young woman and then at the headmistress and, with a nod, followed her. Novalie led the girl to a quieter section of the busy hall and then, turning to question her, accidentally brushed up against her arm. Novalie's eyes rolled into the back of her head, and she fell to the ground. Moonsyrah, unsure what to do, placed the cloak she was carrying under the Prophetess-in-waiting's head and then ran to find the headmistress to help her.

Novalie lay there, conscious but deep within a vision. This one was so real that she could feel the fire licking her skin as she helped a badly burned man down the hall away from her mother's room. She could see a blue-haired man carrying one of the blue girls, and it was from her that the fire was coming. Novalie concentrated on the vision, trying to memorize every detail so that she would know what to do when this event occurred. She saw that her mother's rooms were engulfed in flames, the man she herself led away was burned across his chest and half of his face, and it was obvious the destruction occurred sometime in the night.

Novalie sat up and took a few deep cleansing breaths. Rarely did a vision take control of her and cause her to blackout and fall. She had learned to stand calmly and breathe through them, but this one was so much more intense than any other she had previously. She sat against the wall and reflected on what she had seen. The feeling of the vision was still with her. Novalie knew she loved the man she helped and that he was destined to be by her side. She knew that her mother had died in the fire and that this strange blue girl, so like herself, was the cause of the destruction. And, if she was correct, since the girl was being carried by a man with blue hair, this demon-born travesty was the one foretold to open the gates of hell.

Novalie opened her eyes to her mother's touch and looked up to see the girl of her vision standing next to her. Seeing them together, Novalie knew without a doubt that this girl was her mothers or related to her somehow. How, she was not sure, but there could be no question that she was.

"Novalie, are you okay?" The Prophetess asked as she helped her daughter off of the floor.

"I am fine. I just had a particularly jarring vision and was not able to remain standing through it, but I am perfectly fine." She straightened her dress and looked at the young girl in front of her.

"Mother, I think that one," She pointed in disdain at the blue girl. "Should be given extra tuition in the Calling. I foresee the need to set her on the right path. I fear that she is more demon than the others."

"Novalie, we will talk of this in my office. Meet me there in two hours' time." The Prophetess turned to the young girl, "Come, I think it is time that you got your own room. There are four available to choose from."

Novalie watched her mother escort the stinking demon born away and then hurried to her room to write down every detail of her vision so she would not forget even the slightest thing. Once in her room, the vision was recorded in her journal. Afterward, Novalie changed her dress and when she went to leave the room, the paintings on her wall caught her eye. She went over to them and looked at the trio. The first was a painting done by Prophetess Alena. It depicted a green landscape that was both something out of your favorite dream and your worst nightmare. In the middle of the painting, a verse had been written:

Nature will rise and become our salvation from Nightmare.
Nightmare will become Dream.
And only Dream can save us from Nature's wrath
and keep her from destroying the world.

Novalie looked at the second painting done by Prophetess Eliana. This one, too, depicted a world of green with nightmare images swirling in the clouds, and the trees were twisted into grotesque depictions of what they should look like. Again, a verse was written in the middle of the painting:

Nightmare will engulf us in darkness.

Nature will kill us all in sorrow.

Is Dream but a distant memory?

The third painting was done by herself when she was 14. It was a picture painted in soft greens. All of the pictures were of the same landscape, but the first was a melding of hopes and fears. The second was of death and destruction. Hers depicted a scene that looked as if healing and peace were just on the horizon. And as with the others, hers, too, had a verse in the middle.

Only Nature can heal Nightmare.

And only Dream can heal Nature.

Novalie had the paintings moved from their original place to her room after she had the third vision in the series. None of the previous Prophetesses had understood the meaning of the first two, and Novalie's was added as it had the same theme and talked of Nature and Nightmares. She had not been able to make any sense of the vision, but as with the first two visions, she had received hers after a visit to the Rainbow Falls. She studied them for a few more minutes and, still not understanding their meaning, left to go to her mother's room. She might have the paintings moved to the small chapel across the Monastery from where her mother's apartments were. She did not want them to be destroyed by the fire, and she knew, somehow, that the small chapel, made entirely of the strange substance brought from Earth with the settlers, would not be harmed in the great fire to come.

Novalie started a pot of tea and straightened the cushions on the couch before her mother arrived. She poured out two cups, sat one in front of her mother, and took a sip from the other cup, settling herself into the high-backed chair across from the couch.

"How is she related to us?" Novalie asked as a way of greeting.

"She was my cousin Syrah's daughter." The Prophetess got a faraway look in her eye, and Novalie could see her mother hold back a tear.

"Why did she not come to us as an infant?" She watched her mother closely.

The Prophetess looked down at her cup, away from her daughter's searching eyes. "Syrah told me that her daughter died, and I did not question it. But that no longer matters. Moonsyrah is here now, and we can give her the tuition that you feel she requires. Now tell me of your vision." She said, putting her cup on the table.

"This girl lets the demons free. I am sure of it. Though her hair was different in my vision, I know she is the one the prophecy, we all hope is never fulfilled, speaks of." Novalie drained her cup, set it down, and then pulled a coverlet off the back of the chair to wrap herself in.

"She causes a fire. A great fire that will consume the Monastery, at least, that is how I interpret the vision I received." Novalie began to tell her mother the details, and together, they talked through possible interpretations, but both women felt that Novalie's interpretation was correct.

"I have helped her pick out a new room so that she is kept distanced from others like her, except her roommate. She has chosen the small room at the top of the tower and will share the apartment with Sameen. Sameen is a good girl, and I think she will be a good friend to Moonsyrah and keep us informed on anything Moonsyrah does that she thinks we might need to know. I have asked her to come to me with any concerns and questions as Moonsyrah is so new to the monastery and may need help adjusting to our way of life."

"I still do not understand why we must have the stinking demon-born girls living within the monastery walls," Novalie replied.

"Because they need protection from those that may wish them harm. Only one is destined to set the demons free, and I, along with the past Prophetesses, do not want to see them hurt because of the destiny of one."

Novalie shrugged her shoulders. She did not care if they were protected or not, and this Moonsyrah was the first she would get rid of if given the choice. "Are you going to give her extra tuition in the Calling?" She asked her mother.

"Not in the conventional way. I have always left attending the meetings a choice for those who reside here. Most people attend one or two a week, but I have never forced them to. I do not want to make the girl attend if she is not inclined, as that may cause her to resent the Calling, and if she is the one who frees the demons, we want her not to resent us. I thought I would have her join us in our morning meditations and learn of the Calling in that manner. I want her to feel free to talk to us so that when the time comes for her to fulfill her destiny, we will know and can stop her from releasing the demons from inside the Myst."

Novalie silently questioned her mother's motivation, feeling that her mother wanted to be near this girl. She was disgusted by what she thought was her mother's true reason for wanting the girl to attend their morning meditations, but she did not speak against the suggestion. Novalie would not treat this girl any different than any of the other blue abominations. They were beneath her and did not deserve the sympathy or care that full-blooded Yidderians did. Novalie decided that while it was her mother's right to treat them as she chose, it was her right to do the same. They were less than, and they were made to serve her in any capacity she saw fit. Novalie made up her mind then and there to make sure that when she was around, the blue girls knew their true place.

Moonsyrah was walking down the hall, following her class, when a girl pointed at her and told her to follow. She had looked to the headmistress and, after receiving a nod to do as the girl asked, followed her down the hall. The young woman stopped and started to say something when she fainted and fell to the floor. Moonsyrah looked around and, seeing no one to help, made the girl comfortable and then ran down the hall and straight into the Prophetess.

"Please, ma'am, I need your help." Moonsyrah grabbed her hand, not noticing the Prophetess grit her teeth at the touch, and dragged her toward the fallen woman. She stood back and watched the Prophetess help her up, and Moonsyrah realized that the young woman was the Prophetess's daughter and could see she was loved by the Prophetess. She waited for them to finish conversing and had to keep quiet when the young woman spoke to her as if she wasn't there.

Moonsyrah then followed the Prophetess down the hall and up several flights of stairs. She reached out to help the Prophetess and stopped when she saw the woman pull her arm out of Moonsyrah's reach.

"I am sorry, my lady. I did not mean to offend you with my touch." Moonsyrah was bewildered by the Prophetess's reaction to her.

"No, it is I who am sorry, my child. You, more so than the other blue girls, increase my sense of unease when you touch me. I am not sure why, but those of you born under the moon of Allura have a slight." She hesitated, "Well, to be honest, you increase our fears with your presence. You all have an energy that is unnerving. I will work to ignore it, as I do not want you to feel uncomfortable around me."

Moonsyrah looked sad. "I am sorry. I did not know. My adoptive mother was never afraid of me, and she allowed me to hug her all the time."

"Adoptive mother?" The Prophetess asked.

"Her last words to me indicated that she was not my birth mother. Where are we going, ma'am?"

"I am taking you to look at a couple of rooms, and I want you to choose which you would like to call your own. I think you are old enough now to move from the dormitories." The Prophetess continued up one more small flight of stairs and showed a lovely room to her that overlooked the maze and then another one that viewed the pond. It was the third room that she was shown that Moonsyrah chose. This one was much smaller than the others, but when she stood on the balcony she saw the wall of blue Myst rising in the distance and felt a sense of peace and welcome as she looked at it. Moonsyrah knew this was her room. She wanted to look at the Myst every day. It called to her as nothing else ever had, and if she listened closely and blocked out the noise around her, she could hear the music of the colored crystals.

"I will take this room." She told the Prophetess, who had followed her into the room. Moonsyrah came back inside from the balcony and knew the room was just right.

"Very good. Now, the room across from the living area belongs to a girl named Sameen. I think the two of you will get along beautifully. She will help you with anything that you need. Now I must go and talk with Novalie, so run along and gather your belongings and move them here. Sameen can show you around the monastery from here so that you do not get lost. I will see you later in the week, and we can discuss the duties that you will be given in addition to your classes." The Prophetess turned to leave and then looked back at her once more. Moonsyrah saw a strange look cross her face and, not wanting to acknowledge what it meant, walked back out onto the balcony to look at the lovely view.

Moonsyrah heard the front door close and left her room to wonder around the rest of the apartment. The living area was cozy, with a large couch and a fireplace. Behind the couch and next to the front door was a kitchenette. Moonsyrah saw that it was well stocked and that she could make her own food there. She liked the idea of eating what she wanted whenever she wanted. She went back into her room and found that it contained a private bathroom with a large shower. She lay on the bed and stared at the high ceiling for a few minutes before leaving to go and gather her meager belongings. Moonsyrah thought that she would also gather a couple of bouquets of flowers to make her first night in the room welcoming.

She walked down the stairs eager to meet her new roommate and decided to gather extra flowers for her as well. Moonsyrah spent a happy couple of hours placing her clothes in the closet and arranging her room just so before she heard her roommate enter the apartment. She went out to meet her and was a bit dismayed that the girl was so much older than her. Moonsyrah had hoped for a friend closer to her own age but decided it didn't really matter how old someone was; it was how they treated others that did.

She handed the young woman the bouquet she had gathered. "My name is Moonsyrah." She said.

"Hello, Moonsyrah, I am Sameen." Sameen took the flowers and put them in an empty vase that was sitting on the fireplace mantel. "I am so glad I have a roommate now. It gets lonely in the evenings. It will be nice having you to share dinner with and discuss our days. Do you have everything that you need? If not, let me know, and I will show you where to get it from." Sameen sat on the couch and waited for Moonsyrah to join her.

"The Prophetess said that you would show me around the Monastery from this room so that I do not get lost, but I do not need that as I have a very good sense of where I am. I do wonder if you can show me around the grounds, though. I have not yet had the opportunity to explore them." Moonsyrah asked the friendly woman.

Sameen smiled. "I would love to show you the grounds. There are so many wonderful things to see and explore. Have you been to the village yet?" She asked.

"No, the headmistress would not allow it."

"It is only Wednesday, but let's explore some of the grounds this week, and we can go into the village this weekend. I have the whole of Saturday free, and that will give us time to explore to our heart's content."

Sameen and Moonsyrah talked for a while longer and then, in agreeable companionship, made dinner together. Sameen treated Moonsyrah as an equal and not as the little girl she had first thought she would be treated as. Over the next few days, the girls became good friends and looked forward to their trip to the village. Saturday morning dawned bright and clear, and it looked like it would be a warm autumn day when the two girls were surprised by the Prophetess knocking on their door.

Moon, Sameen's nickname for her, invited the Prophetess in and offered her a drink which was declined.

"I can see that you two are headed out, and I do not want to keep you, but I have come by today to let you know that I expect you, Moonsyrah, to be in my quarters at sunrise tomorrow for morning meditations. Every morning at dawn, I will expect you to attend the morning rituals, and then you will have classes and attend me as needed throughout the day. I have been needing an assistant, and you will do nicely. I will instruct you in your duties to me tomorrow." The Prophetess made to leave before handing Moonsyrah a small coin purse. "I heard you would be exploring the village today and thought that I would give you a few coins to help you enjoy your day. Consider it an advance on what you will make as my assistant."

Moonsyrah held the purse and, along with Sameen, watched the lady sweep gracefully from the room.

"You must have made quite an impression on her Moon. I have never heard of a blue girl being allowed in her rooms or assisting her in her duties." Sameen gathered her own purse, and the two left the monastery and walked down to the village.

Moonsyrah picked out a beautiful white and pink fabric that she thought would make a lovely comforter for her bed and would match the fabric she had chosen from the monastery stores for curtains. Both girls bought new ribbons from the ribbon shop and then enjoyed lunch at the tea shop. After lunch, Moonsyrah headed down a path that led to the other side of town and smiled at the wall of Myst looming even closer than she had expected.

Sameen stopped Moonsyrah, who was inclined to continue down the path. "No, we cannot go that way. It leads to the Rainbow Falls and they are forbidden. It also leads to a path that will take you close to the Myst gates, and we mustn't go near them. As blue girls, we are to keep away from anything that might entice our demon halves to grow stronger."

Moonsyrah stopped and followed Sameen back into town, making careful note of where they were so that she could some-day make her way back to Rainbow Falls. She had not realized that they were so close to the Monastery, and while the thought of seeing them again brought her much sadness, there was some-thing intriguing about them that made her want to explore them once more. Moonsyrah also knew that she wanted to see the Myst up close and touch it. She did not believe that she was part demon just because her eyes glowed and her hair was partially blue and she definitely did not believe that being at the falls or touching the Myst would turn her into a demon. She brushed aside the memory of the fire that flew from her hands. She told herself that the fire was not real. It was just a trick her mind had played on her. No one could produce fire from their hands.

YEAR 402

"THE DEMONS SHALL BE freed and will walk Yiddera, feeding on those who give into their fears. Feeding on those who do not believe in Y'ddra. They will ravage the land, spreading fear, despair, and hopelessness. As we know, one has been prophesied to release these demons to feed on us." The Prophetess looked up from her reading and stared out at her audience, briefly locking eyes with the young woman with bright blue streaks in her hair before continuing.

"Remember that fear is only in the mind, and those who believe will be protected by Y'ddra. It is important to excise any fear you have so that it might not be used against you. Now let us bow our heads in prayer to the Goddess."

Moonsyrah made a scoffing sound low in her throat and stepped just outside of the door to wait for the Prophetess to finish. She did not like it when she had to attend the Prophetess during one of the morning meetings. Moonsyrah did not hold the same beliefs as the Prophetess and her many followers. Though most of the world was of the same faith, Moonsyrah could not bring herself to believe that demons were real and waiting to be released from the Myst to feed on them. Nor could she accept that the girls, unfortunate enough to have been born while Allura was in the sky, were destined to be the downfall of humanity.

She heard the "amen" and knew it was now okay to go back into the room. Moonsyrah handed the Prophetess her schedule for the day and then, checking to see if she would be needed for anything further, excused herself to tidy the room. Once she had put away the prayer books and straightened the cushions, she hurried out of the room and raced across the grounds so that she might spend some time at the falls.

She came to the waterfall that cascaded down into a massive lake of clear crystals. It shimmered and dazzled the senses in the bright light of day. Even with all the beauty, the place was eerie, and people stayed away from it. It was often said that, though they couldn't figure out why, a person's deepest fears rose to the surface of their minds. Rumors abounded about the significance of the place. All more fantastic than the last. The religious leaders encouraged these rumors to keep people away from the falls.

Only the Prophetess knew that some of the rumors were true. According to the first prophetess, Alena, the demons from the Myst held this place sacred. Not wanting anyone hurt by the evil beings currently locked in the Myst (thanks to Amalie), the current Prophetess enforced the law that forbade bathing in the hot springs.

Moonsyrah was different. Unlike other humans and daughters of the Alluran moon, she did not find the waters eerie. They called to her and bade her to swim in their depths. She felt more like herself here than anywhere else on Yiddera. Moonsyrah entered the cave and, disrobing, reclined in the pink hot spring. She closed her eyes and enjoyed the dreams that this particular pond gave her. The waters seemed to awaken her inner desires yet also reminded her of her own innocence. She lay there for almost an hour before stepping out of the warmth. She slipped into her dress and leisurely walked over to the pool of storms. The color of the bath drew her to it. The aura given off by the purple storm called to her mind, body, and soul.

Tucking her cornflower blue braid behind her ear, she stooped down and picked up a stone from the purple pool. The stone vibrated gently in her hand. She felt as if it was spreading fire through her veins. Only once before had she touched the waters and rocks of the purple basin. She had felt the fire then as well. It was not a good memory.

Seven years ago today, she had visited this place. Seven years ago today, she had plunged her hand into the pool that reminded her of a storm at midnight. Seven years ago, today, her life had changed. Though it was the purple pool that awakened her fire, she feared the green one the most. It had fed the fire running through her and had been the last place she had been before her nightmare began. It was the pool she associated with death.

Now, at nineteen, she no longer feared the power of Rainbow Falls; she reveled in the energy that surrounded her, reveled in the very air that seemed steeped in mystery. She enjoyed the waters of the ponds regularly but still would not enter the purple storm. She knew that it would change her life once more, and she was not yet ready for that. She would also never enter the green pool as it was the most painful reminder of that horrible day. She shook away her thoughts and looked back at the purple crystal she held.

Clutching the sparkling stone tightly in her hand, Moonsyrah headed up the path leading out of the cavern and to the river that created the falls. She meandered the banks of the river until she crossed over it and reached the beginning of the Myst barrier. Putting out a hand, she caressed the soft, slightly damp gate and saw it shimmer and ripple under her hand. Listening carefully, she could make out the slight murmur of sound that seemed to come from inside the Myst. Ever so quietly, she could also hear faint off-key music. The music was compelling and tugged at her mind. It seemed to come from the Falls, the Myst, and somewhere closer to the monastery. She held the crystal closer to her ear and found the music very softly coming from it as well.

With her hand still trailing in the Myst, Moonsyrah called out with her mind and heart.

"Is anyone there? Do you really exist?" Feeling ridiculous for even asking, she listened intently and heard no response. Again, she called out, "Hello, if you are there, please answer me." Briefly, she thought she caught sight of the silhouette of a man, but the silence was absolute. The wind kicked up, and her hair came free of its confines. Moonsyrah closed her eyes and enjoyed the feel of the wind swirling around her. This moment touched her very soul. The magic she perceived in it called out to her, and she briefly felt a surge of the fire within her. She enjoyed the feeling for a few minutes, then she opened her eyes and took in the beauty of the scenery around her before heading back home to the monastery.

Later that night, Moonsyrah stood out on her balcony and looked out into the distance. The evening air was brisk with a hint of autumn in it. The sunset was beautiful. Pinks and oranges splayed out across the sky and made the brilliant blue of the Myst seem darker. It was a lovely contrast of light and dark and made the evening sky look like a painting. The third moon, Allura, was creeping higher in the sky, causing everything to be tinged with its blue glow.

She had chosen this particular room when she was younger precisely due to this view. No other room in the monastery looked out onto the Myst so well. Knowing all she had to do was step out onto her balcony to see the beautiful blue curtain gave her a sense of peace.

Moonsyrah had never told anyone how she felt about the Myst or Rainbow Falls. She knew that if she did, people would consider her stranger than they already did. As it was, she had very few friends. Humans seemed to feel uneasy around her. Even other girls born under the Alluran moon felt slightly apprehensive around her. She had learned to accept this difference, but she did not want to make people any more leery of her than they already were.

Breathing deeply of the night air, she let down the guard that she kept in place around her mind. She called out to the Myst, letting it into her very soul. She felt a moment of freedom in not blocking her mind against unwanted thoughts and ideas. All blue girls were taught to keep their minds locked against the chance that the demons might enter and take over their souls. Tonight, Moonsyrah did not care if demons actually existed or not. She wanted her mind to be free. Feeling reckless, she welcomed the chance of hearing someone, if indeed there was someone out there who could be heard through thought alone.

"Are you there?"

She searched for the sound of voices coming from the Myst and heard none. At that moment, she knew that the demons were not real. The murmurs she thought she heard occasionally must be part of her imagination, for if they were genuinely there, she would perceive them now. Surprised at the disappointment she felt when there was no answer, she left the balcony, set the purple crystal in a bowl on her nightstand, and got ready for bed.

Adym was sitting in front of the glass wall and looking out onto the garden surrounding the house when he heard someone calling out. He sat forward on the yellow and white striped couch and listened intently to the sound. He heard the voice of a woman asking if someone was there. He followed the words and found the mind of the one who uttered them. Adym was surprised to find the voice belonged to the girl from outside of the Myst gates, and in his surprise, he let her see his silhouette within her mind. He stood up and saw the girl with blue braids walk away from the Myst. He felt her disappointment in not being answered.

He left her mind and wondered what this could mean. The blue girl had not called out in several years. Indeed, he had begun to believe that she was not the one they waited for. His heart leaped in excitement to hear her call out to him. Had the time finally come? Was she ready to fulfill her destiny?

Adym searched his own memory and found the image he was looking for. Years ago, when the girl was twelve, she had unknowingly called out to him while at the sacred waters. He had watched as she and her mother had enjoyed the lake below Rainbow Falls. He watched as she tripped, and her hand came in contact with the purple pond. He felt her tremble at the energy that swept through her. He entered her mind and encouraged her to dwell on the fire that coursed through her. Adym was there when she used her gift of fire for the first time; in fact, he encouraged her to use it.

Adym left his remembrance and focused on what happened today. He had looked for this girl's mind since that day seven years ago and could not find it, and now here she was calling out to him. Observing her from inside her mind once again, he watched as she made her way back to the monastery walls. He was with her when she called out to him while watching the sunset. He heard her thoughts as she came to the conclusion that his kind was not real. He watched her until she fell asleep.

Adym called an urgent meeting with the Elders and the rest of the SeiOrhii. He met them within the hour in the council chambers on Zeljani. Adym waited patiently for the Elders to sit on one side of the table and his peers to sit opposite them. He continued to wait until Elder Brecher called him to speak. Then, bowing his head in respect for the Elder, Adym stood up and walked to the end of the table so that all might see and hear him.

"Years ago, I came across a child that I suspected might be the one we have been waiting for." Adym paused at the excited sounds elicited by everyone at the table.

"Son, why did you not tell us this before? Why keep this news to yourself?" Elder Brecher questioned.

"I did not want to get anyone's hopes up." Adym paused in his speech, "Today, I heard her again. I am certain she is the one who will free us. I intend to study her and figure out how best to get her to find the key and unlock the Myst gates. If I am correct, we will soon be roaming the hunting grounds of Yiddera once more." Adym looked around the table and saw hope on everyone's face except for Tayin's. He did not look hopeful. Instead, he wore the same scowl that he always did.

"Tayin, do you doubt?" Adym queried his best friend.

"It is not that I doubt, but I will not get my hopes up until I see that you are right. Once we are free, I will believe you have found the right girl." Tayin stated.

Elder Brecher stood up and held out his hand to silence the crowd. "Adym, do what needs to be done. It is time we were set free. Y'ddra needs us. You have told us how the stones in the lake have lost their color. We need to restore them and heal Y'ddra. We must have access to Rainbow Falls. We must start the sacrifice once again to bring our planet back to her full glory." Elder Brecher paused, "What do you need from us to accomplish this task?"

"I do not know at this time. I will let you know when I do." Adym bowed his head once more and took his seat between Tayin and Raighn.

The Elders adjourned the meeting and, as a group, left the council hall. Adym stayed seated with the other house leaders. They sat in silence for a minute or two before Raighn spoke.

"How do you plan to start with this girl?"

Adym thought for a moment and then answered, "I plan to start simple. I will start by talking to her and observing her. Then, once she is used to me, and I know what she is afraid of, I will use that to get her to do our bidding."

"I will let you get on with it then. I have a blue girl of my own to deal with." Kest shifted into the form of a cave cat and bounded out of the room, heading back to Geltahn. Raighn pushed back his chair, nodded his goodbye, and left for his own home on Lioleta.

"When will you leave the Myst?" Tayin inquired softly. Adym glanced over at his friend and saw the worry there.

"Only when I need to so that I can take her the second half of the key. I do not plan to be out of the Myst for long."

"You are the only one who can exit the Myst, but I worry about how much it drains you. You almost did not make it back the last time you left." Tayin said.

Adym put his hand on Tayin's shoulder. "This time, I will have the key in hand, and the gates will be unlocked. There is no need to worry. Soon, we will all be able to come and go as we please."

Tayin lifted his lips in a grim travesty of a smile. "And the humans will pay for shutting us away."

The two men walked out of the meeting chamber together. Once they reached the Hall of Myst, they went their separate ways; Tayin to Kofira and Adym back to Elynas.

Jack had never purposely sought out Kest before, but today, he needed to have words with the man. Jack walked up the stairs and knocked boldly on the front door. He waited a few minutes, and as he knew would happen from past experience, a Tarikan opened the door and signaled for him to wait. He sat on the chair he was shown to and waited impatiently for Kest to arrive. He was kept waiting for about half an hour before he stood up in frustration and headed toward the door. This was a waste of time, and he didn't really want to be here anyway.

"Then why are you?"

Jack turned and saw Kest walking toward him and knew that he had been kept waiting purposefully.

"Of course you were. I wanted to see how long your patience would last, but then I became curious as to why you would come here and even more so about why you are here to see me and not Diem." Kest sat in the chair across from the one that Jack had recently vacated and waited for his unwanted guest to sit back down.

Jack wore a scowl on his face and briefly thought of just leaving, but he had come here for a reason, and no matter how distasteful this visit was to him, he was here and might as well get on with it.

"It is rumored that Adym has found the girl that the prophecy speaks of. Is this true?" He asked his enemy.

Kest lifted an eyebrow in inquiry, "What does it matter to you?"

"The same as it does to you. Once the gates are open, I am taking my family, and I am leaving. Many of the families here want to go explore the world outside of the Myst, and yes, it is true that some plan to stay."

"None of you will leave unless we allow it, Jack." Kest interrupted.

"And this is why I am here today. Let us go, Kest. I do not understand why you always vote against our leaving, but heed me when I say that it is in your best interest to let us go."

"Is that a threat?" Kest asked in a calmly dangerous voice.

"No." Jack laughed with little pleasure. "It is a warning. I have never made it a secret that I do not like you and that I think that Diem is making a mistake in being with you, but I do understand that you love her. More than your own life, if I am not mistaken. If you do not want to lose her, let us go. She will help us, and I will do my best to convince her to come with us, and you will only make that easier for me if you vote against her wishes." Jack stood up, "On the other hand, go ahead and vote against her. Then she will leave this absurd relationship and return to her family where she belongs."

"Sit," Kest told Jack with command in his voice. Jack sat, wanting to hear what Kest would say.

"Why? Why are you giving me this advice? I know you hope I don't do as you ask, so why bother coming to me with this suggestion?

Jack was quiet momentarily and looked at the man who had taken his heart from him. "Because I understand what it means to lose Diem. I understand how hard it is to see her with someone other than yourself, and for as much as I do not like you and I pray every day that she leaves you, I do not want you to know that pain. Even you do not fully deserve the pain of losing the most important person to you. But Kest, you will lose her if you continue this path." Jack stood up for the last time and let himself out of the house. He did not want Diem to know that he had been there, and for some reason, he was sure that Kest would not want her to know either.

He walked along the road and headed to the area by the river where he had first met Diem and was not surprised to find her there. He sat down next to her, and together, they looked out at the river for a few moments. He took her hand and grinned when she scooted closer to him.

"Do you remember when we first met?" He asked her.

"I do. You were so messy that I thought being near you would get me dirty." She laughed.

"And you were right. The moment I first saw you, I wanted to be friends. I just knew that you were special." Jack said and then was quiet once more. "Diem, the rumors are true that the girl has been found, which leads me to believe the gates will open soon. What are you going to do?"

"Jack, we have discussed this before. I will help you leave, but I will not go with you."

"I know, but I will never stop hoping."

Diem kicked a rock with her foot and then adjusted her skirts around her again. Jack smirked at her habit. He had seen her adjust her skirts to look perfect her whole life, and still, he found it funny.

"I think that once the gates open and Kest leaves to hunt across the world once again, we should quickly gather everyone and meet here by the river. We can have rafts waiting and hidden in this nook. The river would be the quickest way out, and there would be less chance of predators stopping us."

"Predators?" Jack questioned.

"Kest will find out, and he will try and stop us. If he cannot get to us, he will send the animals to do the job." Jack shook his head in acknowledgment of the truth in her words. "I think that you have a sound plan. I will have everyone gather a few personal belongings to take with them and have them ready to grab when the time comes. I will also see to the rafts. I do not want you involved in most of the planning. If you do not know exactly what is going on, then Kest is less likely to find out the details."

Diem looked affronted at Jack's words. "I will not tell him the plans, Jack."

"I know, but he has daily access to your mind, and I want to ensure that he has as little chance as possible of thwarting us. Will you come across the Myst with us?"

"No, I will not step out of the Myst without Kest. I will help you get to the barrier, where I will leave you." Diem squeezed Jack's hand in hers. "Find a beautiful place that you can be happy in. I will miss you, Lela, and the grandkids. Tell them every day that I love them."

"I will, Diem." Jack kissed her cheek. "Now I must leave. I have plans to make. When the time comes to make our move, let me know. We will be ready." Jack left Diem sitting on the log under the willow tree.

Moonsyrah woke with a start. She sat up in bed, barely breathing, and listened intently for the sound that had awakened her. She glanced over at her door and saw that it was closed. She then looked toward her balcony and saw the wind gently ruffling the drapes. It was still dark out, and she should try and go back to sleep, but she knew that she would not be able to.

Hearing nothing but the night sounds, she decided she must have dreamt the quiet voice whispering hello. But she could not shake the feeling that she was being watched. She threw back the covers and got out of bed. Moonsyrah went over to her door and, opening it quietly, looked toward Sameen's room. Sameen's door was closed, so it wasn't Sameen who called to her or observed her. She walked onto her balcony and looked up at the stars twinkling in the light of the Alluran moon. The blue shadow that it cast blocked out the light from the other two moons, causing the night to seem darker than usual. Being on the top floor of the monastery, she knew that no one would be out there, but she felt compelled to look for the source of the voice anyway.

Wide awake, she went into her bathroom and, undressing, stepped into the shower. She let the hot water cascade over her body and could feel her tension slowly slide away. She soaped her long blue-blonde hair and was about to rinse it when she thought she heard a wistful sigh, and the idea that she was being watched intensified. She stuck her head out of the shower and saw that no one was there. She hurriedly finished her shower and, wrapping the towel around her, returned to her room to dress for the day.

Moonsyrah could not understand why she felt this way. Was this sensation leftover from her dream? Yesterday she had called out to the mythical demons to talk to her. When there was no answer, she had been strangely disappointed, and now she thought she was being watched. Was there really someone or something watching her, was it just leftover remnants from her dream, or was she going crazy? She would much rather think herself crazy than start believing that the demons the Prophetess preached of were real. Because if they were real, then it followed that the rest of what the religion spoke of might be true, too. She could not believe that she and the other Daughters of Allura were destined to be the handmaidens of the demons. And worse, that one of them would set the evil things free to feed upon the people of the world.

She braided the two cornflower blue streaks in her hair and tied them back with the rest in the dark rose-colored ribbon that went with her pale pink dress. Once that was done, she headed into the kitchenette and quietly made herself a cup of tea. She grabbed an appleberry muffin and then tiptoed across the living room floor, trying not to make any noise that might awaken Sameen, and let herself out of the apartment. She was halfway down the stairs when she realized that she had forgotten her shoes again. She ran back into the apartment, grabbed the flats that matched her hair ribbon, and left the apartment.

Stopping at the bottom of the stairs, she slipped into the flats and decided to head to the library. It was still too early to present herself to the Prophetess for the day. She walked down two more flights of stairs and across the length of the Abbey to the library. Moonsyrah picked up a light stone and made her way to the back of the large room and into the little alcove that led down another short flight of stairs. Entering the room at the end of the hall, she sat the light stone down on a cabinet and went over to look at the maps of Yiddera hanging on the wall.

Her favorite was the map made by the first humans to set foot on Yiddera. It outlined each of the five continents and was the only map to show the whole shape of each. The original settlers had technology that no one living could even dream of now. They had been able to penetrate the Myst and define the edges of each continental landmass. No one else had ever been able to do that.

While the edges were clearly demarcated, the areas of land and water hidden in the Myst were unclear. These areas were colored blue on the map, but no mountains or rivers were marked through them. It was as if the settlers could somehow see the shapes of the continents but could not see into the Myst itself.

Moonsyrah dreamed of one day seeing the world. She longed to travel to each of the continents, see the people, eat the food, and explore their differences. Yet, she had never been any further than the monastery and its surrounding village. And, if she could not travel the world, she hoped to someday have the chance to explore Alenar, the continent on which she lived. Moonsyrah knew this was an almost empty hope as Daughters of Allura were rarely granted permission to leave the Monastery boundaries.

She reached up a hand and touched the glass that covered the map. She ran her finger down Alenar and touched the tip furthest from where she lived. Moonsyrah wondered what was at the very edge of Alenar. At this thought, an image of a tree popped into her mind. It was a giant tree standing on a rock right next to the ocean water. The tree itself was in full bloom. The leaves were dark emerald green and the size of a dinner plate. Small flowers of an electric purple color were sprinkled throughout the foliage. She had never seen such a tree and could not imagine how it had come to mind.

Moonsyrah stared at the map for a while longer, and the image of the tree remained in her mind until she finally willed herself to look away. She turned from the map and looked at the many books that lined the shelves. One book was open on the table that lay in the middle of the room. She walked over, picked it up, and read about the exploration teams that went to each of the different continents on Yiddera. Next, she read of "The Lost," a group of people who went to Lijiang and were never seen or heard from again. She wondered what had happened to them.

Again, an image popped into her mind. This one was of a group of people who had somehow managed to get through the Myst gates. It showed them scared and trying to get out but unable to leave. The image disappeared as quickly as it had come. Moonsyrah had wondered if "The Lost" entered the Myst, but as no one could even get a hand into it, she had dismissed the notion. The history books speculated that they went down with their ship during a storm, but no proof had been found to authenticate this theory.

Moonsyrah read for a while longer. The history of Yiddera fascinated her almost as much as the maps did. She stopped reading when she realized she had been down in the archives for quite a while and was sure it was time to make her way to the Prophetess' chambers. So, Moonsyrah marked her place in the book, picked up the light stone, and left the room.

On her way to the Prophetess' apartments, she was sure she heard someone whisper to her again. She stopped and looked around, finding nobody nearby. She started walking again when she noticed a shadow of someone behind her. Moonsyrah turned, and as she feared, no one was there. She was beginning to get uneasy so she hurried along the passageway and only felt comfortable once she reached the door that would lead her into the Prophetess' chambers.

She took a deep, calming breath. She did not want Novalie to think she was scared of something, so she sedately entered the room. She joined the Prophetess and Novalie outside in the walled-in meditation garden and began the daily meditation ritual with them. As she relaxed into the exercise, she saw a brief picture of a man in her mind. The vision quickly disappeared. She wondered who he was and then brushed aside these thoughts and relaxed back into her meditations.

As the days passed, Moonsyrah became convinced that she was being watched. She jumped at every little sound and took to peeking around corners and looking behind her as she made her way around the monastery halls. She kept hearing her name whispered softly and thought she felt her braids being tugged on by an unseen hand. Twice, she could have sworn that she felt someone breathe against her cheek. Even more unsettling, her thoughts did not seem to be entirely her own. All the fears she never realized she had would surface often. Pictures of places she had never seen would pop up in her mind when she thought of them. They were memories of places once seen or things once done, but they weren't her memories. She began to wonder if someone had taken up residence in her head. This worried her because the Prophetess said the demons could overtake someone's mind. The Prophetess also warned the Dimoni that their mind was at greater risk of infiltration by the demons because of their likeness to each other.

Sameen kept asking her if she was all right, but Moonsyrah could not answer as she was unsure. How could you tell if you were all right if you weren't even sure what thoughts were your own? Then, one evening, after her classes had commenced, she headed up to her room when she heard a very distinct voice call her name. It was not the whisper she had been hearing, but it was the same voice. Looking behind her, she saw no one. Scared, she ran the length of the hallway and entered her apartment, locking the door behind her. She then hastened into her own room and locked the bedroom door as well.

Moonsyrah leaned her back against the door and calmed her racing heart. This was becoming silly, she thought as she made her way to the balcony to sit on her meditation mat. Maybe if she meditated, she could get to the bottom of why she felt she was being watched and whose voice she thought she heard. Closing her eyes, Moonsyrah cleared her thoughts and concentrated on the problem at hand. While in repose, she realized that she had never put her mind guard back up after letting it down on her birthday. That was one week ago, and all this had started the next day. Moonsyrah tried to raise the protective barrier when she heard a laugh and felt something pressing against her effort to block her mind.

"No. Now that I am here, you cannot raise the barrier against me again." The male voice said as he gently pushed against her mind.

Moonsyrah opened her eyes in shock and stood up quickly looking around for the person who was talking to her. Seeing no one, she leaned over the edge of the balcony and tried to ignore the notion that she had heard the voice from inside her mind, not from the outside world.

The dark, honeyed voice laughed again. "I said no." And again, she felt a push on the barrier she was trying to place.

Feeling ridiculous, Moonsyrah asked out loud, "Are you the one who has been watching me?"

"Yes." Was the answer she heard.

"Why?"

"I want to learn about you." The voice caressed her mind and left Moonsyrah feeling disturbed. She pushed away from the railing and sat down on the floor, hugging her knees to her chest.

"It is all in my head. There is nothing really there. I am imagining the voice." She whispered to herself over and over again. The voice laughed once more, and Moonsyrah had the oddest sensation that someone had sat down next to her. She scooted a few inches away and, for the first time, prayed to the goddess the Prophetess believed in. She prayed that the voice would go away. She prayed that she wasn't going crazy. Then, Moonsyrah quickly prayed that she would prefer to be crazy than to hear the voice of one of the demons, as she feared might be the alternative. An unseen hand covered hers as if in comfort, but this only made her worry about her sanity. How could she feel a hand that wasn't there?

She remembered the last words her adoptive mother had said to her: "You are demon born." She felt as if her hold on reality was slipping. Moonsyrah started laughing quietly at first and then with increasing hysteria. Her laughter was accompanied by hot tears. She cried and laughed until she wore herself out and fell asleep outside under the evening sky.

She woke cold and cramped on the hard balcony floor just as the sun was starting to peek out from behind the mountain range that encircled the monastery grounds. She stood up and stretched her aching back and limbs. Moonsyrah looked out across the valley at the Myst and felt a sense of peace envelope her. She had always enjoyed the sunrise as it hit the Myst and caused it to glitter and sparkle in various shades of blue. She stood there for a moment, enjoying the quiet of the morning and of her mind.

"This is my favorite time of day as well." The male voice whispered in her mind. A whisper so quiet it was not much more than a breath. Moonsyrah closed her eyes against the intrusion and, if she was honest, against the feeling of rightness that it brought to her. She pushed away from the wall and entered her room. Trying to convince herself that the voice was part of her imagination, she chose to ignore it and muttered to herself, "It is only in my mind." She washed her face and quickly got dressed for the day. If she hurried, she could make it to morning meditations with the Prophetess. Today, she felt as if she needed the introspection.

Moonsyrah made it to the Prophetess's chambers just in time to follow her and Novalie into the meditation garden. Sedately, she sat across from the Prophetess and lit the candle that would help guide them in their reflection. Moonsyrah stared at the candle's flame and felt herself relax and enter into a state of peace and calm. She reflected on the past week and what it might mean to be hearing a voice in her head.

She sank further into her meditation and remembered another time in her life when she had heard voices. She heard them not just when she was at the falls or near the Myst but also when she was a child. No, not them, just him. She had heard this voice before. It had belonged to the man in the yellow room. Moonsyrah had convinced herself, then, that she had created an imaginary friend; now, she hoped it was a symptom of her descent into insanity. She would not believe the voice was that of a demon. They simply could not exist.

"You do not really believe that. Admit to yourself what you know to be true." The voice gently admonished her. He laughed again. "Do not be afraid."

Moonsyrah gasped aloud, and her eyes opened wide. She found the Prophetess and Novalie staring at her. Novalie with scorn and the Prophetess with questioning concern.

"I am sorry to interrupt your meditations. I will leave you to finish undisturbed." Moonsyrah stood up and let herself back into the living room of the Prophetess' quarters. She busied herself making the tea that was taken every morning after the meditative exercises. She set the table with dishes and fresh fruit, adding an assortment of muffins to the fare. As she went about her tasks, she noticed the presence was still in her mind.

She highly suspected that the voice did indeed belong to one of the demons that she did not believe in. But not wanting to admit it, she preferred to convince herself that she had conjured up the voice for some reason. She figured that if he was not real, she could talk to him without fear of reprisal, but if he was real, the implications were more than she could handle.

"You would rather think yourself delusional than think that I am real? That does not sound logical." The voice paused a moment. "Would it be so bad to learn that you are not imagining me?"

"Yes." Moonsyrah emphatically answered out loud just as Novalie stepped into the room. An embarrassed Moonsyrah dropped her head and pulled out a chair for Novalie and then one for the Prophetess. She then sat down at the table after pouring tea for each of them.

The Prophetess shook out her napkin and set it in her lap before speaking. "Moonsyrah, are you feeling okay? You have seemed a bit off this week."

"Off? She has been acting paranoid all week. Looking around corners, jumping if you so much as talk to her, and not attending to her duties properly." Novalie stated matter-of-factly and without regard to Moonsyrah's feelings.

Moonsyrah disliked Novalie, and her dislike was reciprocated. Moonsyrah looked up at Novalie, and anger flitted across her face. She did not care that Novalie was the prophetess-in-waiting; she did not appreciate being talked of as if she was not here.

"Novalie, mind your tongue." Reprimanded the Prophetess. Moonsyrah grinned behind her napkin as a blush spread over Novalie's beautiful face.

"Tell me what has been bothering you lately." Commanded the Prophetess.

Moonsyrah quickly thought about what she could say. However, she did not feel that she could tell the Prophetess the truth, at least not with Novalie in the room.

"I have been having bad dreams and not sleeping well. I am sure it will pass." Moonsyrah sipped her tea and hoped the Prophetess would buy her excuse.

"My dear child, you should have come to me. I have a blend of tea that will help you sleep without disruptive dreams. Novalie, will you please get the tin from the cupboard and put some in a bag for Moonsyrah." The Prophetess bit into her muffin and missed the look that Novalie gave her.

Novalie scooped out some of the blended tea, tied it up in a pretty little bag, and then handed it to Moonsyrah. She was not happy about acting as a servant for a blue girl, but she must do as the Prophetess bid her. Moonsyrah thanked her and tucked the bag in the pocket of her dress.

"Now, today, we have much to do. Moonsyrah, I want you to stay behind after breakfast; I need to talk with you. Novalie, go about your duties as usual but remember we are meeting with the council of spiritual advisers this afternoon, so please make sure everything is prepared for that. Please gather my notes and set them on my desk so that we may review them before the meeting." She stood up and placed her napkin on her plate, signaling that breakfast had concluded. She waved Novalie out of the room and went to the couch, gesturing for Moonsyrah to take a seat in the chair opposite her. Moonsyrah watched as Novalie left, and once the door was shut, she sat on one of the beautiful green high-backed chairs across from the green and gold couch on which the Prophetess sat.

"What is really wrong, my child." The Prophetess asked as she adjusted her black skirt around her ankles.

"Mistress, why do you believe that there are demons who live in the Myst? Do you only believe because of what the past prophetesses have said?" Moonsyrah sat forward with an intent look on her face.

"You do not believe in what our religion or our history books teach. Why do you ask this now?" Curiosity filled the Prophetess' question.

"Our history books are rather vague on whether the demons exist or not, and they rely heavily on what the reigning prophetess believed and wanted to have recorded." Moonsyrah took a big breath before continuing. "I have recently experienced something that has made me question my own beliefs. Maybe I have disregarded the idea that you are correct too lightly. Do you believe that the demons are real, or are they just a myth as I suppose them to be?"

Moonsyrah watched as many emotions crossed the Prophetess's face.

"When I was younger, I received a vision of the future at a time when I did not expect to. It was startling. I will not go into details, but suffice it to say the vision not only confirmed my faith in demons but also that the prophecy of them being set free will happen in my lifetime."

The Prophetess gave a sad frown, "Moonsyrah," she paused for a moment, "What is it that has made you ask?"

Moonsyrah felt a tension in her mind that was not her own. She felt more than heard the voice ask her, not to mention that she heard him. She reflected on what it would mean to keep the voice a secret. If she was going crazy, she did not want the Prophetess to know. Still, if she was hearing a demon, she felt it was her responsibility to tell the Prophetess. She listened as a passionate "please" echoed in her mind.

"The dreams have made me question many things in my life, and the existence of demons is one of them. It is nothing to worry about. I will drink your tisane before bed, and I am sure it will help me sleep and clear my mind." Moonsyrah made to stand up when she felt the Prophetess grab her arm.

"If you are hearing voices or think you are dreaming of the demons, you will let me know, won't you?" Again, concern for Moonsyrah was evident in the Prophetess' voice.

Moonsyrah swallowed and gently removed the Prophetess' hand from her arm, "Of course," she lied and then left the Prophetess to sit and wonder if she was telling the truth.

Novalie watched Moonsyrah leave before she walked back into the room from the Prophetess' office.

"Do you believe her?" She questioned.

"It is not becoming to listen to conversations that are not intended for you." The Prophetess scolded her daughter.

"I do not know why you put up with her. She is impertinent and a stinking Alluran moon-born Dimoni. Why do you have her as your assistant? So many others would love to take her place, others who are not tainted with the blood of demons."

Novalie sat down on the chair that Moonsyrah had recently vacated.

"It is not your place to say who I can or cannot choose to serve me." The Prophetess frowned at Novalie. "You will be the next Prophetess, and you really must contain your dislike of those whom you will be caring for. The Daughters of Allura are under our protection and care."

"I have never understood why we shelter them in the first place. The prophecy states clearly that one of them will open the Myst gates and let loose the demons to feed on us. And, if I heard correctly, you have had a vision that this will happen in your lifetime. So why not just kill them all? No one would miss them." Novalie crossed her legs and leaned back into the comfort of the chair.

"Have you ever thought that maybe kindness to the daughters of Allura could keep the prophecy from coming true? That maybe it is our disdain of them that makes one choose the demons over our kind?"

"Hmm, well, If I were the reigning prophetess, I would make them disappear. If they are not allowed to live, then they cannot release the demons. So, this seems like a more efficient way to keep the prophecy from reaching fruition." Novalie smiled, "I could take over that task for you."

"You think it is that easy to kill someone, even a blue girl?" The Prophetess looked thoughtful. "I had the same thought once. Though it is sometimes called for, it is much harder to kill than you would think." She stood up and walked toward her office. "Come, enough of this conversation. It is time to start the day's work."

Moonsyrah did not hear the voice again for the next two days. The presence, though still in her head, was quiet as if it was thinking. She was unsure of what to make of it but enjoyed the silence. She could go about her classes and daily life without worrying that she would answer the voice aloud in front of others.

On the third day, the Prophetess sent her down to the archives to retrieve a rather ancient and hard-to-find text. She had also requested that Moonsyrah tidy up the room while she was down there. Moonsyrah talked Sameen into helping her, and together, the two girls searched the dusty shelves for the wanted book. Moonsyrah reached for a book on the highest shelf and could barely touch it, even while standing on her tiptoes, when the voice spoke again.

"Hello." Startled, Moonsyrah stumbled and went down in a shower of falling manuscripts, dust, and whatever else lived on the top shelf.

"Are you all right, Moon? Did you get hurt?" Sameen rushed over to her friend and helped her up.

"No, I am not hurt." Grumbled Moonsyrah.

Sameen started laughing and pointed at Moonsyrah's dress. Moonsyrah went over to a mirror and saw her dress was covered in dust and ink. An ink pot had fallen off the shelf and painted her dress and hair black. Across her nose was another splash of ink, making her look quite comical. She laughed along with Sameen and suggested they take a short break from their task. Sameen agreed and went over to the bag of fruit that Moon had brought with her. She tossed Moonsyrah a peach and busied herself with trying to decide what piece she wanted.

Moonsyrah caught the peach and bit into the juicy globe, the sticky syrup dripping down her chin. Time seemed to stand still as Moonsyrah thought she felt someone suck the nectar from her lips. She closed her eyes and enjoyed the sensation of teeth tugging on her bottom lip, then realizing what she was doing banished the thought from her mind. She heard laughter ringing in her head, and then, once again, there was silence. Moonsyrah looked at Sameen to see if she had noticed anything weird, but Sameen had her back to Moonsyrah.

Moonsyrah finished her snack and, wiping her hands on her already dirty dress, went back to searching for the book. Finally, she found the slender volume tucked between two much more substantial texts.

"This is the book you are looking for, isn't it?' Asked the voice as he reached for it.

She ignored the question and the fact that she had watched the book move forward on the shelf as if someone was pulling it out for her to see. Moonsyrah scooped up the text and put it in her knapsack, and with Sameen's help, the two girls quickly straightened the room.

"After you take that to the Prophetess and clean up, do you want to explore the maze? Sameen asked as they left the library archives.

"Yes. I would like that. I will meet you there in an hour." The two girls parted ways.

An hour later, a clean Moonsyrah met up with Sameen, who suggested they split up and see who could reach the fountain at the center first. Moonsyrah liked that idea and took off down the first left turn she came to. She could hear Sameen laughing as she went toward the right. Moonsyrah enjoyed the quiet of the maze. She liked that you could be just a few feet away from someone else and not hear them.

She headed down the path when an image popped into her mind. She saw herself taking the next right instead of continuing straight and then turning left. The way she knew from experience would take her to the heart of the maze. She decided to follow the image and then the image that appeared after that. She followed the path laid out in her mind until she realized she was hopelessly lost. She turned around in a circle and tried to remember which way she had come from. As she stood there looking about in consternation, she heard the deep, honey laugh.

"I wondered if I could get you to follow the path I laid out for you."

"You got me lost," Moonsyrah replied back without thinking.

"So, you are talking to me now?" The voice queried.

"As you do not actually exist, I see no harm in answering myself when no one else is around." Moonsyrah walked a little bit further and turned into what eventually led to a dead end.

"Why did you not tell the Prophetess about me?" The question was full of surprised confusion.

Moonsyrah sat on the grass and leaned against the hedge. "Well, I do not want anyone to know that I have become unhinged."

"You are not unhinged. I keep telling you I am not part of your imagination." The voice insisted.

Speaking as if there had been no interruption, Moonsyrah continued. "Well, I think you are, and since I am already crazy, I have decided to embrace my insanity and enjoy the ride." She smiled. Picking a blade of grass, she held it in her fingers and played with it.

"Do you have a name, or have I not created one for you yet?" She asked the voice.

"If I were a figment of your imagination, wouldn't you already know the answer to that?"

"Hmm, no, I don't think so. I think that is part of the craziness." Moonsyrah stood up and walked away. "I have been here a long time. Sameen will be wondering where I am."

"Take the next two lefts, go straight, and then take the third right. That will get you to the center." The voice faded from her mind. As she reached the first left turn, she heard him faintly respond to her previous question.

"Adym. My name is Adym." Moonsyrah smiled and softly repeated the name as she continued through the maze.

"Moonsyrah, finally. I have been waiting here forever. What took you so long?" Sameen went over to her friend and walked beside her as they circled the fountain.

"I took a wrong turn while daydreaming and became hopelessly lost. I am sorry I kept you waiting. Though it looks like you won." Moonsyrah hugged Sameen.

"The fountain is beautiful, but it is getting late, and I am a little chilly. Let's find our way back to the entrance together." Sameen started down the lane she knew would take them out of the labyrinth. The two young women made it back to their rooms just minutes before the monastery doors were closed for the night.

When Moonsyrah lay down to sleep, Adym entered her mind and listened to her restless thoughts. He watched as she struggled to understand what was happening to her. He watched as her mind showed her the truth of what he was and who she was destined to be. She fought against the idea. However, deep within her mind, he saw this truth was not as abhorrent to her as she felt it should be. He knew that she was aware of him there with her, for as she drifted to sleep, she focused on him for a brief moment. He whispered her name and a soft goodnight and watched as she physically settled down into a peaceful sleep.

He now knew what she was afraid of. But he also knew that if he pushed her fear, she would not respond as he wanted her too. Instead of playing on her fear of who she might be, the one from the prophecy, he would help her learn the truth and get her to accept that part of her. He would get her to want to set him free. It would be a novel challenge for him to get a human to listen to him without the use of fear.

Adym sat outside on a tree trunk in his garden as he continued to contemplate this blue girl. He pulled back from her mind and thought how attracted he was to her, not just to her delicate beauty but also to her mind. Her desire to please the Prophetess and do what was expected of her was fascinating. But he was attracted mostly by her excitement over learning, her joy of life, and her capacity to love. She had a rebellious streak in her that he was sure would eventually lead her to fulfill her destiny. Adym was anxious to watch the change he knew would soon come about in her. The change that would inevitably lead to his people walking out of the Myst for the first time in almost four hundred years.

It was Moonsyrah's day off from her duties with the Prophetess, so she grabbed herself a small snack, quietly left her apartment, and headed out of the monastery grounds. She skirted the edges of the village so as not to be seen and headed up the path that would lead her to Rainbow Falls. She walked the dirt road under the hanging branches of trees until she came to a fork in the road, where she chose the one that would go up the side of the mountain. The path was rocky, but she walked it with ease. Finally, she arrived at the top, where the river flowed before tumbling down the rock face and into the lake.

Moonsyrah found the narrowest part of the river and carefully made her way over the rocks which formed a sort of bridge over the river, so that she could reach the opposite bank. Once there, she walked the few yards it took to get to the wall of Myst.

For a while, she walked silently beside the barrier, not touching it but enjoying the slight tingle it elicited. Then, after a time, she ran her hand against it as she walked and enjoyed the ripples that appeared and the feeling of familiarity it gave her.

It smelled like Adym. Startled at that thought, she pulled her hand away. How could she think that? Adym was imaginary, a creation her mind made up to drive her crazy. She ran her hand through the Myst once again. It released a pleasant aroma, like the air just before it snowed or rained. It was the same aroma that caught her nose when Adym was around.

Briefly, she thought about what Adym had told her. He said that he wasn't a figment of her insanity. That only left one other option, an option that scared her and yet intrigued her as well. She could not yet bring herself to believe it.

Moonsyrah walked back across the river and down the lane that took her behind the falls where the hot springs bubbled. Once she entered the half-circle cave, she sat down on a boulder and took off her shoes and dress. She laid the gown carefully on the rock so that it would not get wet and then stepped into the pink pool. Leaning her head back and closing her eyes, she let the warmth of the water relax her tense muscles. She was about to drift to sleep when she heard a little splash in the water next to her.

Moonsyrah looked toward the sound and saw the shadow of a man sitting in the pool with her. The shape was distinctly that of a person, but she could not make out any of his features except his eyes. The shadow had eyes that glowed a dark blue. The glow was faint, but it was definitely there. She reached out a hand and touched the face of the shadow, making out the curve of his cheek and jawline. Moonsyrah dropped her hand and gazed at the figure. Her mind had taken one step further to make her believe that Adym could be real, or had it taken that step to encourage her belief that she had lost her sense of reason?

"Someday, I will have to find a way to convince you that I am made of actual flesh and bone." Adym leaned his head back against the rim of pink stones. His arms stretched across its length.

"He is only an illusion. He is not here." Whispered Moonsyrah under her breath.

"I cannot perform illusions. That would be Tayin's ability." Adym whispered quietly back to her.

His voice was in her mind. She did not hear it coming from next to her like it would if he were real. She chose to ignore him, even though she was curious as to what her imagination meant by that statement. If he was real, she would not hear his voice in her head but through her ears.

"True, unless I am telepathic. In which case, I can talk to you in your mind and hear you in mine." Adym caressed her shoulder with his hand as he said this.

She could feel him stroking her skin lightly. It was just a hint of a touch, barely perceptible, except that where he touched her skin, it left a trail of sensation that she could not describe. Moonsyrah unconsciously scooted closer to the shadow and leaned into the caress. It made her think thoughts that she had never had before.

Adym ran his hand up her neck and threaded his fingers into her hair. Drawing her head back by her hair, he leaned in and kissed her neck, just below her ear. He heard her sigh softly in reaction. Adym then lay kisses across her jaw until he reached her mouth. He breathed softly against her lips.

Moonsyrah was overwhelmed with her awareness of him, of the feel of his touch, of his scent. She tilted her head forward and met his lips with her own. The sensation of her mouth on his was more than she thought she could possibly imagine. And, for the first time, Moonsyrah let herself entertain the idea that he was actually beside her in the pool. This thought made her uneasy, and so she went back to assuming he was an aberration brought on by her state of mind. She heard him sigh in frustration and then let go of her hair.

"Close your eyes. I am getting out, and I do not want you to see me." She slid away from him and sat across the pool from him.

"Make up your mind. If I am part of your imagination, what does it matter if I see you naked? You do not believe me to be real, so it should not bother you to walk around without your clothes on in front of me." He paused for a moment, and wickedness crept into his tone. "Show me that you honestly think I am a figment of your fantasy by getting out of the pool."

Moonsyrah sat there deliberating her options. She was starting to accept his word that he was a physical being, kind of. She could not prove he was or was not. She took a deep breath and started to exit the hot spring, quickly turning her back on him. She went over to her dress and saw it flutter a few feet away from where she had laid it. She shook her head and hurriedly grabbed up her dress before it could move again and threw it on. Triumphantly, she looked at him.

"See, I honestly believe you are not here."

"Liar." He said.

"I am not."

"Telepathic, remember? I can see that you are not sure what to believe about me." Adym said. "You have a nice backside, by the way."

Moonsyrah's eyes widened. She stared at him for a moment more and saw his eyes glow a bit brighter. She took a step back, forgetting that a cluster of rocks was behind her, and tripped over one of them. She heard Adym laughing, and with a gasp, she righted herself and raced to the path that would lead her back home.

A few days later, Moonsyrah dropped her belief that Adym was part of her imagination and began to accept that he was one of the Myst demons. A demon that made her heart speed up and her breath quicken. She was deep in the forest when her acceptance began.

In the furthest corner of the monastery grounds, right next to the evergreen forest, was an old A-frame building. This was the residence of the original prophetess while the Abbey was being built. Around it was a rock fence that had a gap in the very back of it that Moonsyrah could just fit through. She had found it in the first year that she had arrived at the monastery. The forest beyond it was thick and dark, and you could quickly become lost if you strayed too far from the fence.

Moonsyrah liked to sit on a fallen tree trunk with just the barest hint of the stone wall in her sight. She sat here in the peace and quiet of the place. The monastery was often noisy with activity. The many acolytes, artists who came to learn, visitors, and the staff kept the building from ever being completely quiet. Here, the thousands of trees dampened sound.

The sun was beginning to set, and the wind whistled softly through the trees. Moonsyrah heard an owl hooting somewhere close by. She always felt at peace here in the mountain woods. She breathed deeply of the air and found it scented with pine and the slight tang of autumn. Moonsyrah felt Adym seconds before he placed a hand on hers. She sat there and guiltily enjoyed the sensation of his skin on hers.

"It is not safe to be out here by yourself." Goosebumps covered her arms as his voice wrapped around her.

"I am safe enough. There is no one here but me." Moonsyrah replied. She heard him laugh seductively.

"I am here." Adym's image became more clearly seen as he said this.

"Ah, but you are not really here. You are just a voice in my head, a being I have created in my imagination. That makes you safe." Moonsyrah hoped this was true.

"Can you not see me?"

"I can, but seeing is not always believing. You can see things that are not there. For example, many plants, if ingested, can cause you to hallucinate." She explained.

Adym turned to look at Moonsyrah with exasperation.

"Can you not hear me?" He asked her.

"I can hear you." She paused for a moment, "in my head."

"Can you not feel me?" Adym reached out a hand and caressed her shoulder and neck.

Breathlessly, she answered yes.

"Can you not smell me?" Adym leaned in and blew against her parted lips. He followed his breath and brought his mouth up to her own. "Or taste me?" he kissed her softly, and then when he felt her shudder against him, he deepened the kiss. Exploring her mouth with his tongue.

Moonsyrah pulled back slightly, "I can." She answered with a riot of emotions coursing through her.

"Then am I not real? If all your senses tell you I am here, why do you choose to believe I am not?" Questioned a puzzled Adym.

"I am not ready to handle the alternative." Was her honest reply.

Adym shook his head in acceptance of this reason and sat with her in silence for a while. Then he took her hand, pulled her until she stood up, and led her further into the woods. The sky was darker here under the trees, and the silence was more encompassing.

"I understand why you do not want to accept the reality of who and what I am, but someday I hope that you can. I need you, too." Adym took her in his arms and kissed her again. He ran his hands down her back and then cupped her nicely rounded buttocks in his hands. She tipped her head back as he nipped her neck with his teeth and then kissed each spot to ease the sting.

Moonsyrah's mind reeled with all the new feelings and the beginnings of her acceptance.

"Do you still think it is safe to be out here alone, with only the voice in your head?" Adym asked as he pulled her closer to him. His voice was like a drug entering her body. It held her as captive as his arms did.

He ran his hands up her back and untied the lacing that held her bodice on. She could feel the hard planes of his chest pressed against her breasts and the feel of his arousal against her. This felt so real. How could it not be? Her body burned where he touched her and ached with a newfound desire.

"I don't know." Was her breathy reply. He turned her in his arms and pulled her back against him. His hand made its way up to the curve of her breast. He tweaked the nipple in his fingers, and Adym moaned deep in his throat at her response.

Moonsyrah began to feel afraid. Not of him but of what she was feeling for this being that she could no longer be sure was just part of her imagination.

"Your fear is as sweet as you are," Adym whispered as he ran his hand over her flat belly.

"Please." She murmured into the darkness of her fantasy.

"I want you," Adym growled low in the back of his throat as he pulled away from her. "But I do not want to continue until you want me for who I am and not because you think I am some fantasy."

Adym walked her back to the fallen tree and let go of her hand, pointing at the break in the wall that she had come through. "Go before I change my mind. Go before I show you how unsafe I can be."

"Maybe you are right, and it is not safe out here with you. I will go." Moonsyrah re-laced the bodice of her gown. "But I do not want to leave," she confessed, "nor can I stay. I fear what I might allow you to do. No, I fear what I want you to do. I fear that you are not just in my head, and I no longer care what that means."

Moonsyrah stepped over the wall and walked around the side of the old inhabitance. She stopped before she reached the front and whispered, knowing he could still hear her.

"If it is not safe to be out here with you, then what makes anywhere safe? You are with me always."

"You are safe from me because I could never intentionally hurt you. Now." Moonsyrah heard the words drift across the night air. She was not sure why, but she believed him. She walked a bit further and then stopped once more.

"Hearing can also be deceptive," Moonsyrah said as if an afterthought to their earlier conversation. "I once believed that I could hear music in the colored crystals. But as we all know, music does not come from rocks." She started walking again and did not hear his surprised intake of breath.

Adym gazed out his window, thinking of the past few days. There was something about this girl that bothered him. He could not quite pinpoint what it was, but something was not what he expected. He clasped his hands together behind his back and paced before the wall of glass. He walked back and forth until, finally, it hit him. He knew what it was about her that bothered him. He must talk to Kest.

Adym hastened to the Hall of Myst and entered the doorway that led to Kest's home on Geltahn. He stepped through the door and was hit by hot, humid air. He was never entirely prepared for the moist heat of Geltahn. Kest met him at the end of the hallway and led Adym to the veranda, which overlooked the river that ran across the whole of Geltahn. After waving for a servant to bring an iced mint drink, Kest invited Adym to talk.

Adym, seated in a low-slung chair across from Kest, glanced over at the stately woman that sat down next to him. Diem was always near Kest. Since Kest had met Diem, the two were never far apart; it was as if the two had bonded, but Adym knew that was not possible. Diem was an allurmonuhra, a girl born of the Alluran moon, the only one born within the Myst. It was impossible for a SeiOrhii to bond with a human, even if they had attributes of an Alluran. Or so he presumed.

"Diem, is it possible for me to talk with Kest alone?" Inquired Adym.

"Of course, Adym," Diem said, then she gracefully stood up and left the veranda in a swirl of brilliant red skirts. Both Adym and Kest watched her exit. She was a beautiful woman and a pleasure to look at. When she had closed the screen behind her, Adym turned his attention back to his friend.

"Tell me, does she see into your mind? I mean, genuinely see, as another Alluran can? Not just images that you wish her to see, but can she delve into your mind and pick out memories on her own?" Adym sat his drink on the side table and waited intently for Kest's answer.

"I have told you all many times that she does. Not one of you wants to believe that a woman such as her can have the abilities that we have." Kest looked at Adym, "That is why I thought she might be the one we were waiting for."

"She is not, as I tried to explain to you when she was first noticed. She cannot leave the Myst any more than you can. The one we waited for had to be born outside of the Myst if she was to have access to the key." Adym sighed. He picked up his cup and absently took another sip of the refreshing drink. Peering out at the landscape, he watched as a family of agile antelope leaped over a row of bushes to disappear into the trees that ran along the river's bank.

He turned back to Kest. "I could not imagine the possibility that Diem could access your mind, but now I think that I am having the same experience." He leaned forward and placed his hands on his knees. "Moonsyrah is the one we have waited for. She can hear me and talk back, not just verbally but telepathically as well. She can see images that I do, images that I have not given to her, but ones that pop up in my mind. She doesn't know that she can access my memories. She found an image of the humans locked away with us. I did not show it to her willingly."

Adym stood up and leaned against the veranda's rail. Quietly, he whispered his next question. "Have you bonded with Diem?"

Kest went over to stand next to his friend. "No, but only because she will not accept the bond."

"So, it is possible then?"

"Yes." Kest hesitated for a moment before asking, "Adym, why do you ask?"

"I find her fascinating. I do not want to leave her mind." Adym pushed away from the rail and went back to the chair. Then, taking a seat, he peered up at Kest, "I have gone to her in spirit form. But, I," Adym hesitated as if embarrassed to admit what he was going to say. "I want to be with her, not just in my spirit form. I want to physically be next to her, to touch her, to taste her. To know her as I know no one else. It is as if my heart does not beat properly unless I am with her."

Kest eyed Adym with understanding. He knew precisely how Adym was feeling. He chuckled softly. "The bond has started; I feel for you. But you cannot leave the Myst without great risk to yourself. You must wait to leave until you are very sure that she will find it and then give you the key. It is the only way for you to get back and for us to be free."

Kest walked over to Adym and placed a hand on his shoulder. "Adym, be very sure of what you think you are feeling before you act on it. So much rides on what you do next. The Korsyon will try to override everything else but its call. I do not envy you this task and for Y'ddra to spring the Korsyon on you at this time is unfair."

Adym stood up, thanked his friend, and headed home, deep in thought.

Moonsyrah was down in the garden gathering flowers for the Prophetess's table when she tentatively called out to Adym. It was the first time she had initiated their conversation, and she was nervous about doing so.

"Adym, are you there." She put a fresh-cut flower in her basket as she waited for his answer.

"Yes, I am here." Adym stayed in his own body and answered her only with his mind.

Moonsyrah chewed on her lip for a moment, not sure what question she wanted to ask first. She put another purple rose in her basket and wandered over to the lilies that grew a few feet away.

"What are you?" She lowered her eyes and looked with seemingly great interest at her basket of freshly cut blooms.

"You know the answer to that."

"Tell me plainly, as if I did not know." She whispered.

"I am an Alluran. Your people call mine demons." He answered.

Moonsyrah ambled through the garden deep in thought. She cut a flower here and there as she went. The sun rose above the tall garden walls before she spoke again.

"Why can I hear you when others can't? How can I see you and feel you if you are locked in the Myst?"

Adym watched as she put a flower to her nose and smiled at its spicy scent.

"Why do you believe me now?" He queried.

"I have always believed, as you well know, but I have not wanted to. I would have preferred to believe I was insane and you just my beautiful phantasm, but." She paused and then, her voice faint, continued. "I cannot deceive myself any longer. I want you to be real. I want to know that I am not crazy, that the person I am beginning to long for is flesh and blood. Even if that means he is a demon."

Adym's heart beat furiously in his chest. She admitted she cared for him. He knew it shouldn't matter, but it did. He appeared in front of her, more solid than he had ever been before. Touching her face, he gently lifted her chin so that she was looking up at him.

"You can hear me because I want you to, but I am not sure how you can talk back to me telepathically. I have never experienced this before with one of your kind since the gates closed. You can see me because I have traveled to you." Adym kissed her quickly and then let go of her chin.

"I am the last Alluran with the gift of, I think you humans call it teleportation or telekinesis, I am not sure which. Maybe it is both. I am the only Alluran that can leave the Myst. It is hard and takes much out of me, but I can do it." He took a step back from her. "It is easier to go through the barrier in my spirit form, which is why I seem to you not much more than a shadow or a ghost."

Moonsyrah circled around him and went back to picking the colorful blooms.

"I have been told by the Prophetess that if I begin to hear voices in my head, I should tell her. I am not sure how, but she knew that I would begin hearing you. That I would start to converse with a demon. She has told me that I need to let her know because she believes that she can help me banish you from my head. That if I don't, I will be the one to release your evil onto the world and my people."

Adym was silent. He did not want to do anything that would make her quit talking to him. He let her wander the garden and slowly walked along behind her.

"Though I am starting to look forward to our conversations, I do not want to bring fear to everyone." She stopped abruptly and turned to face Adym. "I need time to figure things out. To understand. Can you give me time to think without you being in my head?

"I will give you anything that you ask," Adym faded from her sight but stayed in her mind, "my Beloved." Then he vanished from her mind as well.

Moonsyrah felt an emptiness that she was not anticipating. She had gotten used to Adym always being on the edge of her mind. She thought of their talk and realized she had seen more of him than she had before. He was tall, with dark blue hair and matching eyes. He was beautiful.

Over the next few days, Moonsyrah was astonished at how empty she felt without Adym. She was surprised that she had become used to him being with her and comfortable with it. She missed him.

Moonsyrah kept herself busy by taking extra classes at the monastery school. Moonsyrah was very talented with textiles. She could weave, dye, and sew any type of material into anything that she imagined. She especially loved to design and create clothing, but she was quite good at anything that required sewing and design.

Moonsyrah did this in addition to her work with the Prophetess. She hoped that by distracting herself, she would accomplish two things. First, she would be so busy that she would not accidentally let it slip to the Prophetess that she was hearing Adym. Second, she would be able to think things through clearly as she lost herself in the peace of working with fabrics. This worked to some degree.

As Moonsyrah sat at the loom weaving fabric for a dress she was designing, she concluded that it did not matter that Adym was one of the demons the Prophetess spoke of. She needed him. The silence she felt in her mind without him there was overbearing, and her heart did not beat quite right now that he was not with her. Moonsyrah wasn't sure why, but she knew that her future was entwined with his and that she was destined to be with him.

Once she acknowledged this and accepted him for what he was and not a figment of her imagination, a sense of tranquility enveloped her. Being with Adym had a rightness to it that she could not explain. It was as if she finally understood that he was part of her, and she could not be happy without him. Though she knew what he was she couldn't help the attraction she felt for him or the love she was starting to feel.

But she knew that she was failing to convince the Prophetess that everything was as it should be with her. During their times together, the Prophetess would make comments that led Moon-syrah to believe that the Prophetess knew she heard the voices of the demons. How she knew, Moonsyrah could only guess; she was the Prophetess, after all.

One evening, after classes had ended and her evening duties with the Prophetess were done, Moonsyrah headed out to the old chapel at the edge of the grounds by the dark forest. The A-frame building was two stories tall with an attached structure on the side used as the living quarters for the prophetess who lived when it was built. Now, it lay empty.

The windows were beautiful stained-glass depictions of the three moons in their different phases in the night sky. The top story of the chapel had thick glass windows that let in little light. It was a beautiful building that showed signs of neglect and age. Inside the chapel, the floors were covered in limestone. A wooden spiral staircase was beside the entrance and led up to the second floor. Five rows of pews lay between the door and the altar at the back of the room. Across from the altar was the entrance to the prophetess's quarters. This room was simple and contained only a dresser and an old bed frame. This room was also floored with limestone, but the rocks were beginning to sink in some places and lift in others. It was evident that, at one time, the room had flooded.

Moonsyrah entered the chapel and climbed the stairs leading up to the next level. She came here tonight to be alone and meditate on what she should tell the Prophetess and what questions she wanted to ask of her. It was peaceful here, and Moonsyrah knew that no one would bother her. She placed a light stone on the floor and sat on the decaying rag rug next to a bookshelf full of damp and forgotten books.

A storm was coming, and she liked to watch the rain beat against the windows and hear the wind whistle through the trees. It was a bit spooky, but Moonsyrah enjoyed the tingle of fear that the storm produced in her. She wrapped her cloak more securely around her shoulders and started her meditation ritual. She took a deep breath and closed her eyes, letting the sound of the first raindrops relax her. Moonsyrah was deep in thought when a pine tree scraped against the window and startled her out of her trance. She opened her eyes and saw that the storm was in full force and didn't look as if it would stop any time soon.

She stood up, went over to the bookshelf, and rummaged around to see if anything was still readable. She pulled a couple of badly damaged books off the shelf and set them on the rickety table next to it. A red leather-bound book, small enough to fit in a pocket, was wedged between the second book and the wall.

Moonsyrah pulled it off the shelf and saw that, though damp, it was still readable. The journal was written in an old Earth dialect, and the handwriting was small and cramped. It was penned here on Yiddera as the month and date names were Yidderian. Moonsyrah sat back down on the rug and pulled the light stone closer to her. She was able to read the writing, though some of the words were smudged.

Catromis, 34, 04. Terrible things have followed us to the new continent. We have been here for two years and had hoped that in leaving Kruger and the landing city now called Anchorage, we would have left the horrors behind us. It was thought that the happenings in Anchorage were caused by something that we might have eaten, but now we know that is not so. Now, there are whispers of something evil lurking in the beautiful curtains of Myst. It is the evil creatures that live there that are causing these terrible things to happen.

There have been three more deaths this week. Nightmares continue to plague us, and a few followers report seeing ghosts of those who have recently died. People keep disappearing. Some of them are returned; the lucky ones do not. Even the animals on this planet act strange. People are living in terror. If things do not change soon, I do not know how we can survive on this planet. The Prophetess

Alena told of a vision that one would lock away those in the Myst, and our troubles would cease until another would set them free once more. We did not believe her when she said that others inhabited this planet with us, but now, it seems the only explanation, and we can do nothing except wait for the one to come who will bring us peace from the malicious happenings surrounding us.

On a happier note, construction on the monastery continues, and many of the small outbuildings that have already been established are filling with those who follow the Prophetess. Surprisingly many healers have come to make their home here as well.

The village down the road is growing quite big. A tea shop has just opened, and tomorrow, a few of us are going to enjoy a visit and a refreshing cup of tea.

Einmis, 01, 05. *It has been ten months since we last celebrated the day we landed on Yiddera, a full year. Tonight, we will kick up our heels within the new monastery. It is not yet fully built, but the Prophetess Alena states that we must be in the new auditorium. We have called the holiday Ontscheppen, a name for landing and disembarkment, a word contrived from an old earth language. I am not sure which. It is a week-long holiday that will be celebrated with feasting, dancing, and homemade gifts for those we love. The* decorations are to be quite lavish, and the food will come from all over the planet. The gathering will be welcomed by all.

We have many people who live here now, and they have worked hard to build the monastery and its surrounding village. The Prophetess has let it be known that she will be opening the monastery up to include a school dedicated to the creative, performing, and healing arts. I look forward to being part of this future.

We are hoping to finish the Prophetess's quarters soon so that her child will have the honor of being the first baby born within the new Monastery's walls. It is almost complete, and with luck, the weather will hold so the workers do not have to finish during the bitter cold of one of the many snowstorms this area experiences.

Issmis, 38, 05. Yesterday, I saw that Amalie had come all the way from Kahlali to visit with the Prophetess. I was surprised to see her. The last I heard was that she had disappeared and hadn't been seen for over two years. She brought with her a small backpack. Amalie and the Prophetess Alena went into the chapel where I could not see them, so I am unsure what was in the pack, but Amalie held it as if it were very precious. I also heard Amalie tell the Prophetess that she had taken a key from the demons in the

Myst. I do not know what else was said, but are these terrible fears coming from demons? I am not sure that I believe in demons.

__Issmis 40, 05__. It has been over three weeks since any more accidents have occurred, and the disappearances have ceased. I am beginning to wonder if the key that Amalie brought had anything to do with the new peace that has enveloped Yiddera. I have tried to ask the Prophetess about this, but she hushes me and tells me that no "key" was brought to her by Amalie. Maybe I misheard them when they spoke of it, but I am sure that I did not. Oh well, I will follow the will of the Prophetess and say no more of the key.

__Sedemis 02, 05__. It is once again the time of the third moon. The moon, Allura, turns the world blue and mysterious. We still have peace. No more are we plagued with nightmares, disappearances, and fear. Now, we only experience those common everyday fears that all humans are subject to. Maybe Amalie was right, and those that live in the Myst are demons. The prophecy must have come to pass. Someone has locked them away behind the shimmering blue barrier. But why would the prophecy also state that someday, one would arrive and set them free? Who would want to release the demons to once again bring their torment down upon us?

Atumis, 24, 06. Tomorrow, I move into my room in the new building. I will miss my little place up here in the attic of the chapel. I will be sharing my new apartment with three other women. It has four rooms that surround a living room and a kitchenette. It will be nice to have someone other than the Prophetess to talk to as she is not given to verboseness.

Moonsyrah finished reading the small journal and tucked it into the pocket of her cloak. She wondered who had written it. She also speculated on what Amalie had brought with her to the prophetess. What was the key? It was often said that the Myst gates were locked. Was this key that was written about used to lock the gates? It was known in the history books that a woman named Amalie was the one who locked the gates and made the many years of peace they now enjoyed possible.

Moonsyrah looked out the window and saw that the storm was still raging outside. Lightning flashed across the sky, and the rain poured down harder now than it had even just a few minutes ago. She turned off the light stone and settled down on the rug for the night. Then, tucking her cloak around herself, she fell asleep to the sound of the wind howling through the trees.

The following day, Moonsyrah woke to a bright, crisp autumn morning. The rain of the night before had cleansed the air and made everything smell fresh and new. She raced to her rooms, quickly changed her clothes, and met Novalie and the Prophetess in the meditation gardens. After the morning ritual and the following repast, she inquired if she could have a few moments of private conversation with the Prophetess. This was granted, and Novalie was sent on her way.

The two women stayed seated at the table, drinking their morning tea. The Prophetess waited for Moonsyrah to begin the conversation. They sat there in silence for several minutes until Moonsyrah figured out what she wanted to ask first.

She leaned forward and placed her elbows on the table before saying, "Tell me everything you know about the demons, please."

"You have asked this before. So again, I ask you why the sudden interest?" The Prophetess countered.

Deciding to tell the truth or at least part of it, Moonsyrah replied, "I have heard a voice. I think it might be just part of my imagination, but you did ask that I tell you if I started to hear voices." Moonsyrah paused, "You mentioned that I might be hearing one of the demons, and I want to know why. Why do you think I would hear them, and how can I hear them if they are locked in the Myst? Why not another blue girl? What do these demons look like?"

The Prophetess looked into the face of the girl sitting in front of her. She wondered how much she should tell her. Should she begin by explaining how she knew that Moonsyrah was the one who fulfilled this terrible prophecy? The Prophetess decided that she could not tell Moonsyrah exactly how she knew that Moonsyrah was the one. She could not speak of her birth without letting secrets be known. Secrets that she did not want to share.

"Which question would you like answered first?"

"How did they come to be locked in the Myst?" Moonsyrah leaned even farther forward in anticipation of the answer.

"A young lady was taken by one of the demons, as you should have read in your history books. She was kept for over two years and, in that time, figured out not only how to kill one of the demons but how to keep them in the Myst and out of Yiddera as well. I do not know exactly how this was accomplished, but once she escaped, the vile creatures never bothered us again." The Prophetess looked thoughtful. "Though if you get near the barrier, you can feel them. They bring our fears to the forefront of our minds."

"Why do they do that?" Asked Moonsyrah.

"The demons feed on our fears. Or so we were told by the girl who was taken."

"Was the key that Amalie brought to the monastery, those hundreds of years ago, what locked them in?" The query was innocent enough, but Moonsyrah saw a look of shock quickly cross the Prophetess's face. It was so quick that Moonsyrah was not sure she had really seen it.

"Key? What key?" The Prophetess prevaricated.

"I found a book that mentioned that Amalie had brought a key to the Prophetess Alena."

"No book has ever mentioned that a key was brought here. It cannot, as this is simply not true." Lied the Prophetess.

Moonsyrah took the small red journal out of her pocket and handed it to the Prophetess.

"It is in here. Read it, and you will see why I think there is indeed a key." Moonsyrah handed the book over and leaned back in her chair. She quietly drank her tea as the Prophetess read the brief account.

"Well, clearly, the writer misheard. She must have assumed there was a key." The Prophetess paused. "The conversation was overheard, and maybe she thought they were talking about a key.

It makes sense that she would conclude a key was used as we call the barrier a Myst gate and say the demons are locked away."

"But what if she wasn't wrong? What if there is a key? This might be what is used to release the demons." Moonsyrah insisted.

"I do not know of any key. If there was one, the knowledge of its existence would have been passed down from Prophetess to Prophetess. And it hasn't been. This key that was written of was a misunderstanding. It just isn't so." The Prophetess said with finality.

Moonsyrah wished to argue this point but decided it was best to drop it if she wanted her other questions answered.

"Okay. Then, if they are set free, how will we know?" She asked.

"That is an easy answer. This world will be overrun by fear, as it was when humans first landed here. Nightmares, disappearances, creatures of the night, and unnatural storms will hound us. There will be deaths and people tortured who will wish they had died. This is how we will know." The Prophetess took a sip of her tea. "Now, a question of my own? Why do you want to know what they look like?"

"It is said that the Dimoni are marked by the demons. That our hair color and our glowing eyes are the same as the demons. How do we know this? I was under the impression that no one had seen the demons."

"Some people, in the beginning, claimed to see beings with blue hair and eyes that glowed with blue fire. It was believed to be the ravings of people gone mad with fear. When the first blue-eyed, blue-haired girl was born, we knew that these people might have actually seen them. And then," The Prophetess, coming to a decision, stood up and said she would be right back.

Moonsyrah waited impatiently as the Prophetess walked into her bedroom. She came back a few minutes later with a large sketch pad in her hands. It was decidedly old and looked as if it had been flipped through many times. The Prophetess sat it on the coffee table and gestured for Moonsyrah to join her there. Moonsyrah did as she was bid and sat down beside the Prophetess on the couch.

"No one but the other Prophetesses have seen this book. Novalie has not even seen this book yet. What I am going to show you must not be talked about. Is this understood?" With her hand on the book's cover, the Prophetess waited to open it until Moonsyrah nodded her head.

Inside the book were drawings of many unusual flowers and plants. Pages upon pages of them. They all had descriptions of their medicinal or cooking use at the bottom of the page. Moonsyrah read a few and saw that many of the recipes were still used by the healers to this day. She came to one that briefly spoke of having the ability to lower the rate of healing in someone, but it was unclear who as the word was smudged, though it looked as if the word started with an S. Moonsyrah briefly wondered what the word could be before she decided to move on. It was obvious that Amalie must have been a healer or, at the very least, a botanist. Towards the end of the book, Moonsyrah noticed that the sketches were no longer of plants but of people. People with blue hair. The strange thing was that these were drawings of men, not women. No man had been born on Yiddera with this coloring. Moonsyrah dropped to the floor and looked closely at the pictures.

The first was of five men standing around laughing. They looked much like humans except for their coloring. One of the men had their back turned so you could not see his face, only his back. The man's back had blue spots running up his spine and across his shoulders. Oddly, this did not detract from his physique but enhanced it.

Moonsyrah turned the page and, on this page, saw the drawing of the face of just one of the men. He had long blue-black hair and contrasting eyes, the aquamarine color of water. Somehow, the artist managed to show the raw sexuality of the perfectly sculpted man. He was a man that no woman could ignore. Above the face, a storm cloud with rain and lightning had been drawn.

The next face was friendly with a laughing smile. This man had vibrant, electric blue hair that was unruly. He looked as if he was a bit wild and up for anything. Again, the skill of the artist was shown as, somehow, she had conveyed that this man was always in motion. Next to his picture were several small sketches of different animals.

The next one caused Moonsyrah to gasp as she reached out to touch it. This face had the dark blue hair and eyes of Adym. He even had the perpetual five o'clock shadow. This was a picture of Adym. It had to be. But how? This picture was drawn over three hundred years ago. She gazed at the image for a moment longer as at least a hundred more questions ran through her head. Moonsyrah lingered over this picture, hungry to take in every detail of Adym's face. She looked at the other drawings on the page and saw that in the corner was the symbol for infinity. In another corner was a small drawing of a stick figure stepping into a circle, and then there was one that showed the figure coming out of a circle.

The Prophetess had heard Moonsyrah's gasp and paid close attention to the girl as she looked at the drawing. She watched the almost loving way that Moonsyrah touched the page. She wondered at this but chose to ignore it for now and concentrated on the face, herself, for a few moments of time.

"The next page has the last face on it." The Prophetess turned the page for Moonsyrah, who looked as if she would continue to stare at the previous one forever.

"The last face? But there are five men?" Moonsyrah came back to the present and looked at the page.

"Yes, but she did not draw them all. I do not know why." The Prophetess watched as Moonsyrah looked at the artwork. This sheet had two faces on it, one with a smiling laughing countenance and the other a look of rage and maybe grief. Both were identical in coloring; it was only the expressions that were different. It was amazing how the artist could show such contrasting emotions on the same face. Across the paper were water stains. Moonsyrah thought they looked like tears.

Moonsyrah looked closer at the drawing. In the corner of the page was a circle: half white and half black. Each side had a bit of the opposite color in it. Below the yin and yang was another design, this time of a sun and a moon. And below that was written *"My Korsyon, My Nightmare."*

Moonsyrah looked up at the Prophetess. "I think this is a symbol meant to represent day and night. I wonder what it means in the context of this picture. And what do the words mean?"

"Amalie never told us what the little pictures by the faces meant or the meaning behind the words, but we do know that these are four of the demons that she was taken by. We do not know why she only drew four of the five from the first picture." The Prophetess shifted her position on the couch and patted the seat next to her. Moonsyrah got off the floor and sat on the soft cushion.

"Prophetess Alena kept a diary. In it, she speculated that Amalie could not bring herself to draw the one she had killed. She also wrote that Amalie never wrote down the names of the men. Just that she called them demons."

Moonsyrah scooted a bit farther down the couch from the Prophetess. "Why do you think that I am destined to fulfill your prophecy? What makes you think that I am the one to set them free?"

"A bit over nineteen years ago, I had a vision. This vision was enough to convince me that you were the one."

"But I wasn't even born yet." Interrupted Moonsyrah.

Continuing through the interruption, the Prophetess finished her thought. "This vision took place on the day of your birth." The Prophetess reached out to touch Moonsyrah but then pulled back. "I honestly hope I am wrong, but I do not think so. And if I am not mistaken, you, too, know that you are the one."

Moonsyrah turned her eyes away from the Prophetess's stare. She was beginning to think that the Prophetess was right. That she was the one spoken of in the prophecy. She talked to a being who claimed he was what the humans called a demon. He told her that he lived in the Myst. And she just saw his picture in a book that was drawn centuries ago. But Adym could not be evil. She had never felt any fear of him. She knew it was time to invite him to talk with her again. She missed him and had so very many questions that only he could answer.

Moonsyrah thanked the Prophetess for showing her the sketches and asked if she could be excused. The Prophetess nodded and took the book from her as Moonsyrah had picked it up to take it with her.

"May I look at the book again some other time? I would like to read more about what was written under the plants."

"Someday, perhaps." The Prophetess answered and then watched as Moonsyrah walked out of the room, deep in thought.

Novalie was given the duty of planning the new theater. She had sat down with the designers and together had created a building that would be the envy of all other theaters. It was to be four stories tall, and at the top was a room made entirely of glass and intricate metalwork. This would serve as a conservatory for rare and beautiful blooming plants and a place to have fancy dinners and lunches. She planned on creating a small clearing in it that would allow a small music group or a dancer or two to perform for the guests. Novalie thought this would be an impressive place to meet with donors.

The rest of the building would contain a large stage. One that many plays and performances could be held on without feeling cramped. It would have a spot that held a full orchestra, and it would have enough seating for a thousand people. She had also incorporated private boxes for those who wanted to remain unseen. The theater they used now was old and becoming shabby, and Novalie planned to give it a face-lift and attach it to the new building. It would serve as a place to practice upcoming shows, and it would also contain many dressing, costume, and storage rooms. The stage and seating would be removed so that an indoor marketplace could be held in the winter months.

All in all, Novalie was proud of what she had come up with. The current Prophetess thought it was too much, but as she had left Novalie in charge, she allowed the extravagances. Today was the day that she got to walk through the finished building. She had the seamstresses and painters working for months, and finally, it was time for her final walk-through. Novalie smiled in anticipation of seeing her creation in its finished state. This spring, she would hold the festival in this building, and it would be the most magnificent festival the monastery had ever put on.

She entered the building and was delighted at the beauty she had achieved. Her legacy as the most influential Prophetess was starting. Novalie wanted to be remembered throughout history as the Prophetess who did the most good for the Calling. She would raise money and send out missionaries to other countries to bring more people into the fold. She would refurbish all the chapels and churches to the grandness the Calling deserved. Novalie ran her hand over the soft velvet curtains that hung on the side of the stage and found herself clinging to the material to keep herself upright.

A vision passed through her that almost brought her to her knees. This one included a blue girl; she could not make out her face or her coloring, but she knew the girl was demon-born. She was dancing on this stage, and a demon watched her from above. The vision ended quickly, but the incited feelings of excitement, discovery, and foreboding it gave her remained. She knew that this would be an important moment in time, a moment that would change her. The vision showed Novalie that she had permitted both to be there, but why she would ever allow a Dimoni to perform for the Calling on her stage, in her theater, was a mystery.

The beasts would not be allowed to enter this building for anything other than to serve her in a menial capacity. Never would she allow one of them to step foot on stage in front of an audience, and never would she knowingly allow a demon to attend a performance. The vision must be metaphorical, but for what, she was unsure. As soon as this tour was completed, she would write the vision down and study it at her leisure.

She felt the weakness caused by the vision leave her body and straightened her dress before continuing her tour of the great building. Only visions of the Alluran-born girls brought her to her knees. Why, she wasn't sure. She started up the stairs to the conservatory and made a vow that when she was the Prophetess, the blue girls would be put in their proper place and not allowed to sully the Calling in any way.

Moonsyrah snuck off to the falls as soon as she got the chance. She raced down the path that led to the pools and, kicking off her shoes, dangled her feet in the bubbling heat of the yellow-orange basin. She enjoyed the tickling sensation that the waters gave her. It reminded her of the effervescence of champagne and made her feel giddy.

She sat on the high ledge of the pond, kicking her feet when she reached out to Adym. She waited a few moments and was not surprised when he sat down next to her. She could see him more clearly today than before. His bare feet swung next to hers, and his bare chest caught her gaze. Moonsyrah reached out to touch him and marveled at the crispness of his chest hair against her hand.

"Why can I see you more clearly today than I have before." She asked as she tugged gently on him.

Putting his hand over hers, he answered. "The falls are closer to where I am, physically, so it does not take quite as much energy to come here. Because of this, I can be here more solidly. And, while that is part of the reason, the truth is you can see me better because I want you to." He guided her hand to his lips and kissed her palm. "I have missed you."

"I have missed you too, Adym." Moonsyrah scooted a bit closer to him and leaned her head against his shoulder.

With some hesitation, Moonsyrah whispered, "How old are you?"

"Does it matter?" Was the reply.

"No, not really." Moonsyrah kicked her feet and watched the water splash on the opposite bank. "I have seen a drawing. It was created well over three hundred years ago, and it looks exactly like you. But I don't understand how it can be?"

Adym wrapped his arm around Moonsyrah and kissed the top of her head.

"The way we count the years, I am 31. The way you count the years, I am three thousand one hundred and fifty-two." Adym laughed at her gasp of surprise. "I am of an Alluran race called the SeiOrhii. We do not age, and we do not die from natural causes. The oldest of us is four hundred and sixteen."

"Oh. Then I guess the picture was of you." Moonsyrah was saddened by this for two reasons. The first was that if the picture was of him, then maybe it was true that he and his kind were responsible for the wickedness that plagued the settlers. Second, she would grow old and someday die, and he would continue to exist. The thought of him holding someone else and talking with them as he did her caused a sense of jealousy to build in her that she did not know she was capable of.

Moonsyrah scooted a little way from him. "Along with the drawing of you and, I assume, a group of your friends, I also found a journal. In the diary it talked of the demons that caused fear and terror in the human settlers. It talked of unexplained deaths and disappearances and people going crazy." Moonsyrah looked Adym full in the face. "Was this done by you?"

"Yes, among others." Adym sat still and waited for her to digest this.

"Why?" She asked.

Adym was not sure how she would take the answer. He did not want to tell her anything that might cause her to decide not to release him from the Myst, but he did want her to know everything about him. Adym wanted her to love him for who he really was, as he now knew that he loved her.

"The SeiOrhii are not necessarily the demons that you believe; however, we are a powerful race of Allurans who thrive on fear and violence. We feed on other's fears and pain. The fear we gather from the Yidderians keeps us healthy, strong, and powerful. Since our beginning we have needed fear to maintain our longevity and our abilities."

"Can you live without it? Maybe not forever, but for a while?" Moonsyrah interrupted.

"No. Like you, we have to eat, or we cannot go on," Adym stated. "Moonsyrah, I will not lie to you. Even if we could live without it, we would not choose to. Our strength is tied to it. Our very nature requires us to feed on others. But, Moonsyrah, we, I, enjoy it. I cannot change who or what I am, nor do I want to."

Moonsyrah thought about this and then nodded her head. "I think I understand." She scooted back towards him and stood up, pulling on his hand to join her. She walked hand in hand with him to the edge of the pink pool and then, letting him go, removed her dress. She stepped into the waters and submerged herself until her breasts were under the water. She asked him to join her. She watched as he undressed, entered the calm water, and sat across from her.

"How did you get locked in the Myst? The diary writer thought that a girl named Amalie might have brought a key to the prophetess of the time. Is it because she took the key that you cannot leave your home?"

Adym swam across the spring and settled himself in front of Moonsyrah. He stared at her as he placed his hands on her shoulders. "You know of the key? Do you know where it is? Can you bring it to me?" He asked intently and with a sense of urgency.

"I only know it was speculated that there was a key, but I do not know where it is or what it looks like." Moonsyrah stared back at him just as intently. "Adym, even if I did, I am not sure that I would find it for you. I am not sure I can be the one who releases you to feed on my friends. Surely you can understand this."

Disappointment flashed across Adym's face. "I do. But I will change your mind."

"You can try." Moonsyrah leaned in and kissed him. He took her in his arms and ran his hands along her back and over her firm, round buttocks. He pulled her close, and she could feel his hardness next to her very center. She shivered with longing and desire. Adym placed his hand between the two of them and stroked her until she was sure she would melt. A tightness spread over her, and she clung to him just to stay standing. Moonsyrah wasn't sure what it was, but she suddenly felt like she needed something. Adym slipped his finger inside her and felt her tight passage squeeze against his finger. He growled low in his throat and bit her neck. She moaned in response to this and then again as he slid his finger in and out. Tension was building in her, and Moonsyrah felt like she was a fire about to burst into flames. Adym kissed her and swallowed her screams as Moonsyrah was wracked by the waves of her pleasure.

It could have been a few minutes, or it could have been a few days. Moonsyrah was not sure, but finally, the flames of her pleasure subsided and cooled. She followed Adym to the water's edge and out of the pool. She allowed him to help her dress, and then, together, they walked to a small enclosure at the edge of the waterfall's massive cave that enclosed the hot springs.

"Tell me about your friends." Moonsyrah requested of Adym as she brought one of her hands up and slightly behind her to play with Adym's shoulder-length hair. She twisted the lock in her finger as she leaned her back against him.

"What would you like to know?" He asked, his eyes closed in relaxation. The haze from the spraying water and the cool air acted as a pleasant curtain around them.

"I am curious about them. I saw the faces of four of them, but the fifth had his back turned in the picture I saw. I wanted to know a bit more about those faces." Moonsyrah dropped her hand from his hair and placed it on his, which sat lazily around her waist. "Tell me about the sexy one."

Adym laughed. "That would be my cousin Raighn. Women seem to love him. Though I am not sure why. He tends to take what every female offers and then sends them on their way with-out a thought or care. I do not think he will ever settle for just one of them. He is stubborn and thinks his way is always the right way. He can be volatile but is usually even-tempered." Adym paused before continuing, "You are similar to him in some ways."

"In the good ways, I hope, as you speak as if you do not like him very much," Moonsyrah replied.

Adym thought about that for a moment and then kissed her shoulder. "My cousin and I butt heads often. I have never thought about whether or not I actually like him. What I meant, though, is that you are an elemental like him. He has control over the elements. He is the strongest elemental that we have ever had. You seem to have the ability to control fire."

Surprised, Moonsyrah turned in his arms to look up at him, "How do you know that?"

"I can see it in your mind and feel the fire coursing through you. I think you might be able to eventually work with other elements, but I am not sure. Time will tell. You are unique. As far as we know, no other allurmonuhra has gifts such as we do."

Moonsyrah turned back around and settled herself against him once more. "What of the one with electric blue hair?"

"Kest is always up for a good time. His gift is communication with animals, and he can change his shape into any animal he chooses to become. He loves to roam as a giant Rex or as the fierce ageetah. He is fun to be around, but he cannot stay still for long. He is a bit of a loner, and interestingly, he is Raighn's best friend. Two more opposite people I cannot imagine."

Adym shifted against the hard stone floor and placed Moonsyrah's legs over him and her body next to his. He watched as she picked up a stone and played with it in her hand. He was right she did have some basic control over the elements. Adym watched as the stone glided over her hand and between her fingers, at times not in contact with her skin but following a pattern that he saw her create in her mind. He wondered if she was controlling the stone or the air around it. He smiled again and began running his hands over her long legs.

"And the one with two faces? One smiling and laughing, the other angry and maybe grieving? The artist cried as she drew his face."

Adym stopped his caress and asked a question of his own. "You said that in one of the drawings, there was a group of five men, correct?"

"Yes, but she only drew four of them. Though one face twice with two very different expression expressions on it."

"No, she drew both of the two remaining men on one page. Tam and Tayin were twins. I assume the artist was a woman named Amalie." Adym looked at Moonsyrah for confirmation.

At her nod, he continued, "Tam is the one who laughs and smiles. Tayin is the one who is angry."

Moonsyrah dropped the stone back onto the ground and sat up, pulling her legs close to her body. "You said they were twins?"

"Amalie and Tam were lovers until she murdered him, left the Myst, and locked us in." Adym's voice hardened as he spoke.

"I am sorry for your loss." The two sat in silence for a while, Moonsyrah not sure what to say and Adym remembering Tam's death. Finally, Moonsyrah broke the silence with another question.

"Tell me of Tayin."

"He is my closest friend. He was always the gentlest of us all."

Moonsyrah interrupted Adym, "but he is the one with the angry expression?"

"Yes." Adym continued. "He was always the first to offer help when needed. He was the best of us." Adym paused for a moment, a look of sadness on his face.

"Tayin adores children and gives them the best dreams. He is responsible for teaching them about our history. He embeds little historical facts into their dreams so that they learn as they sleep. He is a dream walker." Adym stood up and grabbed a blanket that Moonsyrah had placed inside the cave earlier. He walked back over to her and wrapped the two of them in its warmth.

"But the death of Tam changed him. Twins are rare amongst the SeiOrhii. If one should die, the other knows instantly, as the one twin's gift will pass to the one left living. Often, the death of one drives the other mad, and they take their own life. Tayin let revenge and anger take over, and he now lives so that he may make Amalie's decedents suffer for what she did to Tam." Adym took Moonsyrah's hand in his and placed the other on her cheek.

"My Beloved, if I had to give you a reason not to set us free, it would be Tayin. He is the most powerful of us all. With his brothers' gift of illusion, he can make dreams and nightmares come to life. He can make entire villages of people live the same waking horror. He can kill dozens of people at a time with his ability, and he will once he is free. He has no love for the Yidderians. My gentle friend has turned into the demon that yours think we are."

Adym leaned in and kissed his beloved softly and then with increasing pressure. He lifted his lips the barest hint from hers. "But even saying that, I hope you set me free."

"I don't know how," Moonsyrah whispered.

"I can teach you how." He saw the hesitation in her mind, "when you are ready to learn."

"Moonsyrah, I want you. I want to be inside you the next time you come undone, but that pleasure will have to wait." He said as he kissed her neck and cheek and then whispered in her ear, "I will be as patient as I can be. I will wait for you to make the decision to find the key, but I hope you do not make me wait too long." He pulled her to a standing position, squeezed her tightly against him, and then released her to walk back to the monastery without him. "I must get back. I have expended much energy, and I need to find nourishment."

Moonsyrah watched as Adym faded from her sight. While he was not there in person, she could feel him still in her mind. Small and unobtrusive but always there.

"Ethan and I are going to meet up with a few friends and have a picnic by the skating pond. Do you want to come?" Sameen asked an obviously distracted Moonsyrah.

"Hello? Yiddera to Moon. Are you paying attention?" Teased Sameen as she took a book that Moon was about to throw away and placed it on the shelf where it belonged.

"Oh, sorry, Meen. I was thinking of something else entirely. My mind was not here." Moonsyrah smiled and finished tidying the living room. "What did you ask?"

"Do you want to go on a picnic today by the pond? This is one of the last few sunny days we are going to get." Sameen put her basket on the counter and placed a few of the cakes Moon had made yesterday in it, along with several sandwiches that she, herself, had just made.

"No. I am going down to finish a project that I started on the loom and then make my way to the archives." Was Moon's answer.

"You are always looking at those silly maps. You know that you will never have the chance to travel. We cannot leave the Monastery. It just isn't allowed." Sameen picked up her basket and made her way to the front door. "Well, if you change your mind, you know where I will be."

Moonsyrah watched Sameen leave the apartment. She knew that Sameen was right. She would never get to see the world, but it did not hurt to fantasize about it. She put on her shoes and followed Sameen out the door. Then, deciding to skip her weaving project for the day, she headed straight to the archives. Moonsyrah settled down on a beanbag, a pile of books and maps spread out around her, when she felt Adym join her. He sat on the cushion behind her and wrapped his arms around her midsection.

"What are you looking at today?" He asked.

Smiling, she pointed at a map of Kahlali. "I was imagining that I was here, exploring the village that lays just below the Myst. I wonder if it is cold there? If it has the same seasons as we do?"

"They have four distinct seasons. It is spring there right now. The flowers are starting to bloom, and the surrounding forest trees are bright with new leaves."

Moonsyrah turned to look at Adym. "You have been there?"

He laughed and squeezed her closer. "Many times. I was there not too long ago. Tayin lives there, and we visit together often. Right now, he is probably sitting on a bench amongst the flowers and listening to music, brooding over the unfairness of life."

Moonsyrah snuggled against Adym. Her back touched his bare chest. He never seemed to wear a shirt or shoes, come to think of it. She leaned her head against his shoulder. "Tell me about it."

He kissed the top of her head, "What if I take you there instead."

"You can do that?" She whispered in awe.

"Well, kind of. I can take you there in my mind. I cannot take you there physically yet. But someday, when I am free to walk around the whole of Yiddera, I will take you anywhere you want to go. Today, we can explore Kofira as I know it. It won't be quite like visiting it in person, but close." He told her to close her eyes and let him have control of her mind. It took some work, but finally, she let him have control of her thoughts. She felt almost as if they were one. It was a unique and pleasant experience. She felt more than heard him say, "Let me show you Yiddera through my eyes."

Moonsyrah was delighted that she could smell the air and feel the grass under her feet. She had expected this to be more like watching a play. It seemed so real. She saw the forest that Adym told her about. She saw that the leaves were still a tender green, and the flowers were just about to burst into color. The air smelled clean and new, as if it had recently stopped raining.

Adym pointed out a couple of animals, indigenous to Kofira, that she had never seen outside of a book. She gasped at the size of the purple hawk that flew over her head. Its wingspan had to be six feet from tip to tip. She turned in a circle, trying to see everything at once. Adym laughed and stopped her before she made them both dizzy. They walked through Kofira together, exploring at Moonsyrah's leisure.

The pair was lost in their travel when the Prophetess stepped into the room. Her eyes widened at what she thought she was seeing. Moonsyrah, her eyes closed, sat on the grey beanbag, and wrapped around her was the shadow of a man. His eyes were glowing a brilliant dark blue color, and he was gazing down at Moonsyrah in what might have been love and maybe possession. The Prophetess clutched her heart as it started to beat erratically. She closed her eyes, took several deep breaths, and then walked out of the room. The Prophetess paced the hall for several minutes, trying to reconcile what she had seen with what she knew to be true.

Moonsyrah was, without a doubt, the fated one. Not that she had ever doubted this, but to be confronted with it so blatantly was a shock. The Prophetess took another breath and headed back into the room.

Adym had seen the prophetess enter the room, and he knew that she had seen him wrapped around Moonsyrah. He also knew that she would soon enter the room again. He decided to give the prophetess something to worry about. Seeing the lady reenter the room, Adym instructed Moonsyrah to keep her eyes closed, and he spoke out loud for the first time since he had met her.

"We are one, and soon, not even the Myst gates will keep us apart," Moonsyrah questioned Adym about his words. Laughing, he replied in her mind that he just couldn't help himself. He released her mind and faded back into his self, his shadow no longer visible.

"Moonsyrah, I was wondering if you could assist me." The Prophetess blinked as she saw the shadow vanish from sight, and Moonsyrah snapped her eyes open in surprise. Moonsyrah stayed seated but sat up straighter as if she no longer had anything to lean against. Understanding flowed through her at what Adym had done. She was surprised by it as she had thought he would still not want the Prophetess to know she was talking to him.

"She saw my shadow holding you. I just gave her something to fear." He answered her unspoken query.

Moonsyrah was aggravated by his little game with the Prophetess but even more so for being brought back to the archives. She was enjoying her trip with Adym. She heard him tell her that there would be other trips at other times. She smiled and looked up at the Prophetess, who was a strange white color.

"Of course, I will assist you." Moonsyrah stood up and, walking over to the Prophetess, asked her if she was okay, knowing that what the Prophetess had heard and saw was the cause of her obvious distress. Moonsyrah chose to act as if she had no knowledge of what had just transpired. She would let the Prophetess initiate the conversation she knew would come from Adym's words.

"I am fine. I had a bit of a shock a minute ago and am not quite recovered." The Prophetess made to loop her hand through Moonsyrah's offered arm but stopped herself before touching the girl, and together, the two walked out of the dimly lit room.

"What was it you needed help with?" Moonsyrah walked sedately at the Prophetess's side, up the stairs to the library, and out into the hall.

"Actually, I was wondering if you would like to take a trip with me? I was going to the falls to gather some of the verbena that grows around the lake. I was hoping that you would go with me." This was not what she had initially needed Moonsyrah's help for, but the Prophetess now thought that getting Moonsyrah alone and having a good heart-to-heart with her was called for. She needed to know how long Moonsyrah had been communicating with the demon and how close she was to finding the only way to release them. The Prophetess knew that Moonsyrah loved the falls and would be more apt to talk freely with her there.

Moonsyrah was confounded at this request. The monastery grounds provided a plethora of different verbena species. Orange, lemon, and grapefruit were among the many flavors they grew. Why would she want to go to the falls to gather what grew wild there? Hesitantly, she answered. "Yes, but are you sure that you want to go all that way when we have several varieties here?"

"Yes, I require some time away from my duties. I know that you often sneak away to the falls and this time I would like to go with you. Go and get ready, and meet me in twenty minutes by the village gate." The Prophetess turned and headed in the direction that would take her back to her rooms, leaving Moonsyrah to wonder what was going on.

The women walked companionably on the path to the falls. The leaves had turned colors and were starting to drop from the trees in preparation for the approaching winter. They arrived at the lake in good time. Moonsyrah took the basket from the Prophetess and started cutting the ripe verbena plants that the

Prophetess selected. Moonsyrah surmised the Prophetess had brought her here for a reason. The silence amidst them was beginning to get to her, and when the basket was almost full, the Prophetess finally spoke.

"How long?"

Perplexed, Moonsyrah stopped her gathering and asked, "How long what?"

The Prophetess studied Moonsyrah to see if she really had no idea what she was referring to. Then, she walked over to an area by the lake water, spread out a blanket, and beckoned Moonsyrah to join her. Once settled, the Prophetess expounded on her question.

"How long have you been talking to the demons?"

Moonsyrah bent her head down and idly played with a loose thread on the blanket. Moonsyrah had promised Adym that she would not tell anyone that she talked to him, but how could she lie to the Prophetess, who obviously knew that she was in contact with Adym after today's events.

Moonsyrah gazed out over the calm sparkling water and answered without looking at the Prophetess, "I have only answered once or twice." She felt that this answer might not worry the Prophetess to much. Moonsyrah was no longer concerned that

Adym would be disconcerted by her admission to the Prophetess that she spoke to him.

"Moonsyrah, they are dangerous, especially for you. They will find your fears and play on them until you give in and free them. Or worse, one of them might make you believe that it loves you." The Prophetess saw Moonsyrah blush and knew she was right in suspecting that this demon had convinced this naïve girl that he loved her. Trying to convince her otherwise might be difficult.

Moonsyrah did not answer the Prophetess but continued looking at the lake with its waterfall of colors flowing down on it. She didn't know what to say.

"Please be careful. Do not give yourself and your soul to a being such as those in the Myst. It will only lead to pain. Pain for you when you find out that the demon tricked you into releasing it and pain for the people of Yiddera that the demons will feed on." The Prophetess placed her hand on Moonsyrah's and patted her gently.

"Prophetess." Moonsyrah finally looked at her, "How do you know that they are all evil? Why do you think of them as demons?"

"The one taken by them called them demons, first. Amalie lived with them for a long time and learned their true nature. She spoke of their unwholesome desire to feed on our fears. Amalie told us that once set free, they would hunt us down and kill us all just for the pleasure and strength they receive from our terrors. She was haunted by them for the rest of her very short life. She lived in hell and eventually took her own life to be free from their torment." The Prophetess paused, "Moonsyrah, I do not want that for you."

"The picture, the one of the two faces. There were tears dripped on it. I do not think that Amalie cried just because she killed one of them. I think she cried over that picture because she loved him. That face was hard for her to draw without feeling the pain of leaving him. If I am correct, then they cannot be all evil." Moonsyrah waited for the Prophetess to consider this. She watched as sadness filled the Prophetess' eyes.

"My child, I can only ask that before they convince you to set them free, you will come to me and tell me why you have chosen to comply with their wishes and not with mine. Please do not let a false idea of love fool you into doing his bidding."

They sat together in silence as the Prophetess took out sandwiches and iced rose tea from her bag. She knew that she had to think of something to say that might sway Moonsyrah's decision in her favor. Knowing that all the daughter's born during the presence of Allura were curious about their parents, she decided to try and work something into this. Very few of them heard from their parents once they were brought to live in the monastery. Most parents wanted nothing to do with the changelings. But that did not stop each girl from wanting to know about her parents and where she came from. The Prophetess decided that this might be a way to get Moonsyrah to once again think about what releasing the demons would mean to the humans.

"Have I ever told you of your biological father?" The Prophetess casually asked in-between bites.

"No." Moonsyrah swallowed. She had always wondered about her birth father. What had he been like? Was he anything like the man who raised her, or was he kind and caring?

"You are like him in many ways. He was blonde, tall, and thin as you are. He traveled across the world making maps." The Prophetess spoke as if remembering him hurt.

"He made maps?" Moonsyrah was intrigued. She leaned in toward the Prophetess so that she would not miss a word.

"Yes, he was determined to map each of the little villages and towns spread out over each continent. Ephraim loved exploring, writing about what he saw, and mapping out the areas where people lived." She paused her story, "He died in one of the many violent storms common off the coast of Kruger. The ship went down just outside of the Myst that lies there." The Prophetess quit talking as her throat swelled in grief. She took a moment to gather herself and then continued. "He would have loved your inquisitive nature. He would have just plain loved you."

Moonsyrah was happy to hear that her father would have loved her. Once she learned that those who raised her were not her biological parents, she had been curious to learn about those who were. She suspected she knew her mother but had often wondered who her father had been. Unlike the other Dimoni she was raised with an adoptive family and not in the monastery. If her suspicions were correct, she knew why she was kept from the monastery but did not understand how her mother could have made that decision.

"Why did my mother give me to another family instead of to the monastery as other blue girls are?" She looked intently at the Prophetess.

"For two reasons. First, her husband was not your father, and she did not want others to find out that she had been unfaithful to him. After their first daughter was born, he had an accident that rendered him unable to have more children. So, your presence would have been hard to explain. And second, she was ashamed that she gave birth to a blue girl. She was more concerned about her reputation than she should have been." The Prophetess answered as honestly as she could.

"Oh." Moonsyrah frowned, "If she was here with me right now, would she still be ashamed?"

"That is hard to answer. Ashamed, no, but disappointed that you are talking to demons, yes." The Prophetess put away her now empty cup and gathered up the remains of the picnic. Then, she stood up and asked if Moonsyrah would please fold the blanket. Once this was done, the two women meandered up the path until they arrived at the colored pools of heated water.

"Moonsyrah, all mothers love their children. Parents who have a living child born under Allura love their daughters, but it is hard for them. Your differences scare most people, which is why those like you are brought to the monastery. Your father would not have cared. He would have loved you even if you had two heads, but he would be disappointed in you if you intentionally let free something that would hurt others." The Prophetess looked as if she had more to say about Moonsyrah's father but chose not to.

"Moonsyrah, I know that I cannot tell you what to do, but I ask you to think seriously before you make a decision that cannot be undone. Remember the day your adoptive mother died. Think how you felt after what happened to her. Think how you felt when demon magic flowed through you. Do not let that happen to any more innocent people." She looked at Moonsyrah, who was staring at her in shocked surprise.

"You know what happened that day? How"

"My dear child, you told me a few weeks after you arrived at the monastery. You were so distraught that I gave you a drink to ease your mind. You slept for three days after that, and it seems that in that time you forgot you had told me. I tried to bring it up once, but you would not talk of it. I remember you telling me that what had happened was a secret that you would never tell a soul." The Prophetess said no more for the day she was told this story was the day that Moonsyrah had found the key. She did not want to risk bringing that particular memory back. Those three days of sleep seemed to have worked in erasing it from her mind.

Moonsyrah walked a bit ahead and thought of the father she never knew, the mother she could never acknowledge, and the mother who had died because of her. Absently, she walked out on the bridge that spanned the width of the purple storm. She did not know that her hair blew around her and that the glow of her eyes intensified. She sat on the stone walkway, deep in thought, not knowing that little flashes of fire sparked around her.

The Prophetess was shocked for the second time that day. She watched Moonsyrah sit on the bridge, calmly unaware that she was causing a microstorm to blow around her or that fire leaped from her fingertips. This was even further proof that Moonsyrah was the one chosen by the demons. She shuddered at what she saw but was amazed by it as well. The Prophetess proceeded to watch for an endless amount of time. Mesmerized at the frightening beauty of the girl that sat before her. As she watched, an oft-seen vision flashed through her mind. She could see herself sitting on her couch across from a blue-haired demon, conversing. She watched as he rose and, bending over her, took her life. The Prophetess shook her head and called out for Moonsyrah to join her for the walk home. She knew that events were coalescing and that she did not have much more time in which to figure out how to stop a four-hundred-year-old prophecy from coming true.

Moonsyrah left the Prophetess at the entrance to the Monastery and found herself absentmindedly walking toward the forest by the old chapel. She sat on the ground with her back to the wall and thought of all that the Prophetess and Adym had told her over the past couple of months. She let her mind dwell on how she felt about the information and tried to make sense of all the emotions that coursed through her.

She smiled to think that she was like her father, who the Prophetess so obviously loved and respected. She wondered if she had ever come across any of the maps that he had drawn. She would have to look for them down in the archives. Moonsyrah knew that even had he been alive, she would not have been raised with him. Even though the chance that they might have met would have been slim, it was still nice to know that he would have loved her. Though he no longer walked Yiddera, she did not like the idea that he would be disappointed in her for caring for a demon.

As for her mother, Moonsyrah knew that she could never acknowledge their relationship, but she was glad to know that her mother was not ashamed of her. However, she did not like knowing that her mother was disappointed in her. She wanted to make her parents proud and show the world that the Dimoni were not inherently bad. Moonsyrah did not want to be responsible for allowing the demons, locked away in the Myst, to become free and feed upon those she called friends. If she followed her heart, both of her parents would be disappointed in her, and that was an uncomfortable thought.

Adym. Moonsyrah frowned. What would she do about him? Her feelings for him were more intense than anything she had ever felt before. She wanted to be near him, to touch him, to love him. Adym set her heart to racing. She could not imagine a life without him. His mind and hers seemed to be one at times, and she could swear that she felt his heart beating next to hers. It felt right that she be the one to bring him out of the Myst.

Did she have to choose between the mother she could not acknowledge and the man she loved? It seemed that in order to keep everyone safe and happy, she would have to keep Adym locked in the Myst. But this did not make her happy. If he was locked away, she could not be with him. However, she knew that the safety of the Yidderians was more important than her own happiness.

She saw that the sun was lowering in the evening sky and knew she should head back into the Monastery. Moonsyrah stood up, shook the pine needles from her skirts, and headed out of the forest. As she walked, she once again thought of her family.

The Prophetess was right. Moonsyrah did not want what happened to her adoptive mother to happen to others. She did not mean to unleash fire upon her. She was still not even sure how that had happened. The Calling stated that the Dimoni were cursed by the demons, and the Prophetess spoke of the Alluran-born girls having markings like that of the demons, so maybe the fire was a demon thing. Adym had said that it was.

She did not want to hurt others and did not want to see the fear on her friends' faces like she had seen on her mother's when she used her demon gift. Seeing fire spring from her hands and hurting someone she loved was her worst memory. Her guilt over causing the fear and pain she saw on her adoptive mother's face was heart-wrenching. Maybe it was best to listen to the Prophetess. Letting the demons free, if she was the one destined to do this, did not seem like the best idea. Even if it meant that she could not be with Adym.

Moonsyrah made it back to her room and picked up her needle and thread. How did one go about making everyone happy? It seemed that no matter which path she chose, someone was going to be hurt. She knew Adym wanted her to look for some kind of key, and the Prophetess wanted her to block him from her mind. She did not want him gone from her thoughts, but until she knew more, Moonsyrah felt it was important to hold off looking for the key Adym searched for.

Not necessarily happy with her decision but determined to adhere to it, she put her thoughts aside and concentrated on her sewing.

"That crafty bitch." Adym paced his house, up one hallway and down the next. He was fuming and impressed with the tactics that the Prophetess had taken to turn Moonsyrah away from him. He had known that the Prophetess would try and stop Moonsyrah from releasing him, but to play on her love of a father she never knew was low. And even lower still to use Moonsyrah's memory of her gift awakening as a means to keep her from releasing him.

The words spoken by the Prophetess had made Moonsyrah take a step back from him and ponder on what an unknown and dead parent would have wanted her to do. He was losing the battle. The person who meant more to him than he meant to himself was choosing against him, and now, to top it all off, the council demanded his presence for an update.

Adym stopped his pacing and, heading into the Hall of Mysts, entered Zeljani. He was the last to arrive and had barely seated himself before the Elders made their frustration known.

"It's been several weeks." Elder Elcrys said as she pounded her fists down on the table. "Why are we still locked in here? How is it that you have not made her release us yet?"

All eyes were on Adym, waiting for his reply, but he had no real answer to give. What could he tell them? That he wanted the girl to choose to set him free? That while he knew they all depended on him to quickly finish this task he was dallying because he loved the Yidderian girl? Would they just nod their heads in understanding that he was giving Moonsyrah time to work out how she felt about him? Not likely.

"Well?" Elder Brecher asked. "Why has it taken so long?"

Adym glanced around the room and saw that they all expected a reasonable answer. He sighed and then finally responded.

"She does not know where it is. It is proving harder to find
than expected." There, that was a decent answer. Adym glanced
at Kest and knew that he was not buying it, and neither, it
seemed, was Tayin.

Elder Brecher stood up from his chair and paced behind the
rest of the Elders, his arms folded behind his back.

"Can you estimate how much longer it may be?" He paused
in his pacing and looked back at Adym. "I am sure that you
realize we are all becoming impatient. We thought that once we
had located the one that would set us free, it would be but a
matter of days until we could gather once more at Rainbow
Falls."

Adym stared at the Elder and then bowed his head in respect.
"I am not sure." He held up his hands to silence the now grum-
bling crowd. "I am not sure, but I will do whatever I can to bring
about our release as soon as possible. I, too, want to leave the
Myst. I promise that as soon as I can get her to find the key, I will
let you all know." He surveyed the room once more. "I know that
you are all counting on me, and I assure you that this task will be

completed as soon as possible. We have waited this long. Please be patient and know that I am doing all that I can to arrange our release."

The council, though obviously unhappy with this answer, nodded their understanding and dismissed the meeting.

Adym stood up and tried to escape the room before any of his peers could corner him. He knew that Kest would be the one most likely to understand why he procrastinated, but Adym did not want to hear his opinion on how the Allurans were more important at this time than the girl was. Raighn would just look at him in disdain and then go back home, glad that Adym had been reprimanded for the delay by the Elders. His cousin was not his biggest fan. Tayin would be the worst. How could he look into Tayin's eyes and tell him that he had fallen for a Yidderian? Tayin would be the least likely to understand, with good reason, but Adym did not want to contend with Tayin's temper today.

He made it back home and was heading to the conservatory when he heard the footsteps of Tayin and his not-so-happy thoughts. Adym sighed, allowed his friend to pass him, and, following behind, waited for the coming argument with his closest friend.

Tayin walked past Adym into the conservatory and waited impatiently for Adym to follow him into the room.

"You look as if you could use a drink," Tayin said as he went over to the side bar and poured himself and Adym a drink. He handed one of the glasses to Adym before sitting down on the couch.

"The Prophetess is convincing Moonsyrah that she should not release us. I am not sure how to change that." Adym ran his hand through his hair and sat down heavily in a chair next to the sofa.

"Why are you giving her a choice? Just make her get the key and give it to you." Tayin stated matter-of-factly.

"She knows of the key but not where it is hidden," Adym replied

"Does she know how to find it?" Tayin inquired.

"She doesn't know she does." Adym stared out the glass in his hand. "She can hear the music. She just doesn't know what that means."

"Dammit, Adym. It is your duty to make sure that she finds the key. If she can hear the music it makes, what have you been doing these past two months if not showing her the way to free us?" Tayin stood up, walked over to the window wall, and looked out at the evening sky.

"She knows of the key, but I will not force her into this decision." Adym sighed in frustration.

"Why the hell not?" Asked Tayin, his temper bubbling to the surface.

Adym walked over to stand next to his friend. "I love her, Tayin." He said simply.

"She is human! How can you love such a creature? Did you not learn anything from Tam's experience? You cannot trust them." Tayin shouted at Adym.

"She is a daughter of Allura, not a human, and I love her." Adym turned toward Tayin, "I need her to want to set me free. I need the choice to be hers."

Tayin shoved Adym against the wall, "Listen closely, my friend. This does not just affect you. It affects all of us. What you think you need is irrelevant." His handsome face filled with anger as he moved closer to Adym. "I promise you this. If you do not show her how to interpret the music tonight, I will find her through your mind and wrap her in so many nightmares that she will find the key just to get me to stop. I will make her life an unimaginable hell."

Adym pushed away from Tayin. "Do not touch her." Anger filled his voice. "My best friend, you might be, but I will kill you if you touch her."

Tayin shoved Adym again, "Tonight, Adym. I will give you tonight. But tomorrow is mine." Tayin stormed out of the room and left back to Kofira.

Adym slammed his fist into the wall and yelled in frustration, knowing that Tayin would be true to his word. So, Adym, fueled with rage at both Tayin and the Prophetess, angrily called out to Moonsyrah, commanding her to meet him at the falls. Tonight, he would show her how to find the key. No longer would he wait. He would bring her mind into his and make her recognize the music that would lead her to the key.

Moonsyrah was in her room embroidering flowers on the dress she had finally finished sewing when she saw an image of the falls flash in her mind. She set her sewing aside and went out onto the balcony to look in their direction. The sky looked like a storm was coming, the Myst took on an eerie glow in the evening light, and the rumble coming from the falls was louder to her this evening. There was a tension in the air that mimicked the anxiety she was suddenly feeling. Again, the falls flashed through her mind, and she heard Adym calling to her. Without much thought to the coming storm, she grabbed a blanket and threw it around her shoulders, then headed out of her room. Moonsyrah hurried along the halls, hoping not to run into anyone as she left the building. A few yards away from the monastery, she looked up and thought she saw Sameen standing by her window, watching her. She decided it didn't matter and continued walking.

She left the monastery grounds and reached the path that led to the falls. It was starting to get dark and windy from the coming storm, so she sped up. She made it to the falls as the first furious drops of rain came down. The falls were slippery, and she walked gingerly past the pink and yellow pools and around the bend of the green hot spring till she reached the midnight purple one. There, she saw Adym standing, anger covering his handsome face. His thoughts matched the fury of the storm, and little flickers of her own fears flashed in the back of her mind. She warily invited him further into her mind so that she could see his thoughts. The images intensified, and she worked to shut them out.

"Why?" she asked him, "What have I done to make you angry?"

"You have made me lose sight of something important. Something I should have already accomplished." Adym reined in his thoughts. He pulled her to him and made himself more solid and less shadow as he kissed her fiercely and bit her lip. She pulled away and touched her mouth with her fingers. His mood and the tension she could feel fit the energy of the storm. She knew that he had brought her here for a reason. She looked at the storm beyond the falls.

"I do not think I will ever understand how I can feel for you as I do, knowing what you are, but even with your anger, I can't help it." Moonsyrah paused, "Adym, I love." She started, but Adym interrupted her. "Do not say it yet. You must first understand what that means to both of us. There is a bond beginning between us, and once the words have been said, there will be no going back for either of us. I need you to be very sure that you know me before you say the words. Once said, they cannot be unsaid." Adym's voice was rough with emotion and anger.

"But Adym, I do know you."

Adym interrupted her once again, "No, you do not. I am not the hero in your fairy tales, Moonsyrah. I am the demon of the story, the one you were warned about. You know I am; you have been told repeatedly by the people you love. I have told you how I grow stronger and more powerful when I bring fear to others. I enjoy it. I revel in the pain I cause. Moonsyrah, I am the demon that your people believe me to be. Do not expect me to be other than I am." Adym forcefully pulled her mind into his.

Images of Adym and the others from the sketchbook flashed through her mind. She saw Adym and his friends kill people with their minds and laugh at it. She saw the fear that the first humans to encounter him had. She felt Adym's enjoyment of their terror and anguish, and she felt him grow strong with it. Her mind rebelled against the horror of the images that he showed her, but her heart still ached for him. Her body still wanted his touch.

"Adym, what do you want from me? I know there is something other than these images. You could have shown me these at any time. You did not bring me here to scare me. Tonight, there is an urgency. I can feel it in your mind." She said instead.

"Our destinies are intertwined. Yours is to find the key and mine is to guide you to it. I need you to find the key tonight. I need you to bring the prophesy to a close. I no longer have the option to wait for you to come to terms with your part in all this."

Adym sighed deeply before he entered her mind farther than he had ever been and pulled her into his without her permission. She fought back. The force of his mind pulling hers felt like an invasion. Moonsyrah felt Adym's mind twine around hers in ways she did not know were possible; their minds and souls had become one. Adym's memories were now hers to explore. She saw the reason why he stopped her from telling him how she felt. She knew that the bond would be unbreakable once she accepted it, but it no longer mattered. She still loved him, and in the twining of their minds, the bond had been cemented into place.

Moonsyrah watched images of herself and was shocked to see how young she was in many of them. Moonsyrah saw her first contact with the voice as a child; she saw Adym watching her and her mother swimming in the green pool. She saw him cause her to stumble and fall part way into the purple water and felt the fire flare-up inside of her for the first time. She saw him watch her experience the energy of the green pool, watched her fear of it spreading throughout her body. She saw him in her dreams that night, teaching her to channel the energy she felt from the stones.

Moonsyrah saw him there, with her, when her mother fell from the cliff. She saw him smile when the flames shot from her hands. It was her worst memory and the recurrent nightmare of every birthday eve. To find him there in the background disturbed her but also caused her to acknowledge that she had known that someone or something was with her that day. The memory flooded her senses.

For the first time, she saw past the surface of that event and saw Adym in it. He was the voice that helped her find and control the fire within her. He was the one that caused the branch to fall. He was the one who helped her kill her mother. She had produced the fire, and he had helped by pushing her mother further toward the cliff's edge, causing her to fall in her attempt to escape the flames that ate at her dress. Moonsyrah violently fought to pull her mind back from Adym's; he wouldn't let her. This memory was far worse than the horror he had shown her earlier.

"Moonsyrah, I will not let you go, so quit fighting me. Push past the painful memory and listen to the music of Rainbow Falls. I know you can. I need you to learn their different songs so you can find the one I need." He silenced his thoughts so that she could hear the sounds of the many-colored crystals. He felt her reluctantly do as he asked.

Moonsyrah heard music all around her. The music was like a symphony being performed in a small space. It was deafening. Adym pushed her mind to focus on the gems in the purple pool, and Moonsyrah could hear a soft melody coming from them. The song didn't have many challenges to it, and yet it sounded like the tune was trying to change into something more than it currently was. Then, suddenly, she heard the melody evolve into a full orchestra of sounds. It was complicated yet simple. It made her think of becoming something more than she was. It was like a gentle spring rain bursting into the most violent of storms. It awakened the fire energy within her, and she felt as if she was at the center of the storm.

Moonsyrah was more afraid of it than ever and more drawn to its depths. Her mind felt like it was the storm itself. She could feel Adym pushing her to jump into the pool, but she wouldn't give him that control. Before she could process all the sounds and images she was receiving, she felt him pull her to the green pool, where she heard the music of violins and other string instruments. It was a haunting melody that started out bright with new life and then ended in the melancholy of death. The green crystals repeated the tune over and over again. It was like the song was a circle that couldn't be interrupted. Again, she saw her mother playing in the water and then saw the flames that sent her mother over the edge of the mountain. She closed her eyes against the pain, knowing that this would not block the images from her mind.

"Stop. I do not want to hear or see any more of this." She looked at him as a demon for the first time. Moonsyrah tried to block Adym out of her mind, but he still wouldn't let her go.

"No. Forget the memories you see and concentrate on the music." Adym made her leave the green pool and follow the path to the yellow-orange pool. Moonsyrah heard the flute-like sounds of the crystals that sang of happiness, playfulness, and reckless desire. The song from the yellow-orange crystals tried to dominate all the other music around her. The tune stimulated her senses and her imagination. It was overwhelming and impulsive. She heard the music building to a tempo that made her feel as if she was a predator about to begin a hunt.

Without waiting for Adym to push her, she walked to the pink pool. Here, the crystals sounded like a piano playing a deceptively soft lullaby. It eased her mind into a sense of peace before the music became louder and brought knowledge with it. She could see her dreams in the notes. She could feel her blood heat with desire and longing. The music brought with it wisdom, and this knowledge made her uncomfortable yet confident. The song was filled with all of her most perfect dreams and her most terrible nightmares. The music was no longer just a lullaby of love and naivety; it was intimate and full of sexual desire. Her mind, entwined with Adym's, became hot with the understanding and acceptance of what was between them. She could feel his desire for her and knew he could feel hers for him. Her soul sought to touch him as he touched her, but still, she fought against the attraction, the love she felt for this demon.

Adym led her back down the path. He could feel her hesitate at the edge of the purple pool. He pushed Moonsyrah past the pool and walked beyond the shelter provided by the mountains and into the raging storm. He walked her into the lake of clear crystals and helped her block the sounds of the rain. She heard all the crystals' songs at once. They sang of life and death and every emotion and experience held in between.

"Block out the music you have already heard and concentrate on the tune that is left behind. I need you to hear the music in the blue crystals." She pulled the other songs away from the center of her thoughts and found hidden behind them a low-pitched, slow melody of such intensity it hurt. It was quiet, steady, and melodic. It felt immortal, aloof, and cold. It was beautiful and vibrant; it was order in all things. It was the feel of the third moon. It sang of control and magic. It was the tune that held all the music of the crystals together and made them blend in harmony. She felt Adym unravel his mind from hers, and she felt a sense of loss at the distance this put between them.

"Now listen for a song like that of the blue crystals. It will sound as if it is unlocking a secret and as if you are entering another dimension. Listen carefully. Follow the tune. Find the key."

Adym pushed himself to the very edge of her mind so as not to interfere. This she must do herself. She was the one destined to find the key. He could not help her hear its call.

She heard nothing at first and then thought she heard a faint sound in the distance. She couldn't be sure where it was coming from. She walked out of the lake and stood on the shore. The rain was coming down hard, and she could feel her dress plastered against her body. She spread out her arms and let the energy of the storm and the surrounding crystals enter her mind and flood her senses. She felt the power of the songs coming from the Rainbow Falls. She could feel the persistent calling of the Myst just beyond them, and finally, she could feel the direction from which the new song called. This song beckoned her back to the monastery. It appealed to her to find its source. She had heard this one before. This song belonged to the rock she had once held. She tried to unlock the memory of where it was.

Moonsyrah could feel the excitement rise in Adym. She let the song and the memory go. She now had the power to make Adym feel her thoughts. She made Adym feel her desire for him and felt his need for her rise within his mind, and then she forcefully pulled his mind to dwell on the memory she saw at the green pool. Moonsyrah made him feel her pain at knowing that it was he who taught her to kill, even if unintentionally, her mother. She then reached out to him and lightly kissed his shadowed lips. It was a kiss that bonded them irrevocably together in the Korsyon. It was a kiss that spoke of her love. It was also a kiss that he recognized as a goodbye.

"No. Don't leave me." He felt his heart rip in agony. He had forced her to join minds with him. He had made her learn of the music in the crystals. He had shown her how to find the key. Opening his mind to her had been a risk; he knew what she would see there, and still, he forced her mind to open and join his. In his anger with himself over letting his feelings for

Moonsyrah overshadow his duty, he had driven her from him. He knew she could feel his love for her, and yet she was still walking away. He watched as she walked the path that would lead her back to the monastery. He had failed. Moonsyrah could now find the key and release him, but in that last kiss, he knew that she no longer wished to.

Moonsyrah heard nothing from Adym for two very long days and realized the enormity of her decision. Walking away from him left her feeling empty, something she did not understand since she knew now what he was capable of. On the third day, she heard him say her name in question. She ignored him, and she ignored him again when he spoke to her that evening. She heard him every day after that, and every day, she made the decision not to answer him. Every time he talked to her, it became harder and harder to ignore him. Her heart ached for him, beat for him, but her mind was set. He was the demon that the Prophetess had warned her he was. She couldn't keep him entirely out of her mind, but she had learned to block him from some areas within her mind and how to dim his voice in her head. Inevitably, once he realized she wasn't going to answer him, he would go away.

She became melancholy and often found herself gazing off into the distance and reliving that night at the falls. The rush of entirely mingling her mind with Adym's had been intoxicating and scary and left her feeling exposed and vulnerable but oh so powerful, too. The music in the crystals was finally in tune, and it was magical. The feelings they invoked were varied and intense. The feelings mimicked that of those she had for Adym.

She longed to call to him and say she was sorry for leaving, but the memory she saw that night was heartbreaking. She had always felt as if someone was with her, other than her mother, on that fateful day. To learn it was Adym who taught her to channel the energy of the crystals into fire and then guided her to push the image at her mother was devastating. The anger she felt over this betrayal ate at her soul. How could she love a man who had helped her murder her mother? What kind of person did that make her?

She went about life listlessly for a couple of weeks. She did what was required of her, but nothing more. She rarely left her room, and she knew this was causing concern in both Sameen and the Prophetess, but she couldn't bring herself to care. She probably would have continued in this fashion for several more weeks if it hadn't been for the music.

It was a crisp late fall day when the Prophetess invited Moonsyrah for lunch. Moonsyrah had ignored other invitations, but this one sounded more like a command than the others, and so she went. She knew the Prophetess would remark on her melancholy and her health, so she did her best to look good. She dressed in her favorite pink dress, which added color to her face, and re-braided her hair. At the Prophetess' door, she plastered a smile on her face and entered once she was beckoned to come in.

She looked about the lovely, inviting room and noticed that everything was still the same as it always was. Moonsyrah wondered how everything around her could be so normal when everything inside had changed for her. She sat down in the tall-backed green chair where she always sat and waited for the Prophetess to join her. The Prophetess walked across the room and went over to the windows to pull open the drapes as she greeted Moonsyrah. The sun poured into the spacious area, brightening everything it touched.

"Good morning, my child. Please pour the wine while I get the plates." The Prophetess went over to a nearby cabinet and pulled out a couple of plates, placed them on the coffee table, and sat down on her settee. Moonsyrah could smell the cinnamon and cloves that flavored the warmed mulled wine as she poured it into the two glasses. She handed one to the Prophetess and took a small sip from hers. She could also smell the sweet spiciness of the appleberry scones on a tray next to little finger sandwiches of cucumber, dill, and smoked salmon that were to make up their lunch.

The Prophetess looked at Moonsyrah with concern as she sipped her wine. "I have watched you over the past few weeks. You have not been yourself lately, and I wonder what is troubling you. You have not even been to our morning meditations. Are you feeling unwell?" The Prophetess set down her glass and leaned forward to look more closely at Moonsyrah. She looked paler and thinner than usual and had dark circles under her eyes.

"I am fine Prophetess." Moonsyrah brightened her smile and reached for a scone that she didn't plan to eat.

"Do not lie to me, child. I know that something is wrong. Please tell me what I can do to help. I am worried about you." The Prophetess reached across the table intending to put her hand on Moonsyrah's, but the look that flashed in the young woman's eyes stopped her, and she withdrew. She leaned back once again and adjusted her skirts around her to give herself time to calm her suddenly racing heart. Moonsyrah had never looked at her like that before. It was a look of anger and fire. It had the hint of an awakening demon behind it.

"Very well, I have been plagued with nightmares. I am sure they will pass, and I will be back to my usual self soon." Moonsyrah hoped this was true. She took a small bite of her scone, knowing this would please the Prophetess and maybe convince her that there really was nothing to worry about.

"Nightmares? Would you like to discuss them? Sometimes, talking with someone about what worries or scares you can help dispel the nightmares."

"No, I would rather not." Moonsyrah was curt with her answer and hoped this dreadful interview wouldn't take much longer. Maybe if she finished her scone, she could leave. She took another bite, then placed it back on her plate and set it on the table.

The Prophetess raised an eyebrow of displeasure at Moonsyrah. She sat up straight and looked directly into the girl's eyes once again, "tell me, are you still conversing with the demon who speaks with you?"

"No, while he speaks to me, I have never spoken back to him." Moonsyrah lied, trying to lessen the truth of her contact with Adym. "I have closed my mind to him." She said this in an almost convincing manner, though she could hear the sadness in her words.

The Prophetess took a deep breath, "Do not lie to me again in this conversation. When did you start speaking to one of them? More importantly, when was the last time you spoke with the demon?" The Prophetess looked at Moonsyrah with consternation and some concern.

"The night that you and I went to the Falls." Moonsyrah blinked back the tears that threatened to fall. She looked down at her hands in the hope the Prophetess would not notice.

"Is this last conversion what brings you nightmares and has put you in this listless mood?"

"Yes, but I have learned how to reinforce the barriers in my mind against him. When he speaks, I do not speak back. Prophetess, you told me to ignore the voice, and I am. I have also started drinking the tea blend you made me that helps block against bad dreams. I drink it every night before bed. I know you do not wish me to communicate with the demons, and as I do not wish to hear from him either, I keep the block strong in my mind." Moonsyrah decided that since she had made the slip, she might as well tell a part of the truth to the Prophetess, at least the part that would appease her. She could never admit the love she had for Adym to the Prophetess.

The look of concern was back in the Prophetess's eyes, this time tinged with worry. "My child, why didn't you come to me for help? I asked you to."

"I felt I did not need the help. I am able to deal with it on my own." Moonsyrah set her face with a 'this conversation is over' look and picked up her wine to indicate that she had nothing more to say on the subject. As she lifted the cup to her lips, she caught a faint musical sound. A song that she recognized. Startled, she stood up and turned toward the window, accidentally spilling her wine across the seat and arm of her chair. Moonsyrah looked in question at the window. Her mind strained to hear where the music was coming from.

"What is wrong, Moonsyrah?" The Prophetess hurried over to the girl and turned her away from the window. She took the now empty glass from her and placed it back on the table. Moonsyrah looked at the Prophetess, and a memory flitted through her mind. She had heard the music in this room once before. It was long ago, but precisely when she did not know. She knew it was coming from a door hidden behind the curtain that was drawn back from the windows. She couldn't let the Prophetess know she heard the music.

Moonsyrah knew instinctively that the Prophetess would see this as a cause for more concern and give her another lecture on the prophecy and the voices. She might even possibly move the source of the sound somewhere she might never hear it again. And so, Moonsyrah lied. "I thought I heard something knock against the window. It startled me. I am sorry I spilled wine all over your beautiful chair." Moonsyrah knew this lie did not fully explain her actions, but it would have to do. She shrugged away from the Prophetess and grabbed a napkin. She haphazardly started to mop up the spill while intently listening for the music. It seemed to be coming from below the window.

Another memory swept across her mind. The door behind the drapes led to a stairway. She needed to be alone to think of what this could mean and if she should try to find the source of the sound.

"I am so sorry for the mess I have made. I will send in a servant to clean up the spill. It looks like I spilled on my dress as well. I must see to it before the stain sets." Without waiting for the Prophetess's dismissal, she hurried out the door.

She had forgotten all about the key. The key was the whole reason behind that night at the falls with Adym, but her leaving him had enveloped her thoughts completely. She stopped at the bottom of the stairs that led to her rooms. She listened intently for a moment and found the music again. From here, she could barely hear it. It was distant and faint but definitely coming from the rooms of the Prophetess. It grew louder the longer she concentrated on it, and the music gave her new energy. She knew that she must find the key. What she would do with it once she found it was another matter.

For the rest of that day and all the next, she focused on finding ways to follow the music and get back into the Prophetess' rooms without her ever-watchful eye noticing. Only when she once again heard Adym's voice did she block the music from her mind, and like every other day, she ignored his call.

It took her two days to come up with and settle on a plan. Tomorrow, when the Prophetess was making her morning rounds to the many different areas within the monastery, she would sneak into her quarters and look for the key. She would bring a gift of apology for the spill and her rudeness as an excuse to be there should the Prophetess return before she was able to locate the key and leave the rooms.

And so, the next morning, Moonsyrah made her way down to the Prophetess's rooms. She didn't rush, and she nodded politely to the few servants she met along the way. She didn't want to call undue attention to herself. She made it without any problems and knocked softly on the door. Receiving no answer, as expected, she let herself into the rooms. She set her gift of freshly baked cinnamon cookies and an orange-zest-scented tea blend on the table. Standing quietly by the table, she listened for the music. It played loudly in her mind, and called out for her to follow it. Walking across the soft, thick pine green carpet, she headed towards the window. She pulled open the heavy gold-toned drapes and let in the weak morning light. She pulled the curtains a bit further back and found the door from her memory. Moonsyrah looked around her to make sure she was still alone before opening the door.

The stairway was made of stone and was not very well-lit, just as she remembered it. She made her way carefully down them. With every step, the music became louder and more urgent. The bottom of the stairway opened to a sizable stone-floored room that faintly reminded her of the dungeons she had read of in fantasy books. She looked about her and saw that the room was filled with several pieces of art that she recognized as works from Earth. Each piece was an original and worth a fortune. She ignored these treasures and followed the music to a corner in the back of the room, farthest from the staircase.

The corner was lit by a pale blue glow emanating from a dark blue, round stone. It was about the size of a large plum. Its surface looked smooth and perfect. Moonsyrah stepped closer and noticed a crescent moon-shaped hole running right through the middle of it. The music was deafening, and it urged her to pick up the stone. She knew this must be the key to the Myst gates. Moonsyrah hesitated for the briefest of moments before she picked it up and held it in her hands. She could feel the power contained within it. It felt like the magic of the third moon; it smelled like the air before the rain, like the Myst, like Adym. She never wanted to let it go.

Moonsyrah remembered the memory she had tried to find while at the Falls that fateful night. It had been right after she had come to the Monastery. She remembered getting lost in the monastery and hearing music; she had decided to follow it. She remembered descending the stairs and standing in front of this very pedestal. She could remember longing to pick up the stone that sang so beautifully to her. The Prophetess had found her there. She had been most upset at Moonsyrah and told her that she was not to ever touch this particular item. Moonsyrah remembered telling the Prophetess of the slightly off-key music she heard coming from it. She also recalled the Prophetess telling her that rocks did not make music or sing. She was then led to the room above and given a drink that made her forget she had even seen the crystal. She had even forgotten the door that led to the hidden room.

Coming out of her reverie, Moonsyrah slipped the key into a concealed pocket within her brown work dress, and tamping down the music in her mind, she headed back out of the room. She had just closed the hidden door and pulled the curtain closed over it when she heard someone enter the room. She looked behind her when she heard the Prophetess's voice.

"Moonsyrah, what brings you here this morning?" The Prophetess worried over the proximity of Moonsyrah to the hidden door as she made her way to the window.

"I knew you would be back from your rounds soon and wanted to meet you here to give you a gift. I hope you don't mind; I opened the curtains. It looks like it is going to be a beautiful autumn day and I wanted to watch as the sun made its way into your garden." Moonsyrah swept past the Prophetess and headed towards the table. "I feel bad about the way I behaved the other day and wanted to apologize. I hope you like the tea I have made for you." Moonsyrah looked innocent and genuinely sorry. The Prophetess knew the young woman could not have found the door; she had erased it from the girl's memory and, brushing aside her suspicion, thanked her for the thoughtful gift.

"Would you like to share a cup with me?" The Prophetess put on a kettle and got out two teacups.

"If you are not too busy, I would love to." Moonsyrah knew that if she declined, the Prophetess would again get that suspicious look in her eyes. She settled down on her usual chair and grimaced at the ugly stain that her spilled wine had left.

"Would you like me to reupholster your chairs for you? I have some beautiful green velvet that I could use. I could also redo your settee. I have a piece of gold-watered silk embossed with flowers that would look lovely in here."

The Prophetess sat down and poured the hot water over the tea. She smiled as she caught the delicious scent of the herbal blend. "I would like that. Right now, the harvest is upon us, so you may begin after the first of the year." She took a sip of the tea. "This is wonderful, Moonsyrah. You are quickly becoming an expert at making new tea blends." The two women sat there eating the freshly baked cookies and drinking the warming tea.

After she had finished her drink, Moonsyrah politely excused herself to start her day and left the Prophetess sitting on her settee, thinking that all was once again right between them.

Two weeks had passed since she had discovered the key. Two weeks of indecision on what she should do with the key. Two weeks of trying to ignore Adym and keep the secret of the key from him. Her thoughts constantly dwelled on the round stone and what would happen if she gave it to Adym. The indecision was wearing on her. She was exhausted from trying to convince everyone she was okay. Moonsyrah tried her best to put more energy into her daily activities but didn't quite succeed. When Sameen invited her to walk down to the pond to see if it was frozen enough for ice skating, she accepted, thinking it might help put her turbulent thoughts aside for a while.

She put on her warm purple cloak and walked down to the pond with Sameen. They could see their breath in the air and felt sure the pond had to be frozen through. Moonsyrah walked to the edge and tapped the ice with her foot. It felt solid enough, and so she walked out a bit further. She couldn't see through the ice because of how thick it was, and she didn't hear any cracking sounds. She carefully made her way back to the shore to put on her skates.

The scenery was picturesque. The tall evergreens were covered in frost, and the mountain range was snowcapped and peaceful. The air was sweet and crisp. Moonsyrah smiled a genuine smile for the first time in almost a month. She skated out to meet up with Sameen, who was already doing pirouettes in the very middle of the frozen pond. The two young women tried to outdo each other's tricks and found themselves flat on their butts often. Their laughter rang out in the crystal air. They were eventually joined by a few others brave enough to face the cold.

Moonsyrah watched as Sameen entered a game of crack the whip. She laughed as those at the end were sent flying. She skated the perimeter of the large pond twice before she saw Sameen, unable to hold on to the person in front of her, slide across the pond flat on her back. Moonsyrah went and sat on the nearby bench to watch Sameen and the others when a young man came up to her and asked if he could sit. She nodded yes and continued to watch her friend skate.

"Hi, my name is Gavin." The blond, rather good-looking young man said.

"I am Moonsyrah." Moonsyrah scooted a little bit further down the bench from Gavin.

"Why aren't you out there with your friend? I was watching you skate. You are pretty good."

"Oh, I just needed a break. Why aren't you skating?" Moonsyrah asked politely.

"I saw you sitting over here and wanted to say hello. Will you take a turn around the pond with me?" Gavin stood up and held his hand out to Moonsyrah.

Moonsyrah was startled by this and was unsure what to do. People tended to avoid her touch, and they did not offer their hand to her. Her mind briefly flitted to thoughts of Adym and his touch. She quickly pushed aside these thoughts, and hesitantly, taking Gavin's hand, she accepted his invitation.

Hand in hand, they skated around the pond. Gavin was right in saying he wasn't very good, and he often took her down with him when he fell. Laughing, Moonsyrah would help him back up, and they would try again. They made it around the frozen pond a second time before Sameen and a young man met up with them. The four of them skated back to the bench and sat down to take off their skates. Moonsyrah introduced Sameen to Gavin and learned that the two of them already knew each other. Then Sameen introduced Ethan to Moonsyrah.

"It is nice to meet you, Ethan. Gavin, thank you for inviting me to skate with you. I had a lot of fun." Moonsyrah leaned over and gave Gavin a hug. Gavin smiled and hugged her back.

"Would you like to walk with me tomorrow in the maze?" Gavin asked Moonsyrah.

"I would like that." Moonsyrah smiled back and then excused herself and Sameen.

Arm in arm, the two girls left the pond with the laughter of those still skating ringing in their cold ears. Once in their tower rooms, Moonsyrah put on the tea kettle while Sameen stoked the fire back up. The two girls changed out of their damp clothing and sat down to enjoy their warming tea in front of the crackling fire.

"Thank you, Sameen."

"What for Moon?"

Moonsyrah turned toward her friend, who sat cuddled up in a red lap blanket, feet tucked up under her. "For convincing me to go skating. It was just what I needed." Moonsyrah tucked her own blanket more firmly around her legs.

Sameen looked at Moonsyrah and saw the shadows that were, lately, a part of her eyes. "I have been worried about you, Moon." Sameen paused, "I saw you leave the monastery the night of that huge storm. I waited up for you for hours. I saw you come in cold, wet, and crying. I almost went to you, but you looked as if you wanted to be alone and wouldn't appreciate my company. What happened, Moon? Where did you go?"

"I thought you might have seen me leave. I went to the falls. The Prophetess told me I wasn't to go back to them, but I had to. I went there to meet someone. I can't tell you who I met or why I went, but it is over now, and I won't be going back." Moonsyrah's heart ached that what she and Adym had was over. Saying it out loud to Sameen made it seem more final. Moonsyrah closed her eyes to check the tears that wanted to pour down her cheeks. "I am sorry I have been such a bad friend lately."

Sameen smiled, "we all have our hard times. Just know that I am always here for you. You can talk to me about anything. That's what best friends are for." She hugged Moonsyrah. "Now, let's forget this conversation for tonight and decide what you are going to wear for this walk around the maze with Gavin."

Moonsyrah and Sameen both got up from the couch and went to look at what Moonsyrah had in her closet. They settled on a long-sleeved dress that was warm but showed off the small-ness of Moonsyrah's waist.

"Sameen, I am nervous about tomorrow. What if we have nothing to talk about?" Moonsyrah hung the dress they had picked out back up in the closet and sat on the bed with her friend.

"Gavin is a really nice person. He is training to be a healer. He knows a lot about our history, and as you are also interested in history, you two will have plenty to talk about." Sameen stood up to leave Moonsyrah's room. "I do have one bit of advice. Smile and try to have a good time. If you make the decision to be happy and have fun, you will." Sameen kissed her friend on the cheek and left to her own room.

Moonsyrah thought of what her friend had said. How could she be happy when all she could think about was the key, what to do with it, and Adym.

Novalie had seen Gavin sit down next to Moonsyrah at the lake. She had heard their conversation and went stiff with anger that he had invited Moonsyrah for a walk the next day. She had become even angrier when she saw Moonsyrah hug him before she left with that other blue-haired demon girl. Gavin was Novalie's, not Moonsyrah's.

Novalie walked back to the Monastery, no longer interested in skating. She was the next prophetess, and Gavin was her future partner, not Moonsyrah's. She did not like the freedom and lack of discipline that her mother allowed these blue freaks. If she could not permanently get rid of the evil things, then once she took on the mantle of "Prophetess," she would not allow much of what was currently allowed to them. First, she would take away their freedom to associate with others who were not like them outside of classes and other duties. Second, she would make them learn that the only way to redeem their souls was to admit their evilness and devote their lives to the Calling and to the church. She wanted to have complete control over them. None of this treating them as almost equals, such as her mother did. Novalie would not permit them any rights other than those she would give to animals such as the Dimoni were.

Novalie knew why Moonsyrah was special to her mother and was sickened by this relationship she shared with Moonsyrah. She knew that her mother thought that this blue-eyed freak was the one the ancient prophecy spoke of. The evil entity that would release the demons and set them free to feed upon the innocent humans. The Prophetess was actively trying to stop the prophecy from coming to fruition, but Novalie knew that she wouldn't succeed. The prophecy would come true, the world would burn, and out of the ashes, she would rise, with Gavin more powerful than any other prophetess since the first. But for now, she had to make sure that Moonsyrah was dealt with and that she left Gavin alone.

The next morning, Moonsyrah got ready to meet Gavin for their walk. She met up with him at the entrance to the garden maze. At first, she felt a bit awkward and wasn't sure what to say;

until now, Adym was the only man she had ever talked to that wasn't one of her teachers, but Gavin commented on how pretty she looked and with his easy conversation soon made her feel comfortable.

"Sameen tells me you are studying to become a healer. What made you choose to study the healing arts?" Moonsyrah queried.

"I have always wanted to be a healer. I don't know why exactly. I have always been interested in the healing aspects of herbology and in helping others. What about you? What do you study?" Gavin chose a left turn, and they found themselves at a dead end. He leaned against the maze hedge and took Moonsyrah's hand in his. Her first inclination was to pull away, but then she decided there was no harm in holding his hand, so she left her hand in his.

"I am interested in many areas of study. I enjoy geography and am quite good at old Earth languages. If I had to choose only one thing, though, it would be working with fabric. I love making beautiful things, and I find embroidery and sewing relaxing. I wouldn't want to give up geography or ancient languages, though." Moonsyrah tugged on Gavin's hand and started walking again. They talked about many things, and Moonsyrah found his conversation stimulating.

"Do you believe in destiny and prophecies?" Moonsyrah asked Gavin, genuinely wanting to know his thoughts on the topic.

"I believe that destiny can lead you to a choice, but it is up to each individual to make that choice on their own. I do not believe that we are destined to make one choice or the other. Destiny can lead us to the point where the choice is offered. A prophecy can foretell something that will happen, but I do not think they are infallible. A prophecy might foretell that you choose to pick the rose, for example. I believe that destiny will one day lead you to that very rose, but neither destiny nor a prophecy can make you pick it." Gavin let go of Moonsyrah's hand and stood in front of her.

"But if you pick the rose, wouldn't you be fulfilling the prophecy and therefore prove that you were destined to pick it?"

"Not necessarily. Did you pick the rose because of the prophecy? Moonsyrah, you choose who you want to be and what you want to do. There are no predestined answers, only predestined choices." Gavin placed his hands on her shoulders and pulled her closer to him. Moonsyrah twisted out of his hold and started walking the path again.

"I have never thought of things that way before. I have always just believed that the Prophetess's visions were set in stone and that they couldn't be changed. Of course, I do know that she is trying to change one of the prophecies that was foretold by one of her ancestors. Sometimes, I feel that I do not have a choice in my own destiny." Moonsyrah said this quietly and with a touch of sadness.

"You will always have a choice in your destiny."

The two continued their walk and had reached another twist in the maze when Gavin spoke, "I know you don't remember, but we met before, about a year and a half ago,"

"Really?"

"We had a herbology class together. It was the last week of class, and you had cut your finger, and you started to cry. I came over and told you I was a healer and could take care of it for you."

Moonsyrah looked up at Gavin with wide eyes, "I remember. You told me not to cry, and then you went over and mixed some herbs and placed them over the cut. You said that one of the herbs would help with the pain and the other would help stop the bleeding."

Gavin tightened his hand on Moonsyrah's and smiled that she remembered. "The next day, I went to the girls' dormitories to check on you, but I was told you had not lived there for years and had your own apartment. I did not know where to find you and was unsure whether I should disturb you there, so I chose not to check in on you. I figured I would see you in class the next day, but I don't remember you showing up. I later learned that you were an apprentice to the Prophetess. I wanted to talk to you, but I could never catch you alone until yesterday. I have wanted to get to know you since then."

"I don't even have a scar from the cut," Moonsyrah said, ignoring the rest of what he said. The two walked in silence for a while.

"What do you do for the Prophetess?" Gavin inquired as he once again brought them to a stop at one of the dead ends of the maze.

"I help her with odd jobs and do whatever else she asks me to. She is training me in the art of meditation, which I find one of the more enjoyable aspects of the job. I do not enjoy it when I have to attend the evening meetings with her. I think I will attend to her until I am old or Novalie takes over for her." Moonsyrah leaned against the hedge next to Gavin.

"What if you get married? Will you still attend her then?" Gavin absently rubbed his thumb against the palm of her hand.

"I am not destined to marry. I am not sure I would be even allowed if I wanted to. Blue girls are forbidden to have children, and I believe that holds true of us marrying." Laughed Moonsyrah.

Gavin looked at her in astonishment. "Why? Not having the right to have children does not preclude the right to marry. You are a beautiful and smart woman, and I am sure you will marry someday. You will meet a man who consumes your very thoughts and dreams, and you will consume his. Maybe you have already met him."

Moonsyrah knew that Gavin spoke no truer words than this. She had already met the man who would consume her thoughts and dreams, but she was trying hard not to let him. As for marriage, that was not to be. The one that she loved was locked in the Myst, and though destined to decide to set him free, she knew that she would not. She could not let her demon out of the Myst; she could not be the one that lets hell loose on the world.

They reached the fountain at the center of the maze and sat down on the bench. They quietly watched two birds splash around in the water until Moonsyrah laughed at their antics and scared the birds away.

"Moonsyrah, I have enjoyed our walk today. Would you like to walk again with me tomorrow?" Gavin hoped she would. He had an interest in the blue girls, in general, and Moonsyrah, in particular. He thought she was fascinating and beautiful and wanted to get to know her better.

"Yes, this time, let's walk around the pond and watch the skaters."

A cold wind kicked up, and the two stood and hurried to the maze to gain a bit of shelter from the wind. Gavin again picked up Moonsyrah's hand and held it as they walked back toward the entrance to the maze. She liked the feel of her hand in his and then found herself wondering what it would feel like to hold Adym's hand. She had felt his touch and knew he had felt hers, but not fully. She had actually never felt him as flesh and bone, only in his shadow form, which wasn't quite the same. She banished this thought from her mind and concentrated on enjoying this moment with Gavin. They parted ways at the exit to the maze with the promise of seeing one another the next afternoon.

The next day Gavin and Moonsyrah walked to the skating pond and joined other couples skating around on the frozen water. Moonsyrah began to suspect that Gavin could ice skate very well and just enjoyed pretending he couldn't so he could hold her close as they skated. Gavin confessed this was true and then, after a perfect pirouette, proceeded to fall, pulling her down on top of him. She laughed at his antics and helped him back up. Gavin led her to the shore of the pond and helped her untie her skates. They walked over to the nearby bench and sat for a while, watching the other skaters play.

Novalie watched as Gavin and Moonsyrah played on the ice, and the more she saw, the angrier she became. She watched as they sat on the bench, laughing together. Enough was enough. Novalie walked over to the pair and seated herself between them.

"What a lovely day for skating, isn't it?' Novalie innocently inquired.

"Yes, it is. Are you joining the skaters?" Gavin asked the beautiful but intimidating woman. It was a bit awkward to be sitting with the "Prophetess-in-training." He moved a bit further along the bench to give her more room.

"What do you want, Novalie?" Asked a perturbed Moonsyrah. "I know it must be something, or you wouldn't willingly sit this close to me."

"Actually, I do want something." She turned to Gavin, "I was wondering if you could meet with me later and help me make a tincture for headaches. I have been plagued with one for a few days now, and I heard you were very good at medical herbology. I saw you sitting here and decided to enlist your help." She placed a hand on Gavin's knee and looked at him expectantly.

"Of course, Lady Novalie. Where would you like me to meet you?" He asked

"I will send a servant to your quarters shortly to lead you to my rooms." Novalie stood up, "I will see you soon." She walked away from the pair, knowing she had upset Moonsyrah and would soon have Gavin's attention.

Gavin and Moonsyrah sat in silence for a moment and then continued talking as they put on their shoes.

"Well, I guess I must be going, but I wanted to ask you something first. Moonsyrah, Ontscheppen is coming up, and I was hoping you would allow me to escort you to the celebration festivities."

Gavin's cheeks were flushed, and his brown eyes sparkled in the winter light. Moonsyrah replied that yes, she would like to go to the dance with him. Gavin picked up Moonsyrah and twirled her around in happiness. He set her back down on her feet, and together, they walked back to the monastery, making plans for the coming celebration and what they would do tomorrow.

Moonsyrah thanked him for the walk and then headed up the stairs that led to her rooms. She looked back and saw that Gavin was watching her from the bottom of the stairs. She blushed and continued to her room.

Early the next morning, Moonsyrah met with the Prophetess and Novalie for morning meditation. She enjoyed the peaceful ritual, and closing her eyes, she focused on relaxing her muscles when she saw a snow-covered valley. She looked down on the valley from somewhere very high and could barely resist uttering a sigh of delight over it. She stopped herself in time and then quickly shut the image out. She knew it was Adym's way of telling her he was thinking of her. She focused on the meditation, and when the bell rang, she got up with the other two women and went in to break her fast.

"How is your headache, Novalie?" Moonsyrah asked. She did not actually care but was interested to see why she had really asked Gavin to come see her.

"Not that it is any of your business, but it is now gone. Gavin is a wonder with his tinctures." Novalie poured herself a glass of juice and offered one to her mother. The Prophetess held out her glass and waited as it was filled.

"I did not realize you were feeling unwell, Novalie." She said as she picked up the pitcher Novalie had set down and poured a glass for Moonsyrah.

"It was only a mild headache. I am fine now, but I think I might ask that healer; Gavin is his name, isn't it?" She looked at Moonsyrah with a smirk and saw her nod her head yes. "If he would mind giving me lessons in herbology. I feel I could learn much from him."

Moonsyrah wondered what game Novalie was playing but decided not to cause an argument by asking. She finished her breakfast and then excused herself to go about her day. The Prophetess granted her this request and waved her out of the room.

Two weeks passed and Moonsyrah and Gavin went walking almost every day. On the days that they couldn't be together, Gavin would pop in to say hi to her in between classes. The time passed quickly, and Moonsyrah found herself looking forward to their time together.

The past two weeks would have been perfect if she could have forgotten about Adym, but for whatever reason, he was more in her thoughts than ever. At night, when she was alone, she found herself gazing out at the Myst and wishing she was there with him. Adym was overwhelming, intriguing, selfish, and oh-so incredibly sexy. The way she felt when he was in her mind was beyond compare. The way she felt when she was with him was amazing. She felt powerful, capable, and wanted as she had never truly felt before. But Adym was one of the forbidden. A demon, a being that would bring pain to her world, had indeed already done so.

Gavin, on the other hand, was a good person, kind, caring, and handsome. She enjoyed his company. He always had something interesting to discuss or fun things planned for them to do. He was pleasant to be around. Yet the more time she spent with Gavin, the more confused she became. The more time she spent with him, the more she longed to be spending that time instead with Adym.

How could spending time with Gavin make her long to be with Adym? Was this why she sought Gavin's company? Why did she feel Adym's heart beat next to hers still? Moonsyrah had thought that by leaving, she could weaken the bond between them but this didn't seem to be happening. She had left him because of what she saw in his mind. How could she want to be with Adym, knowing what he was capable of? How could she long to forget her reasons for leaving and be with him again? The nights without him were getting longer and longer. And it was getting harder and harder to ignore Adym when he called out to her.

Adym sat slouched on his couch, drink in hand, for two days after Moonsyrah left him. There was no reason for him to ever get back up. His heart had left him when Moonsyrah walked away from him. He would sit here until he faded away. He would drink to numb the pain of losing her. He would drink the years away, waiting for her to grow old and die so that he might follow her in death and his pain would finally end. Human lives were short. But this pain would make it feel like an eternity. Maybe he would do as Raighn did and pass the time with the drug entasi. Maybe it would help numb him along with the drink.

Tayin found Adym sitting on the couch, stinking of Oaken Whiskey and looking as if he hadn't changed clothes or washed since he last visited. In disgust, he took the glass out of Adym's hand and sat it on the side table.

"I have given you one day more than I told you I would. Why are we not yet free?" Tayin looked down at his sodden friend.

"We will never be free, Tayin. I showed her the way, and she turned her back on me." Adym reached over for his glass once more, only to be intercepted by Tayin.

"You do not need any more of that." Tayin sat on the arm of the couch Adym inhabited. "Why did you not make her find the key as I told you to?"

Adym stood up in anger and leaned over Tayin. "It was on your advice that I pushed her into finding it. It was under your threat that I forced our minds to become one. It was that which made our bond cement and our minds to share thoughts." Adym turned away from Tayin and walked to stand in front of the glass wall that looked out to the edge of the Myst.

"I lost her. She has chosen not to set us free." He whispered in pain.

"I do not understand how you can bond with a human, and for this, I am sorry for you, but why do you not make her bring you the key?" Tayin asked again.

"I can no longer make her do anything. She can block my thoughts, my powers, my ability to make her do anything. I can no longer appear to her as I once used to. She can keep my shadow self away." He rubbed his hand over his face. "Forget it, Tayin. We are never going to be free. I have failed us all."

Adym heard Tayin send out a message to the council to call for an emergency meeting. He felt Tayin's hand grab his arm in a vice-like grip and pull him toward the Hall of Myst. He thought about refusing to go and briefly pulled back but gave up because he knew that the council must be told. He might as well get it over with and take whatever punishment they chose to give him due to his failure. Adym felt Tayin release him once they reached the conference room. He entered and stood in the shadows, watching as other members appeared and sat down. Tayin pushed Adym and then followed him as he took his seat at the table.

"You called a meeting to report an update, Tayin." Elder Brecher spoke.

With respect, Tayin bowed his head to the Elder before speaking. "What needs to be said should be told by Adym. It is his news. I called for this meeting on his behalf as he was not inclined to do so." Tayin turned and looked at his friend until Adym threw up his hands in defeat and started talking.

"I have failed in my mission. Moonsyrah will not set us free." He held up his hand for silence and continued, "It is no longer in my power to make her."

Adym glanced at the council and was not surprised by their faces of anger and confusion. He stood up and placed his hands on the back of his chair. He looked at each one of the members until he came to Kest. It was easier to admit this next part while staring at the only one who might understand his reasons.

"I have bonded with the one that was destined to set us free. We are one in mind and heart. I cannot make her obey me now. I no longer have the power to make her do anything." He paused to take a deep breath and closed his eyes for a brief moment. "She has made the choice to remain with the humans and not set us free. Moonsyrah has decided that we are the demons her people think we are, and she does not want to be the one that lets us free to feed on her people."

Elder Brecher spoke, disappointment in his every word. "I am sorry for you. The bond is unbreakable, and bonding with a human, even a blue girl, is hard to fathom, but as it has happened, it cannot be undone. You do know what this means to your future?" He saw the small nod from Adym. "The bond may make her think again about setting us free. She will start feeling the pain of separation from you. This may make her change her mind."

"Son, keep trying to bring her around. The prophecy told by the human so long ago was confirmed by Y'ddra. It will happen. We must try to get over our disappointment that it will not be soon and learn to be patient." Elder Elcrys stated. "But we will not be patient forever. This prophecy needs to come about. We are in need of a bigger feeding pool. Use your bond to encourage this girl to let us free." The Elders got up from the table and left the room.

Adym looked up at Raighn's voice. "Cousin, you do know that freeing us still will not free you from the punishment of bonding with one that is not SeiOrhii? You have given up im-mortality for this woman."

"I know." He walked out of the room and back to Elynas without another word.

For the next several weeks, he tried to speak with Moonsyrah, but she refused to answer. He could feel her confusion, her doubt over her choice. He could feel her longing for him. He let his longing and love for her infuse his mind and knew she felt it. Adym also knew that it made it harder for her to ignore him, but she was a stubborn woman and kept shoving him to the back of her mind.

He saw the day that she met the human weakling and accepted his invitation to walk. His anger filled both his and Moonsyrah's minds. He watched as day after day she continued meeting this Yidderian. Adym felt her grow close to the man. Every day, Adym tried to speak with her, and every day, her resolve strengthened against him. Adym let her feel his love for her and his anger for her attachment to this lesser being.

Sitting on the peak of the highest mountain on Alenar, Adym could see the ocean from where he sat and knew that Moonsyrah would love the view. He tried to reach out to her once more. He entered more fully into her mind and saw that she was in meditation. Adym sent her the image of the valley, which was beautiful, with the rising sun reflecting on the snow and the ocean in the background. He felt her appreciation of the view, and then the instant she shut down the image. Frustrated, he yelled into the wind. Taking a deep breath, he stood next to the ledge and let himself fall into the nothingness that would take him home.

He had made a decision. It was a decision that he knew there was no coming back from. A decision that would change his life. He sent for two of the humans that had been locked in the Myst with the Allurans. He fed deeply on them, bringing about both of their deaths as he needed the strength he could garnish from the fear they felt at the moment their lives faded. He left them where they fell and headed to Kofira. He went into the room that housed the historically important relics and picked up the piece of the key that the Allurans had retained. Before Tayin found him there, he hurried back to Elynas and toward the gates of Myst that separated him from Moonsyrah.

He stepped out into the side of Alenar, which he had not physically entered for so very long, and looked back at the Myst separating him from his home. Adym fell to his knees in agony and weakness as soon as he passed through the gates. This passing was much harder than he had ever experienced, and he knew that he could no longer return to the Myst.

He saw Tayin running toward the barrier. Adym watched as Tayin placed his hands on the solid surface and heard him ask why.

"It is the only way that I can help you. I can no longer live forever, and so I choose to be near her." He told his friend. Adym could see the pain in Tayin's eyes. He knew that Tayin was feeling the pain of his choice but also reliving the moment that changed his own life so many centuries ago.

"You cannot make it back through. You can no longer return without the key." Tayin whispered in a voice rough with emotion.

"I know, but I can feed freely out here and maintain my strength so that I may find a way to free you." Adym turned to walk away, "Goodbye, my friend." He left the Myst behind him and walked toward the cabin he had given Nicollete. He was already feeling the strength gained from the earlier meal leaving him. His mind went silent, and he could not hear the voices of his people, and though he could still feel her heart, even Moonsyrah's mind faded from his. This separation of minds from his beloved was agony. Never had he experienced such pain, and never in his wildest dreams had he thought it possible that his mind could become separate from hers once they had become one. He would need to find food again to be able to finish what he left home for. He would rest for a moment and then go into the village and find sustenance. He needed strength so that he could hear his Korsyon again.

Moonsyrah was skating around the pond when she felt the loss of Adym. She fell to her knees in pain and anguish. She shook uncontrollably and was helped up by Gavin and Sameen. Gavin carried her to her apartment and laid her on the couch.

He brushed her hair back from her face and asked what was wrong. Moonsyrah shook her head and cried. Sameen and Gavin left her to go and bring back Ethan, and since he was already a master healer, he might be able to figure out what was wrong with Moonsyrah.

Once alone, Moonsyrah cried out Adym's name and found no answer. He had left her. She had wished he would but had never even imagined that not having him there in her mind would hurt so much. It was actual physical pain. Her body felt as though half of her had been ripped away. She lay there with silent tears running down her face as the healer arrived and tried to find what was wrong with her, knowing he would find nothing. How could he? This was beyond anything they had ever known or seen. She felt Ethan lift her head and made her drink of the tisane he put to her lips. She felt it sweep her away into silent oblivion.

Moonsyrah woke 36 hours later with a sense of loss but thinking maybe it was for the best. Without him constantly in her head, she might learn to live without him. She could learn to be happy once again, maybe. The pain in her heart would eventually fade. At least, she tried to convince herself it would. The hole where his had been might never go away, but she also tried to persuade herself that this emptiness was something she could learn to live with.

She got out of bed, showered, and dressed for the day. She went down to the Prophetess' rooms and joined Novalie and the Prophetess in morning meditation. As usual, Novalie was her charming self, and she grumbled about having Moonsyrah participate in the morning ritual. Moonsyrah ignored her and tried to heal the emptiness inside her through self-visualization and meditative introspection. After the much-needed meditation, the trio sat down to their breakfast.

"Moonsyrah, I had heard you were sick. Are you feeling better?" The Prophetess inquired as she spread jam on her scone.

"I am fine now. The induced rest was very restorative." She answered. She helped herself to some of the snowfruit juice she was partial too.

"What made you scream like a ninny in the first place?" Novalie smiled at Moonsyrah, letting her know she did not particularly care. She was just asking to make the Prophetess think she did.

Moonsyrah smiled back at Novalie and accidentally, on purpose, knocked over the jug of juice onto Novalie. "Oh, so sorry. I am so clumsy this morning." She looked anything but sorry.

"Honestly, Moonsyrah." Novalie stood up and wiped the juice off her robes. "Now I must change." She stormed out of the room with a look of disgust on her face.

The Prophetess watched the exchange and, once Novalie left the room, spoke once again to Moonsyrah. "That was an effective way to distract her from the fact that you did not answer her question." She took a bite, chewed, and then addressed Moonsyrah once again. "What did make you fall?"

Moonsyrah had hoped that the distraction would make the Prophetess forget the question, but she wasn't to be that lucky.

She thought carefully about what to say. "I just got a sudden headache that was excruciating. I am not sure why." She took a drink to help cover up the small blush that always spread over her cheeks when she lied.

"Hmm. I am not sure I believe you, but I will let it go for now." The two had just finished eating when a freshly robed Novalie came back into the room.

"There has been another death, Prophetess. This one was a young man. He was found embedded in the rocks at the edge of the village." Novalie perched herself on one of the green chairs. Moonsyrah leaned back in the one with the wine stain and once again thought she should start reupholstering it, ignoring the conversation of the others.

"Embedded? Like the last one?" The Prophetess looked seriously at Novalie.

"Yes, just like the last one. As if the rock formed around him. I do not understand how this is possible." She turned to Moonsyrah. "Since your little 'episode,' there have been four deaths. Each is done in ways that we cannot explain. Do you know why this is?"

"I cannot embed people into rocks, idiot." Moonsyrah glared at Novalie. Her heart started pounding. She might not be able to but she was pretty sure she knew who was capable of such a feat.

"If I were the prophetess, I would strike you down for that." Novalie's face went red with anger.

"Well, thankfully, you are not." Moonsyrah regarded the actual Prophetess. "What do you think is the cause?" She did not want to entertain the thought that was beginning to form in her mind. She knew Adym's powers. But as he was locked in the Myst, how could it be him?

The Prophetess sought the answer Moonsyrah held in her eyes. She was silent for several moments. "I think." She looked at Moonsyrah intently once more. "That the prophecy is about to come true. It was foretold that curious deaths would start appearing before the release of the demons. The one chosen to set the demons free will soon fulfill her terrible destiny."

Moonsyrah turned away in discomfort and then, clearing her throat, answered the query she beheld on the Prophetess' face. "What if the chosen has cut all ties with the demons and has decided not to set them free? Would this not belie the reason you have set upon?"

Novalie broke back into the conversation, "Surely the chosen would have no choice as she would be destined and have no control over her fate. Did you set one of them free, dear destined one."

"Why do you both believe that I am the one the prophecy speaks of? I have done nothing to either of you to warrant such a belief about me." Moonsyrah was shocked that Novalie held the same thoughts about her as the Prophetess did.

"I have seen the future results of your deeds. I know that you are the one that brings about the fire." Novalie crossed her hands over her knees. "I have recently been shown a vision that the one that is destined to fulfill the prophecy lives now. Other images in the foretelling have helped me to realize that it is you the prediction speaks of."

"And you, Prophetess?" Moonsyrah looked appealingly at her.

"Suffice it to say that I have known you were the one since the moment I met you." She answered in sorrow.

"You are wrong!" Moonsyrah jumped up and left the room.

She ran out of the monastery and along the path that led to the old chapel at the edge of the grounds. She leaned against the wall of the old stone building and sank to her knees. She had left her love to save everyone. She had chosen not to be the fulfillment of the prophecy. She was not responsible for the deaths that were happening. Adym couldn't be either, as he was locked safely away behind the barrier. She had to find a way to change the minds of the two women. Surely, she had a choice in her own destiny. She sat there until the evening air became too frigid for her to be outside any longer. She slowly made her way back to her quarters. She sat in front of a freshly made fire and lost herself in the flames.

The next few days were filled with more deaths. Each was perpetrated in an odd manner. Each death was accomplished in a way that could not be explained. Fear took hold of the monastery and the village. Moonsyrah walked among the grounds and saw people huddled together and heard them whispering with fear over what was happening. She walked into the village and caught a glimpse of someone in the shadows that reminded her of Adym, but this could not be. Her heart beat louder, and a second beat matched her own, a beat she thought had been forever lost to her.

She followed the route she saw the person take. She came to a dead end between two buildings and, looking around, saw no one. She headed back onto the main street of the village and searched the faces of every dark-haired man she saw. Knowing she would not see the face she looked for, she finally stopped the search and went about her business.

She entered into the store that sold the buttons she wanted for the dress she had almost finished for Sameen. She made her purchase and left wondering if the Prophetess would let her look at the sketchbook again. She wanted to see if anything written or drawn in there could explain what was going on. She admitted to herself she also wanted to see Adym's face again, even if only as a drawing. She walked back to the monastery and, receiving no answer, let herself into the empty rooms. She set her purchases on the couch and entered the Prophetess' bed chambers. She found the book in a chest of drawers and, holding it close to her heart, took it out into the living room with her.

She curled up on the sofa and opened the book. She looked at the beautifully detailed flowers and herbs and read each description under the drawings. She came to a drawing of the

Moonflower. This was a beautiful white flower that, as far as she knew, only grew in the Prophetess' meditation garden. She had several of the beautiful plants lining the wall that surrounded the enclosure. Written underneath this flower, along with its scientific name, was what it was used for. This flower, the author wrote, was the only one that could make a SeiOrhii vulnerable. Again, she could not make out the smudged word, but knowing Adym, she guessed the author had written the word SeiOrhii. The flower could weaken them enough that it could be used to bring about their deaths.

This worried Moonsyrah. While she did not want the Allurans set free to hurt her fellow Yidderians, she also did not want Adym and his friends hurt or even killed. That the Prophetess had the knowledge to bring about the deaths of those she called demons troubled her. Moonsyrah knew that the Prophetess would not hesitate to use this if needed. She continued looking at the flower before realizing it did not matter if the Prophetess had this knowledge as the demons would never be set free and, therefore, could not be harmed by it.

She finished reading about the remaining plants and finally came to the picture that she was longing to see. Adym's face was there in perfect detail. The artist had captured his personality in her art. Amalie was very talented and it pained Moonsyrah to think that this woman had known him well enough to capture his essence in a simple drawing. As odd as it seemed, Moonsyrah was jealous of anyone knowing him this well, even a woman who was long dead.

Moonsyrah ran her hand over the picture and admitted that she was glad that she at least had this picture of him. Her heart cried out with longing, and she felt tears fall down her cheeks and splash on the page. She understood the artist's pain over the loss of her love. Her tears would forever be marked on the drawing of Adym as Amalie's were on the page of her heart's love.

She stayed looking at the picture for a few minutes more before getting up, closing the book, and placing it on the table in front of her. She did not want anyone to find her there. She would be unable to explain away the tears that flowed freely down her face. Moonsyrah took a deep breath and told herself to stop crying. She had made the decision to leave Adym. She had made the decision to leave him locked away. She must learn to live with that choice.

Moonsyrah left the room, walked through the darkening halls, and became aware that she had not read anything that would explain or confirm her idea that Adym was responsible for the recent deaths. Part of her was relieved by this, but another part also knew, deep down, that he somehow was the responsible party. Moonsyrah wondered if the Prophetess would cancel the upcoming celebration in light of all that was happening. How could anyone enjoy a celebration when there was someone out there killing their friends, neighbors, and loved ones?

The Prophetess was giving one of her nightly sermons. These had become so crowded she had started holding them in the sanctuary, usually reserved for ceremonial days. This evening, her lecture was on overcoming the fear everyone felt. She preached on the importance of everyone putting their trust in Y'ddra and believing that these trials and tribulations would soon pass. Moonsyrah wondered if anyone, besides herself and Novalie, knew that the Prophetess did not believe that this would soon pass but would, instead, soon become worse. She was surprised to hear the Prophetess say that the celebration of Ontscheppen would take place as planned. She encouraged everyone to participate this year and bring joy to the world in these dark times.

Moonsyrah left the sermon determined to enjoy the upcoming festivities and to ignore the accusing looks that Novalie sent her way and the sad ones sent to her by the Prophetess.

As the days passed, more and more deaths were reported, and Moonsyrah was convinced that somehow Adym was behind them. She worried that she was the cause in some way. How could she enjoy the upcoming celebration if she was the reason these poor people were dying? If she was the one who was to release the demons, and the prophecy spoke of mysterious deaths occurring before the release, then how could she not hold herself responsible? Moonsyrah chose to maintain her belief that she could choose her own destiny. She had already lost so much in order to keep the prophecy from reaching fruition. She was not content to believe that she was fated to do it anyway.

Walking along the monastery halls she could hear the fear of the people mingling with their excitement over the upcoming holiday. Maybe the Prophetess was right to keep the celebration as scheduled. It seemed that Ontscheppen was something the people needed to help ease their fears. Moonsyrah caught their enthusiasm and couldn't help but also become excited over the preparations that had already begun for the holiday.

"Sameen, the Ontscheppen celebration is in two days, and I still have to put the finishing touches on your gift. If I am to go out with Gavin tomorrow, I need to work on your gift for a while tonight. Have you finished making yours yet?" Ontscheppen was a holiday that celebrated the humans landing on Yiddera. The landing took place on the beaches of Kruger, a continent on the other side of the world, on a hot summer day, but being a holiday that was celebrated worldwide, those here on Alenar celebrated it in the middle of winter. It was honored at the monastery with the exchange of homemade gifts, an evening of music, dancing, and a bountiful feast. By this time tomorrow, the monastery would begin smelling of freshly baked bread, warm spices, and the delicious smells of sweet and savory pies.

"I finished weeks ago, Moon. Since you have been spending so much time with Gavin lately, I had ample time to make my gifts. You will really like the one I made for you."

"I can't wait to see it." Moonsyrah gathered up the cups, took them to the kitchen, and rinsed them out. She went back into the living room, folded her pink lap blanket, and laid it neatly across the arm of the couch. "I am going to my room to work on your gift for a while before bed. Goodnight, my dearest friend."

"Goodnight Moon."

For the rest of that evening and most of the next day, Moonsyrah worked on finishing the yellow lilies she was embroidering down the sleeves and across the neckline of the dark maroon dress she had made for Sameen. When she finished, she neatly folded it and wrapped it as nicely as she could, adding a big yellow ribbon around it. She set it next to the gift she had for the Prophetess. She briefly wondered if she should have made one for Novalie, but as the gifts were traditionally given to people you loved, she could not bring herself to make one for her nemesis. She just hoped that she would arrive early enough, to visit with the Prophetess, that Novalie would not yet be there.

Moonsyrah then went to work in the kitchen making chocolate-covered appleberry caramels that she planned to give as gifts.

Once finished with the caramels, she put them in the refrigerator to keep them fresh. In the morning, she would box them up for the Prophetess and Sameen.

Humming to herself, she went into her room and out onto the balcony. The snow was falling thick and fast, and though she couldn't see the Myst through it, she looked in its direction. Her day had been pleasant, but she found that, as always, she missed Adym. While she could now once again feel his heart, his absence from her mind was still physically painful. She missed sharing her thoughts with him. Missed knowing he was always there with her. If she closed her eyes, she could almost imagine him holding her while they watched the snowfall. She tried to shake this thought from her mind but found it hard to let go. She had once thought that it would make life easier if he was gone, but she was finding that this was not so. The opposite was true. The longer she went without talking with him, the harder it was. She felt as if his absence was draining her energy and life. She stood there for a while longer, enjoying the snow, lost in her thoughts. Finally, she went inside, and pulling the balcony doors closed behind her, she whispered goodnight in spite of knowing he was not there to hear it. She added wood to her fire and then tucked herself under the thick, down-filled pink and white comforter.

YEAR 403

ONTSCHEPPEN MORNING DAWNED BRIGHT and clear, and Moonsyrah woke to the sunshine streaming in through her windows and balcony doors. She stretched, got out of bed, pulled on a warm dressing gown, and went to stand in front of her window. The snow had quit falling and covered the grass. She gazed at the brilliance of the sun on the pure white snow. It was bright enough to bother her eyes. She turned away from it and changed into a long-sleeved dress of a chocolate brown color with pink buttons on the bodice. She slipped into a matching pair of slippers and then, picking up her gift to Sameen, went into the living room. She was glad to see that Sameen wasn't up yet. She still needed to box up the caramels she had made the evening before. She placed her wrapped package on a small nearby table and went to work filling the candy boxes. Once done, she added a yellow bow to Sameen's box and a green bow to the one for the Prophetess. She placed both packages on the table and then went over and started a cozy fire. While she was working on the fire, Sameen came into the room carrying a beautifully wrapped box with her.

"Happy Ontscheppen." Sameen yawned through her greeting, causing Moonsyrah to laugh. Sameen sat on the couch, put the gift on the side table next to her, then tucked her legs up under a blanket.

"Happy Ontscheppen to you too." Moonsyrah scooped up the packages she had for her friend and joined her on the couch. "I hope you like your gifts." Moonsyrah handed the small box of caramels to her and watched as Sameen opened it and popped one of the candy pieces into her mouth. She commented on their delicious flavor as Moonsyrah handed her the next package. Sameen opened it, paper flying everywhere, and unfolded the dress inside, exclaiming over the delicate needlework. She jumped off the couch and held the dress up to herself. "Thank you, Moon. It is lovely. I will wear it tonight for the celebration." She leaned over and kissed Moonsyrah on the cheek in thanks. "Now open yours."

Moonsyrah unwrapped the package and found a delicate wooden box with the phases of the moon carved into the top. She carefully opened the box and nestled inside was a silver necklace with a crescent moon-shaped pendant. Next to the necklace lay a pair of dangle earrings, also in the shape of the crescent moon. The silver work was exquisite, but what made the gifts invaluable was that the moons were made of blue glass. Blue was a hard color to make, and even more unique was the bright cornflower blue that Sameen had used in the glass. Moonsyrah looked at Sameen in wonder.

"I tried to match your eyes. During this past phase of the third moon, I found poppies of just the right color. I had to gather over two baskets of petals to get enough to make the blue coloring agent for the glass."

"They are works of art, and you are truly talented. I will wear them tonight. They will perfectly match the dress I plan to wear. Thank you, Sameen. This gift is a true treasure." She leaned over and hugged her friend.

The girls admired their gifts for several more minutes before deciding to start the rest of their day. Sameen cleaned up the wrapping paper that littered the floor while Moonsyrah folded their blankets. Sameen left to her room to get dressed and hang up her new gown. Moonsyrah carefully put the jewelry back into its box and then put it in her chest of drawers for safekeeping.

"See you this evening, Sameen. Have fun handing out the rest of your gifts." Moonsyrah called out as she picked up the gifts she had for the Prophetess and left the tower rooms. She hurried down the stairs and found Gavin waiting at the bottom.

"Good morning, Moonsyrah. Happy Ontscheppen." Moonsyrah looked at Gavin in the morning light and saw his eyes light up when he saw her.

"To you as well. You are up early." Moonsyrah walked past him and headed down the hall, inviting him to walk with her.

Gavin took hold of her hand and stopped her. "I was hoping to catch up with you this morning. I wanted to ask you something."

"Oh, what is it you wanted to ask me." Moonsyrah adjusted the gifts she had in her arm and waited for Gavin's question.

"I know we haven't known each other for more than a few weeks, but, Moonsyrah, I really like getting to know you, and well, I was wondering if you would allow me to kiss you." Moonsyrah did not expect this question and was not sure how to answer it. She looked at Gavin and found herself saying yes.

He took her packages from her arms and laid them on a nearby table. He then took her face in his hands and leaned down to kiss her. His lips were soft and warm on hers, and the kiss was gentle and sweet. She heard a low, distant rumble in the back of her mind and let out a sigh of pleasure in response to the growl. Gavin, encouraged by the soft sound Moonsyrah made, deepened his kiss. The growl in Moonsyrah's head grew louder, and an ache formed in her mind. She laughed out loud at the sound this time. Her heart filled with delight now that the burning emptiness was gone. Adym was back, and she felt true happiness for the first time since the day the emptiness had appeared and left her in pain.

She pulled away from Gavin and looked up into his kind face. She knew at that moment that it didn't matter how good for her Gavin might be, she was Adym's. She knew what Adym was capable of, and it did not matter to her anymore. Moonsyrah could no longer deny her feelings for him, her need of him. She leaned up on her tiptoes and kissed Gavin once again. She enjoyed the anger she felt coming from Adym. To hear him once again in her mind brought her intense joy. She backed away from Gavin and smiled up at him.

Gavin saw a sparkle in Moonsyrah's eyes he had not seen before. She always had a look of sadness in her eyes, now that sorrow was gone.

"Thank you, Gavin. You have given me the best gift I could have hoped for today, but I must go now, or I am going to be late for breakfast with the Prophetess." Moonsyrah scooped up her packages and headed toward the Prophetess's chambers.

"Moonsyrah, wait." Gavin hurried to catch up with her. "Kissing you is the best gift I will receive today as well." He pulled her closer to him and kissed her again. The ache in her mind caused by Adym's jealousy sent waves of pleasure running through Moonsyrah. She stepped back from Gavin's embrace.

"Gavin, I didn't…" Moonsyrah hesitated and did not correct Gavin's misunderstanding of her words; instead, she let him enjoy the moment, knowing he was going to be disappointed soon. "I will see you tonight at the celebration, my friend." She left him to go his own way and continued down the hall.

The Prophetess opened the door to Moonsyrah's knock, looking quite splendid in her holiday outfit. She was wearing her usual black, but the dress had dark green stripes on the skirt, and a beautiful leaf-shaped brooch was pinned to her bodice. She moved out of the doorway to let Moonsyrah pass and enter the room. Moonsyrah placed her packages on the coffee table and then sat at the breakfast nook positioned by the window. It was beautifully made up with a centerpiece of the purple and white tulips that bloomed at this time of year.

"Thank you for having breakfast with me this holiday morning. I hope you don't mind; it is a simple repast. I felt breakfast should be light, given the many wonderful things we will be eating too much of tonight." She leaned over Moonsyrah, filled her cup with tea, and then filled her own. Moonsyrah helped herself to one of the cranberry-orange scones with sweetened cream and a couple slices of bacon.

"It all looks delicious. Happy Ontscheppen Prophetess."

"Happy holidays to you, Moonsyrah."

"Will Novalie be joining us this morning?" Moonsyrah asked, looking around for the bothersome woman.

"No, we are meeting later. She has chosen to sleep in this morning."

The two women ate in comfortable silence for a while. Moonsyrah poured herself another cup of tea and asked if the Prophetess would like one as well. Her mouth full of eggs, the Prophetess nodded yes. When they were done eating, Moonsyrah helped clean the table and put things away. The Prophetess went over to the refrigerator and took out a pitcher of snowfruit juice. Moonsyrah loved snowfruit. It only grew in the winter. It had a white rind, but the inside was firm-fleshed and bright red. It tasted somewhat like the pineapples that she had only eaten once and that grew in the more tropical regions of the world. The Prophetess poured the juice into two tall glasses and carried them over to the sitting area. Moonsyrah followed her and sat down on her usual chair grimacing at the wine stain that was still quite visible.

She handed the Prophetess her gifts and bade her open them. The Prophetess opened her presents and thanked Moonsyrah for the caramels and the lovely green silk scarf embroidered with palm leaves. She placed it around her neck and handed her gifts to Moonsyrah. The Prophetess's gift to Moonsyrah was two dream pillows, each about ten inches square. The first was done in a material of the palest pink with dots of a darker pink throughout and smelled of lavender, mugwort, peppermint, and bistort. She knew this pillow was for lucid dreaming. The second pillow was dark purple with lavender stripes, and it smelled of clove, bergamot, blackberries, and just a hint of black pepper. This pillow was for protection. She knew the Prophetess gave her this one to protect her from nightmares and to help her avoid hearing the voices of demons. She drew in a deep breath and appreciated the scents coming from both pillows.

"Thank you. The pillows are beautiful and will be used often."

"You look happier today. Have you quit having nightmares?" The Prophetess asked.

"I haven't had nightmares for a while now. I am feeling much better. Today, I came to a realization, a decision, and it has helped to ease the confusion in my mind." Moonsyrah took a drink of her juice.

"And the voices? Are you still hearing him?"

"No. I do not hear anyone calling to me other than those that walk the monastery halls."

"I worry for you, my child. You are destined to bring fruition to a terrible prophecy, one that should never be fulfilled." The concern in the Prophetess's voice was evident.

"I know you worry about me. I know you think I am the one the prophecy speaks of, but Prophetess, even if this is so, it is my choice to fulfill it or not. I have realized that a prophecy doesn't have to become my destiny." Moonsyrah finished her juice and set the glass on the table. "You are my friend and teacher, and you have taught me many things over the past years. You have taught me that I am a woman capable of making her own choices. Please trust me when I say I do not wish to see Yiddera destroyed." She went over to the settee and hugged the Prophetess.

The Prophetess patted her back and said, "I do trust you, Moonsyrah. It is the magic of the demons and the Myst I do not trust."

"I know, but do not worry about me today. It is a holiday, and today is made for fun, not for worrying. Thank you for the gifts and for breakfast. Everything was wonderful, but I must go now. I have much to do to get ready for tonight's festivities."

"Thank you, my child. You enjoy today as well. I am sure I will see you tonight."

Moonsyrah gathered up the pillows and headed back to her room. She put the pillows on the overstuffed chair that stood next to her window, then went to the wardrobe and pulled out the creamy yellow dress she had made for that evening. It was done in an off-the-shoulder style, which showed just a hint of cleavage and had long, tight sleeves. The bodice was decorated with the different phases of the moon, from crescent shape to full and back to crescent. The moons were embroidered in a deep sapphire blue. The skirt was full and twirled when she spun around. She hung the dress up on a hook so that it wouldn't be wrinkled for this evening. She set aside a pair of matching yellow heels and a blue ribbon for her hair.

She looked out the window and saw that the sun was still shining, and the skies were crisp and clear. Before she finished getting ready for the celebration, she wanted to go down to the maze fountain and sit awhile. She bundled up in her purple cloak and put on a pair of mittens. The sun may be shining, but she knew that it was deceptive, and it would be cold outside.

She made it to the maze fountain and took a seat on the stone bench by it. She watched as the fountain's hot water turned to a sparkling cloud in the cold air. She could see it make swirls in the breeze before it fell, frozen back into the fountain.

"Adym." She whispered. She knew the real reason why she wanted to come here was to talk once again with him. "Are you there?"

"Yes, my Beloved, I am." Adym appeared at the very edge of her mind, hesitating, unsure of how he would be received.

"I'm sorry I left you. I shouldn't have." Moonsyrah felt Adym enter her mind more fully, knowing that he now felt welcome to be there.

"No, you shouldn't have. Your leaving has hurt us both." Moonsyrah felt the pain he had also gone through without her as he asked, "Why come to me now? What has changed?"

Moonsyrah stared past Adym and into the whirls made by the fountain. "I left you because of the memory I saw in your mind. I left because I was hurt and confused about what you made me see and hear when you took over my mind. When you left, I felt empty and alone." Moonsyrah paused. "Without you there, I realized that I hadn't stopped answering you because I was angry at you. I was angry at myself for still wanting you despite everything that happened that night at the falls. What kind of person am I to love the man who smiled at my adopted mother's death? The man who planned it so that she could no longer protect me from him." Moonsyrah looked into Adym's beautiful yet different eyes, which gazed at her with need.

"Moonsyrah," Adym started to speak but was interrupted.

"Adym, I need you. I need you here, in my head, if that is all I can get. I need you to love me."

Moonsyrah felt free at the admission. She realized it didn't matter what he might once have done or what he would probably do in the future. She wanted and needed him here with her. Whatever kind of person that made her, she no longer cared.

Adym appeared as a shadow, more solid looking than he had ever appeared before, and stood in front of her. She felt his breath against her lips and his hand in her hair. She closed her eyes and felt his next words on her lips. "My love for you is beyond need. It is my reason for living. It takes all other thoughts but you from my mind. Never leave me again." He kissed her possessively and then withdrew to the edge of the fountain. His shadow faded into nothingness. "You are very cold. You should go back in."

Moonsyrah had not felt the cold once she had started talking to Adym, but now that he had mentioned it, her toes were starting to go numb. She stood up and started to walk back through the maze. "Today is a celebration day. Tonight, there will be dancing and music. Will you be there with me?" Moonsyrah asked as she reached the monastery doors.

"I am not sure that is wise. With all those people around, someone is sure to notice you talking to yourself, and you tend to sigh loudly when I touch you." Adym laughed, relieved that she had chosen to come back to him. He had feared that she had called to him to tell him that she was interested in the boy who had kissed her. Instead, she was telling him she accepted him for who he was and wanted him with her.

"Well, then, I will see you after. Adym?"

"Yes."

Moonsyrah had come to a decision concerning the key. "It is traditional on this day to give a gift to those you love. I have one for you. Tonight, after the celebration, I will give it to you."

"I have a surprise for you as well, Beloved. Till tonight." He appeared once more and kissed her before leaving again.

Moonsyrah entered the tower rooms and started a hot fire crackling in the fireplace. She hung up her cloak and took off her mittens, sitting them on the hearth so that they might dry. She then went into her room and drew a hot bath. While she undressed, she realized she could still feel Adym's presence, in her mind and yet far away. She was comforted to know that he was with her even though he was still locked in the Myst.

Moonsyrah was just putting on the second earring when Sameen peeked her head in the door to see if Moonsyrah was ready to go. She replied yes and then took one last look at herself in the mirror. The yellow dress fit her perfectly. She had curled her hair so that it fell down her back in waves. The blue pieces she had braided and pulled back into a single braid. She felt beautiful and ready for a night of fun. She turned to Sameen and saw her wearing her new maroon-colored dress. She had pulled her hair back into a fishtail braid and added yellow flowers to it.

Moonsyrah followed Sameen back out of her room and down to the auditorium where the festivities were to be held. The room was decorated in greens, whites, and purples. The curtains were bright purple with silver tiebacks holding them open so that people could easily step outside if they wanted to. The tables were covered in dark green tablecloths, and vases of white branches from the snowfruit trees were placed in the center.

Around the stage, where the musicians would soon be playing, stood tall vases that held freshly cut pine boughs and more of the white stems. The room looked magical and smelled of fresh pine but also of the many delicious spices used in their holiday dinner. Moonsyrah and Sameen took a seat at one of the little tables and started telling each other about the different presents they had received that day. Moonsyrah mainly just listened to Sameen, as the only gifts she had received were from Sameen and the Prophetess. She couldn't tell Sameen about her favorite gift, having Adym back. So, she listened and exclaimed over the gifts that Sameen described. While they were talking, Gavin and his friend, Ethan, Sameen's date for the evening, joined them. Food was served, and the musicians started to play old Earth music in the background.

The four of them talked and ate until the signal for the dancing to begin sounded. The tables were pushed back, and the dancing commenced. Sameen was quickly asked to dance by Ethan. Sameen took his hand and followed him onto the dance floor. Moonsyrah could tell there was something serious between the couple, and she was happy for her friend. Gavin asked Moonsyrah if she would like to dance, and she accepted. She felt Gavin put a hand on her waist as he led her out onto the dance floor. Moonsyrah felt a growl of displeasure enter her mind. She laughed lightly and ignored Adym. Gavin twirled her around to the music, and when the next song started, he pulled her closer to him as they continued dancing, this time slowly.

"You look beautiful tonight, Moonsyrah," Gavin whispered in her ear. Moonsyrah felt Adym stir in her mind once again. The song finished, and Moonsyrah pulled away from Gavin's arms.

"You are an excellent dancer, Gavin, but I must excuse myself. I find I am thirsty and in need of some punch." Gavin kissed the back of her hand before letting it go and asked if she wanted him to get it for her.

"No, enjoy the dance. I am going to freshen up after I get a drink. I will see you back at the table." Moonsyrah left the dance floor and headed to the punch table, where she picked up a glass of snowfruit juice before heading out one of the many doors and into the moonlit garden.

"I thought you wouldn't be here with me tonight?" Moonsyrah took a drink of her punch before sitting it down on one of the low walls around the garden.

"I didn't plan on it, but when I felt that boy touch you, I couldn't help but make my presence known. I do not want you to dance with him again. You are mine." Growled an irritated Adym. Moonsyrah could feel his breath against her face.

"This is a celebration, Adym. Weeks ago, I told Gavin I would be his date for the evening. I would much prefer to be dancing with you, but as that is not possible, I am going to dance with others tonight. Besides, he is a nice man to whom I owe at least one more dance before I tell him I cannot see him anymore." Moonsyrah felt Adym's hand tighten around her hair, and his lips touch hers. Her body grew warm despite the cold night air.

"You do not owe him anything. Do not dance with him again. You would not like my anger."

Adym left her before Moonsyrah could form an answer to his threat. She stood there by the wall and picked up her punch once again. Moonsyrah did owe Gavin an explanation, and she wasn't sure what to say to him or how to talk to him without upsetting

Adym. She went back inside and was immediately asked to dance by a young man and then another and another. With each dance, she could feel Adym's tension rise in her mind. Twice, she told him to relax, and both times, he ignored her, and the young man she was dancing with looked at her oddly at her words.

Halfway through the evening festivities, the musicians took a break, and the dancing stopped. One of the dance troupes and a magician took turns on stage entertaining the partygoers. Dessert trays had been set up at the back of the room, and Moonsyrah found Sameen there, choosing which treat she wanted to indulge in. Moonsyrah took a slice of cherry pie and covered it in bourbon-flavored whipped cream. Sameen chose a piece of mint chocolate cake and then followed Moonsyrah back to their table. The two girls were joined by Gavin and Ethan and proceeded to enjoy their desserts and conversation.

"You have some cream on your nose," Gavin stated as he wiped it off for her. Moonsyrah felt Adym slam back into her mind, and she leaned away from Gavin.

"Thank you for letting me know." Moonsyrah smiled politely at Gavin and then took the napkin from him so she could finish wiping the cream off her nose.

The musicians started playing once again, and Sameen and Ethan got up to dance. Gavin asked her if she would like to join him. She politely declined and stated that she would sit this song out. Gavin laughed and said he could not let her do that as she felt him take her by the hand and lead her out onto the floor. Moonsyrah relented and followed Gavin out amongst the other dancers. He pulled her closer to him and brushed his lips across hers. She knew instantly that this was a mistake, and she backed away from him while she tried to pull her hand from Gavin's, but he only held hers tighter. Adym had left her mind, and she could see Gavin's eyes grow round in fear at what she could only imagine.

"Adym, stop it. You are scaring him." Moonsyrah whispered so that others might not hear her. She knew Gavin had, but there was no helping that. Gavin turned pale and gripped Moonsyrah's hand tighter.

Adym's shadow slowly became visible, and Moonsyrah could see the anger starting to glow in his eyes. She could see his hand around Gavin's throat and knew Adym was going to kill him. How it was possible for him to reach outside the Myst to do this and all the other deaths that were occurring, she did not know, but she needed to stop this for Adym's and Gavin's sake. Gavin was already showing signs of fainting. How would she explain what happened if he collapsed right here on the floor? Moonsyrah saw Novalie walking over to where they stood. Moonsyrah was sure Novalie could see Adym's shadow because of the smug, knowing look on her face.

"Adym, let him go now." Moonsyrah was a bit louder this time, and several couples looked at her. Moonsyrah was finally able to take her hand back from Gavin, and the fear started to leave his face. He reached up and placed a hand on his neck where bruises were already forming. He struggled to get a breath. Gavin looked at her in confusion, pain, and fear, then walked away from her. Moonsyrah stalked to the patio doors and into the garden so that she could confront Adym.

"It is just a dance, Adym. There is nothing to be jealous of." Moonsyrah angrily told him.

"I told you not to dance with him again." Adym's anger made her head start to hurt.

"Adym, you are hurting me." He instantly let go of her mind. Moonsyrah could feel that he had left, and the pounding in her head ceased. She took a couple of deep breaths. She left the garden area by way of a side gate and walked around the monastery to the entrance closest to her tower room. She entered the building and walked the darkened hall until she came to the stairs that led her back to the tower. She sat down on the steps and wondered what repercussions would occur after that scene. She was sure to hear from Novalie. That woman loved needling her, and this was something big to pester her about.

Surely, Gavin would tell someone about whatever it was he saw, felt, and what he had heard her say. Eventually, it would get back to the Prophetess, and she would know instantly who or, according to the Prophetess, what she had been talking to. Moonsyrah didn't see a way to fix the problem, so she continued up the stairs to her room. She went out on her balcony, looked out toward the Myst, and called to Adym. She could feel that he was still angry and so taking a deep breath, she started to talk to him.

"Adym, I am not sorry I danced with Gavin, but I am sorry it upset you. We have become friends; I am not interested in him any more than that." Moonsyrah explained as she stared out into the night.

"That boy you danced with is more than interested in you, my Beloved. He believes himself in love with you. And I can see that you care for him." Adym paused and drew a deep breath before admitting, "I am afraid of losing you again."

"I thought Gavin and I might get together and that I could forget about you, but, as you know, today, he kissed me. I heard your anger at his kiss in my head, and I found more pleasure in your anger than in his kiss. I do care for him, but that doesn't matter now. I belong with you and to you. My heart does not beat for him as it does for you. I cannot nor will I ever leave you again." Moonsyrah tried to coax him out of his anger. "Do not be angry anymore. Remember, I have a gift for you, and I would like you to be in a good mood before I give it to you."

Moonsyrah walked back into her room and closed the balcony doors. She stood in front of her mirror and slowly undid the zipper that ran down the back of her dress. Moonsyrah slipped her arms from the sleeves and let the dress pool at her feet. She stood there in her underwear and could feel Adym's anger start to fade away. She stepped out of her heels and enticingly rolled her stockings down her long legs. Adym started to growl again at her, this time in pleasure.

Moonsyrah laughed at him and lay back on her bed against the headboard. She closed her eyes and felt the edge of the bed sink and his breath against her lips. But this time, he felt very solid, not like the shadow she was used to. Moonsyrah opened her eyes and gasped in pleasure that he was really here, with her. He was here in flesh and blood.

"How?" She ran her hands along his bare back and felt the spinal ridges there. She was amazed at the warmth of his skin. She placed her hand over his heart and felt the beat match the one she felt echoing next to hers.

"I can never return to my home now that I have left. But to be with you is worth everything." Adym replied. He leaned over her and kissed her lips with his own, and this first real kiss was ecstasy for them both. She felt him shift his weight and lift her so that she was lying on top of him. He started to run his hands down the length of her body, and she shivered in delight.

"Wait, I still have my gift to give you."

"You are all the gift I need." He bit her lip gently.

Moonsyrah smiled mischievously and slowly brought down the last barrier she held against him in her mind and unveiled the memory of her finding the key. She heard him suck in his breath in surprise and was jostled off him as he sat up.

His voice held a questioning tone and barely checked joy as he asked, "Is this a real memory, or have you learned to play games with your mind?"

"It is real. I would not play games with the key to your release. Before I knew that you had left the Myst, I knew that I was going to set you free. If releasing the demons means I can keep you with me, then release them, I will." Moonsyrah sat up next to Adym.

Adym stared at the woman beside him. He had not failed in his duty to his people. Their bond was true. He could feel the sincerity in her words. She was not playing games; she was choosing to set him free. Against all reason, she had chosen him.

"You are more important to me than any fear the humans may experience from your people's release. I love you, Adym, forever." She went over to her dresser and found the key in the bowl of crystals she had gathered from the Falls. She sat back down next to him, the stone clutched in her hands.

"All I ask is that you give me a week to talk with the Prophetess and finish up a couple of things before you release the others. I want to be there with you when that happens." She handed him the key.

Adym took it and marveled at the feel of it in his hands. After so long, he held the one thing that would bring his people peace and health back to Y'ddra. He placed it carefully on the side table and made love to his Korsyon. As important as the key was to him, he wanted this night to be about the two of them.

Sameen saw the scene between Gavin and Moonsyrah and wondered what had upset him and caused Moonsyrah to leave the dance. She excused herself from Ethan, told him she would meet him in his room later, and walked over to Gavin, who was being helped to a seat by Novalie. Unsure whether or not to question him in front of the prophetess-in-training, she hesitated. She then decided it didn't matter. She needed to know, so she asked him what had happened, and his answer made no sense. He said that in his mind, he could see a man with dark blue, glowing eyes standing in front of him and could feel his hands at his throat. It seemed so real that he could feel the breath leaving his body. The image didn't leave until Moonsyrah told Adym to stop, and she let go of his hand.

Sameen thought maybe Gavin had indulged a bit too much in the punch until he said that the image went away once Moonsyrah spoke the name, Adym. Sameen grabbed Gavin's arm and made him repeat what he had just said. Gavin told her the story again and then left, with Novalie following behind him. Gavin decided he had not had enough punch and needed another glassful to wash away the images that still flashed through his head.

Sameen left the celebration and went out into the garden to find Moonsyrah. She was too late to catch up to Moon, but Sameen followed her footsteps to the monastery entrance that was closest to their rooms. She saw Moonsyrah at the top of the stairs and almost called out to her but decided not to. She was curious to hear what Moon was softly muttering to herself. She saw Moon enter her bedroom, closing the door.

Sameen quietly opened Moonsyrah's door just enough to peek inside when she heard Moon call out to someone named Adym. She had heard Moonsyrah say this name once before. Sameen leaned in closer to the door opening and listened as Moonsyrah told Adym not to be angry and that she had a gift for him. Sameen closed the door a little bit more when she saw Moonsyrah come back into her room from her balcony. She expected Moon to have someone with her but was surprised to see her close the balcony door behind herself.

She watched as Moon undressed, and how this was done caused Sameen to blush and almost leave, but she wanted to see who this Adym was. Where was he? She could still hear Moonsyrah talking to him, but no one was there. She closed the door quietly so as not to be seen and listened to Moonsyrah talking to the invisible Adym as if he were right next to her. Sameen heard her tell him about a key she had found that would release demons on Yiddera.

Sameen shook her head and left to her own room. She wondered if her friend had finally gone crazy. She had seemed to be doing better in the last few weeks since she had met Gavin, but maybe she had finally snapped. The Prophetess had once mentioned that if Moonsyrah ever started acting strangely or talking to someone who wasn't there, she wanted to be informed. Sameen wasn't sure if she should tell the Prophetess yet. Maybe she should just watch Moon for a while. She pulled on her cloak and left to spend what was left of the holiday evening with Ethan.

The Healers Hall was full of classrooms and patients' quarters, while the two floors above housed the healers. Sameen walked up the stairs to the third floor and entered the master healer's wing. The master healers all shared a kitchen and living room, and just like her and Moon's rooms, they all had individual bedrooms and bathrooms. She walked to the fourth door on the left and knocked. Ethan opened the door and smiled when he saw her standing there. Sameen entered the room and sat on the chair underneath the window. She took off her shoes and curled her feet up under her.

"Ethan, tell me what you know about the demons that live in the Myst. Not what the Prophetess teaches but what you know." Sameen looked up into the face of the man she loved, her eyes filled with questions.

"What a serious question for a night that should be full of joy and celebration," Ethan said as he closed and locked his door.

"Well," he began. "I know that they are wicked beings that thrive on the fear of others. It has been passed down through generations of my family that they actually gain health from the fear and pain of others, and this is what gives them eternal life and keeps their magic strong." Ethan went over to Sameen and sat on the floor in front of her. He rested his head in her lap/

"Let's see, I remember also hearing that they have the same hair and eye coloring as you and Moonsyrah. Though they also have blue markings on their bodies, and their eyes are a different shape than yours but have a similar glow to them." He looked up at her. "Why do you ask?"

Sameen ran her hand absently through Ethan's hair. "Tonight, something strange happened between Moon and

Gavin. As you know, she left the celebration rather abruptly after dancing with Gavin. I went and asked him what had happened, and he said that an invisible being spoke to him and then tried to choke him. The hand would not let him go until Moon told someone named Adym to stop." She paused for a moment before continuing her story.

"I then went after Moon to ask her what happened as Gavin's story was odd, to say the least, and because I have heard her say the name Adym before. I heard her talking to someone in her room tonight, but no one other than Moon was in the room. I am worried that she is talking to one of the demons." She went back to lightly running her fingers through his hair.

"No, I am worried that she is doing far more than just talking to a demon. I just can't figure out how since they are supposed to be locked away in the Myst and unable to leave it."

"I do not know how it is possible either, but according to my family's stories, the demons are supposed to be able to invade our minds. It sounds like this is what happened to Gavin and Moonsyrah. You do not think that maybe she has set them free, do you?" Ethan opened his eyes and looked up at Sameen.

"No, I do not think that. She is my best friend, and I think that I would know if she was thinking of setting the demons free."

"The story passed down in my family states that if they are set free, they will kill every one of my bloodline first and then start killing the rest of the Yidderians. I will talk to Gavin tomorrow, and you talk to Moon and we will see what we can figure out. If she is consorting with one of the demons, she is in danger. Together, we will figure out a way to stop the demon from playing with her." Ethan raised his head from Sameen's lap and stood up. He took her hand in his and tugged on her until she, too, stood up. He led her to the side of the bed and, turning her around, started undoing the buttons that ran up the back of her dress.

"This is a holiday, a time of celebration. Let's forget everything else but us." He slipped the dress off Sameen's shoulders and kissed the newly exposed skin. Sameen sighed in pleasure as his hands cupped her small, firm breasts.

"I think that is a great idea." Sameen turned around in his arms and kissed him. All thoughts of Moon and the demons vanished. Ethan was right; this was a night meant to be spent in celebration and love.

The next morning, Moonsyrah and Sameen were working in the archives when Sameen noticed an absent look on Moonsyrah's face and heard her whisper, "Adym." Sameen watched Moonsyrah out of the corner of her eye and saw her close her eyes and smile. Moonsyrah then suggested she and Sameen take a break and meet back here later that morning. Sameen said that was a great idea and she would see Moonsyrah later. Moonsyrah left the archives and headed out into the orchard, where the snowfruit trees were heavy with fruit. Sameen followed discreetly behind Moonsyrah and watched and listened.

Moonsyrah did not realize that Sameen had heard her whisper Adym's name, nor did she know that she was being watched now. She leaned back against one of the trees and picked a ripe fruit.

"Adym, I missed you when you left last night. Where did you go?" Moonsyrah opened her eyes wide and watched as Adym appeared in front of her.

"Nowhere important. Moonsyrah, Allura is soon to show in the night sky. I think that it might be the best time to unlock the gates. The Myst is always at its most vulnerable at that time. Meet me at the falls on the second night of the third moon." Adym ran his hands down Moonsyrah's arms, then, taking her chin in his hand, lifted her lips to meet his.

"That is almost two weeks away." She said when he released her lips. "Are you sure you want to wait that long?"

"I need to gather my strength. I still have not recovered from leaving the Myst. I am going to the next village over to feed. I want to be at full strength for the occasion. Will you miss me while I am gone?" Adym asked in a teasing manner.

"Adym, I love you, and to have you gone for even a day is torment. I will miss you more than you can know. I will meet you at the falls during the Alluran moon." Moonsyrah could see Adym standing next to her, looking at her with love. She knew he was reluctant to leave her, yet she also saw his need.

"Until the third moon, my Beloved." Adym pulled back from her and disappeared.

Moonsyrah stood there for a while still savoring the feel of his thoughts in her mind. She pulled herself out of her reverie and then headed back into the archives. She needed to finish up the task she had been working on and then plan her trip to the falls. The moon of Allura would show in the night sky soon, and she had much to accomplish before then. Moonsyrah was not looking forward to the days without Adym, but she had plenty to do, starting with finding Gavin and trying to explain things to him. She was just about done tidying up the counter when she looked up from her work and saw that Sameen was back.

"Sameen, I need to talk with Gavin. Do you mind if I leave you to finish up with the dusting?" Moonsyrah asked her friend and waited for her answer.

"Of course, Moon." Sameen had not expected Moonsyrah to ask to leave to go find Gavin. After the conversation, she had overheard and what she had seen, Sameen had assumed Moon would find a way to meet up with this Adym again, even though he said he would be gone. Sameen picked up the duster when she saw Moon hesitate at the door.

"I promised the Prophetess that I would reupholster her settee and chairs for her. I thought I would start on that this afternoon. Would you like to help me?"

"I would love to Moon. I have wanted to talk to you about something, and I think that would be a perfect time. I will meet you in the fabric storeroom after lunch." Sameen started her task as Moonsyrah left the archives. This afternoon, she planned on asking Moon who Adym was. She was hoping she was wrong about what she had seen earlier. The man's eyes glowed as hers did, but surely it could not have been a demon. They were locked away in the Myst. Well, at least she thought they were. The conversation she had overheard indicated they were, but maybe one had already been released? Why would Moonsyrah release a demon? And how could she love one?"

Moonsyrah found Gavin in the drying shed, as he often was. He was always in there studying. She had asked him why once, and he told her that he loved the different herbal smells and that seeing the drying herbs helped him remember what each one was used for. She entered the building cautiously; she wasn't sure what his reception of her would be. She walked up to him and quietly said his name. He looked up from the herb he had been studying and, seeing Moonsyrah, took a step back.

"I am sorry about what happened at the dance. Will you walk with me for a bit and let me try and explain?" Moonsyrah's face showed her wariness at being around him and her guilt over what she had caused.

Silently, Gavin put down his pen and paper and headed out of the building. Moonsyrah followed him and found that he was heading down the walkway that would take them to the skating pond. She smiled and thought of how often they had walked this way together. She frowned as she felt Adym stir in her mind. Quietly, she told him to calm down and was surprised when he obeyed. She turned her attention back to Gavin.

"Explain," Gavin said in a terse voice. He slowed his walking down so that Moonsyrah could walk beside him.

"I am not sure exactly how to explain, but I will try my best." Moonsyrah paused to get her thoughts in order. "Before you and I met, I was in a relationship, if that is what you can call it, with someone else. I ended it for reasons that I cannot go into. When I met you, I thought I could get over him."

"Moonsyrah, I love you." Interrupted Gavin.

Moonsyrah looked into his eyes and saw that what he said was true. Adym had told her how Gavin felt about her, but she hadn't believed it until now.

"I know." She replied and walked for a moment in silence before looking back at him in question. "I have always wondered why you were never afraid of me as so many others are. I guess it doesn't matter now, but I am curious."

Gavin looked at her and reached for her hand, but Moonsyrah took a small step back, not allowing the touch. "I guess I was never afraid because I have worked with the blue girls, and I kind of got used to the chilling feel around them. With you, it was a bit harder to ignore, but the more time we spent together, the more I didn't notice it. The more I fell in love with you, the more it didn't matter."

"Oh," Moonsyrah said, lost in thought, trying to come up with a way not to hurt him any further but knowing that what she had to say would. She continued walking slowly next to Gavin and picked their conversation back up. "When you kissed me, I realized that what we had was not to be. When we kissed, I realized that I would never be over Adym. That he meant more to me than any person should mean to anyone. You gave me the gift of clarity. Of seeing what I really wanted despite the consequences. Your kiss was wonderful, but the anger I felt from Adym gave me more pleasure than the kiss." Moonsyrah could see the confusion on Gavin's face.

"Moonsyrah, there was no one else in that hallway when we kissed. How could you know it made this Adym angry?" Gavin stopped and sat down once they reached the bench by the pond. Moonsyrah sat next to him.

"I should have broken things off with you right then, but I didn't. I wanted you to enjoy your day. That night, Adym warned me not to dance with you, but I did anyway. When you took my hand in yours and then kissed me, Adym did not like it. I do not know what image he put in your head, but you paid for my mistake, and I am sorry."

"I saw a demon with blue hair and eyes staring at me and placing his hands around my throat. I couldn't breathe. The image didn't go away until." A dawning look appeared in Gavin's eyes. He quickly stood up and backed away from her again. "It didn't stop until you told Adym to quit. Moonsyrah, are you telling me what I saw was real?"

She reached up and touched one of the fingerprint bruises on his neck. "Did you honestly doubt that it was real?" She sighed loudly when Gavin quickly moved away from her touch, and his eyes reflected his fear of her in them.

Moonsyrah looked up at Gavin and decided to tell him the truth. "Yes, Adym lives in the Myst. And as far as I know, you are the only other person here who has met him. The stories told about the demons are true. I love him, Gavin. I cannot help it. He is everything to me."

"The Calling speaks of this, and Ethan has often told me the stories are real, but I never believed either of them. Now, Moonsyrah, after what I experienced and what you have said, I can't help but believe." Gavin backed further away from her. He was afraid that if he got too close, he would meet Adym again. "How can you love a demon?"

"I don't know. I just know that without Adym, I am not whole. Gavin, I am so sorry for everything. You are a good person, and you will find someone who deserves you. I do not expect you to ever understand or even forgive me. I just felt that I owed you an explanation for everything that happened." Moonsyrah got up from the bench and began to walk away.

"Moonsyrah, wait." Gavin stepped toward her. "I can help you. You do not have to stay with him. He is an evil being, and I think he might be playing with your mind. He has you convinced that you love him, so you might be willing to set him free."

Moonsyrah smiled at him, knowing he would never understand, "Goodbye, Gavin." And she continued walking, leaving him standing there looking at her with mixed emotions on his face.

Moonsyrah went back into the monastery and knew she had done the best she could to explain things to Gavin. She removed him from her thoughts and headed to grab a quick bite to eat before she met Sameen to choose fabrics for the afternoon's project.

While Moonsyrah and Sameen were gathering the fabrics needed for the upcoming work, Novalie walked in. She immediately told Moonsyrah that she couldn't use the gold-watered silk embossed with flowers for the settee and then told them to use the gold crushed velvet that was embroidered with a pattern of green leaves.

Though Moonsyrah was put out by the interruption and the autocratic way Novalie took over the decision on what to use, she liked the idea and thought the material would go well with the green velvet she was planning to use on the chairs.

"See that you get the settee done today. The fabric is wearing on it." She stated.

"But I was going to do the chairs first as the one with the wine stain looks ghastly," Moonsyrah argued.

Novalie frowned at her, "I want the settee done first. Do not argue with me." She stepped closer to Moonsyrah and leaned in to whisper in her ear. "Do it my way, or I will let the Prophetess know your secret." With that, she marched out of the room and left the two girls staring at her back. Frowning at the retreating figure, the two women gathered up the rest of the supplies they would need and headed to the Prophetess' rooms. Without looking at the material and patterns chosen, the Prophetess left the two to do their work and headed out for the afternoon.

The girls started with the settee since it had been decreed that they must. They carefully took off the old fabric and busied themselves using it as a pattern for the new section. While they were working, Sameen decided it was time to talk with Moonsyrah.

"Who is Adym?"

Startled at the question, Moonsyrah dropped her pins and watched them scatter across the floor. She ignored Sameen's question and searched for the pins.

"Moon, who is Adym?" Sameen asked again, helping to gather the loose pins.

"Why do you ask?" evaded Moonsyrah.

"I have heard you talking to him, and I saw you with him in the forest. And Gavin said he heard you speak to Adym. I know of no one named Adym who lives here at the monastery. So, who is he?" Sameen was determined to get Moon to answer her question.

Sighing, Moonsyrah stopped her search for the missing pins and answered Sameen.

"You have heard the Prophetess speak of the ones that live in the Myst." She began.

Sameen picked up a pin that had rolled by her and put it in the jar with the rest. "You mean the stories of the demons? The stories she tells of the evil beings that, if released from the Myst, will eat us all?"

"Yes, those stories." Replied Moonsyrah.

"I do know them, but what have they to do with Adym?" Sameen was pretty sure that she knew, but she wanted Moon to confirm what she believed.

"Well, those stories are true. At least true in the sense that there are beings that live in the Myst. Adym is one of them." Moonsyrah cut the fabric and started sewing the pieces.

"I thought so. But how can you speak to Adym when he lives in the Myst? According to the stories, they are locked in and cannot get out." Moonsyrah was shocked at Sameen's easy acceptance of what she had been told, and her "I thought so" comment surprised her.

"Adym is telepathic, as they all are. He is the only one who can leave the Myst, though it is draining for him, too. His abilities allow him to appear and disappear at will. The others do not have this ability, so they cannot get out."

Moonsyrah looked sad about this, and even though Sameen couldn't understand how Moon could be saddened by demons being locked away, her heart went out to her friend.

"There is a prophecy about the demons. I think it says that a key is needed to release them but that if released, they would destroy Y'ddra and all who live on Yiddera."

"How do you know of the prophecy? You never go to the talks held by the Prophetess." Moonsyrah asked her friend.

"Ethan told me of it." Was Sameen's reply

"How does he know so much about the demons in the Myst and the prophecy? Does he go to the meetings? Is he a believer of the Calling?" Moonsyrah was again surprised at Sameen's words.

"Yes, actually, he is, but his reason for believing is that Ethan says he is the many greats grandson of Amalie. She is the one who locked the demons in the Myst and hid the key. His family has known of the prophecy forever. And unlike most people who only believe because the Prophetess says it is true, he believes because his family has proof. They have a diary written by Amalie that tells of her story. Ethan says that a child of the third moon would start to hear the voices and bring about the release of the demons." She looked in concern at her friend, "They cannot be let out of the Myst, Moon." Sameen put her hand on Moonsyrah's. "Do not let this demon manipulate you into letting him go."

"Adym is not manipulating me into anything. I love him, Sameen." Moonsyrah pulled her hand away from her friends and finished the seam she was working on.

Sameen did not know how to reply to that, and so she didn't say anything for a while. The two girls finished sewing the fabric pieces together and set about recovering the settee. Once they were finished, Sameen revisited their conversation.

"He is a demon, Moonsyrah. How can you be sure that he is not deceiving you into loving him so that you will release him?"

"My love for him is real, Sameen." Moonsyrah decided the conversation needed to reach an end, so she chose to lie to reassure her friend. "I am not the one the prophecy speaks of Sameen. I am with Adym because he loves me, too, not because he wishes me to release him. He has never mentioned a key to me. I do not know where it is or even if it exists."

Sameen knew that Moonsyrah was lying to her, but she let it slide. Sameen pulled out the green velvet for the chairs, and Moonsyrah folded the remaining gold fabric and put it in the basket she had brought it in.

"Sameen, are you still seeing Ethan?" Moonsyrah hoped this would start a new topic of conversation. Sameen blushed and unfolded the green fabric before answering.

"Yes, we have been seeing each other for a few months now. You have been so wrapped up in yourself and then in Gavin that I am not surprised you haven't noticed. He is so kind and handsome. I love the way his eyes sparkle when I enter the room." Sameen gazed dreamily at a vision that only she could see. "He has asked me to marry him. We will, of course, wait until he is done with his training. Though he is already a master healer, he has a year left before he finishes his internship. Once this is complete, we will go back to his home near the forests of Kluane, on Kahlali, if the Prophetess allows me to leave the Monastery. If not we will move into the village here. Moon, he makes me so happy."

"I am happy for you, Sameen. You will make a wonderful wife to a healer, and the different scenery will give you new ideas for your paintings and jewelry." Moonsyrah hugged her friend. "It is getting late. Let's finish the chairs another time. We will ask the Prophetess what day would be best for her to have us finish." Moonsyrah placed the cut green fabric on the end table beside the chair with the stain on it. She placed the basket of sewing supplies under the same table and then, picking up the basket of remnants, left the room with Sameen.

"Sameen, I will take this basket back to the fabric closet and put it away. You can go and spend the rest of the evening with Ethan." Moonsyrah watched as Sameen scurried down the hall, which would take her to the exit that led to Ethan.

When she was done with her task, Moonsyrah headed to her room for what she was sure would be a long night. It had only been one afternoon, and the silence in her head was deafening. She could still feel him at the edges of her mind, but his mind did not feel as entwined in hers as it had once. She went out onto her balcony and looked out at the Myst. She missed Adym.

Today, she had found out that her friends suspected she was the one the prophecy spoke of, and they believed the Prophetess's words that the demons would destroy their world. She didn't think that setting Adym free would destroy Y'ddra or the planet, but she did know this decision would change the world. Moonsyrah gathered comfort from the Myst and then headed back into her room. She whispered, "I love you" and heard the words said back to her as she crawled in bed to sleep.

The Prophetess made her way back to her quarters, hoping that Moonsyrah and Sameen were done for the evening. She opened her door and looked over at the sitting area to see if the young ladies had left yet. What she saw turned her white and caused her to stumble and fall, hitting her face on a side table. The Prophetess stayed sitting on the floor next to the side table and stared at the settee as blood flowed down her face. The settee was covered in the gold material with the green leaf pattern that was in her recurrent dream. The Prophetess distinctly remembered Moonsyrah saying she would recover the settee in gold silk, not a green and gold velvet. What had made the girl change her mind? The settee fabric, the stain still on the high-backed chair, and now the cut she could feel across her nose all indicated that her vision, seen at the birth of Moonsyrah, was about to come true.

The Prophetess gingerly stood up and held the back of the settee until a wave of dizziness passed. She then made her way, shakily, to the bell rope to summon a servant to help her. One of the older maids answered her summons and helped the Prophetess into her room and onto her bed.

"Please go get one of the healers and bring them to me. Tell whoever you get that stitches will be required. Hurry back to help me change my dress and wash up, please." The Prophetess grabbed a hand towel from her nightstand and held it against her bleeding nose as the maid rushed out of the room to find a healer. The Prophetess didn't have to wait long before a healer arrived.

"Good afternoon, Prophetess."

"Hello, healer Ethan. Who is your assistant?" She asked.

"This is Bette. She is going to help me set you to rights." Ethan opened his medical bag and pulled out a cleanser, his stitch kit, and a topical numbing agent. He set the supplies on the dresser top as he addressed Bette.

"Please help the maid get the Prophetess cleaned up, into a fresh nightgown, and back into bed while I wash my hands and prepare a tonic to help relieve her pain." Ethan left the bedroom to give the ladies some privacy. Bette sent the maid after a warm washcloth while she gathered a clean nightgown for the Prophetess to wear. She then gently cleaned the Prophetess's face and helped her to change.

Bette was just getting the Prophetess settled comfortably into her bed when Ethan came back into the room. Ethan handed the Prophetess the drink he had made to help ease her pain and watched to make sure she drank it all. He gave the empty cup to the maid and then applied the topical numbing gel. Ethan then set to stitching the cut across the bridge of the Prophetess' nose. He finished with the fifth and final stitch before asking the Prophetess what happened.

"I was just being clumsy and tripped over the rug." The pain medication started to take effect, and she became sleepy and unable to say more. Ethan pulled the blankets up over her and told her that he would be back in the morning to check on her. The Prophetess listened to him whisper to the maid and his assistant and then heard her front door close behind him. She drifted off into a painless sleep.

Novalie walked through the Monastery the next morning in a hurry to get to her mother's rooms. She was going to be late for morning meditations, and she absolutely hated being late. She had been up late the night before, unable to sleep. Something about the air didn't feel right. Novalie pondered on that part of her visions. The air always felt off when she was either going to have a prophetic dream or when one was about to be played out. Last night, she had no vision, and so today, she wondered which would come true.

She stopped outside the door and adjusted her skirts before walking sedately into the room. Novalie looked around the room and saw that her mother was not up and about in the living space, and the curtains to the garden were still closed. It was unlike her mother to sleep in. She quietly walked into her mother's room and was surprised to see her mother still asleep in bed. She shut the door behind her as she went back into the living room and saw that one of the first-year healers had come in. She waved the girl over to her and sat with her on the couch. Quietly so as not to wake the sleeping Prophetess, Novalie asked why she was there.

Just as quietly, Bette answered, "The Prophetess tripped and cut her nose in the fall. She is being taken good care of by Ethan and myself, but she is not to be disturbed by anyone else. My lady, if you would please leave her undisturbed so that she can get the rest she needs, it would be appreciated."

"Of course. I want her to heal quickly. Please let her know that I dropped by and will attend to her duties so that she does not have to worry about them. Also, please let her know that

I will check on her later this evening." Novalie stood up and left the room after she saw the young healer hurry about her preparation for attending the Prophetess.

Novalie left the room and sat on one of the benches situated nearby. Her mother was not clumsy. In all the years she could remember, nothing had caused her mother to trip and injure herself before. She wondered if this was part of why the air felt different and foreboding. Was it one of her mother's prophecies that was in the works or one of her own? Novalie closed her eyes and searched inside her mind until she found the memory that she was looking for. Her vision of the fire showed her mother with a cut on her face. Novalie had never concentrated on that portion of the vision before; she had always been concerned with getting Gavin out of the fire. Both she and her mother had visions of the night the gates would open, and now it looked as if it was nearing time, but not yet. The air felt as if the time for the gates to open was still a bit of a way off.

Novalie knew that she had to make plans and prepare. The old chapel at the edge of the property would remain safe. She made her way to her room to gather the things that she did not want to lose and that she would need to be comfortable in the old chapel.

The Prophetess woke that morning to a throbbing pain in her nose and a headache. Bette came bustling into the room, bringing with her a poultice that would help ease the pain. The Prophetess thanked the nurse for her help and inquired if Moonsyrah had been in to see her that morning.

"No, Mistress, she has not. Novalie stopped by. I told her that you had taken a fall and needed rest, and then I sent her on her way, but she will be in later to visit with you, and she asked me to tell you not to worry. She said she would take over the tasks that need to be done in your absence." Bette handed the Prophetess a glass of warm milk and a muffin to break her fast.

"Healer Ethan will be by shortly to check on you. If you think you will be okay by yourself, I will leave you for the morning and check back this afternoon." Bette said as she straightened up the room and fluffed the pillow.

"I will be fine by myself this morning. I will catch up on some reading and rest." The Prophetess was feeling sleepy again and wondered what sedative had been added to her morning milk. She placed her unfinished muffin on the nightstand and fell back to sleep.

The next few days passed quickly and with a predictable routine, with Novalie taking care of what duties she could for the Prophetess and Ethan coming to check on her in the mornings, often bringing less experienced healers with him so that they could learn from his care of the Prophetess. She was always given a sedative and an herbal pain remedy, and then she would sleep for several hours. Bette came in the mornings, at lunchtime, and in the evenings to monitor her and bring her something to eat. By the fourth day, the Prophetess was able to get around on her own without feeling dizzy, and she dismissed Bette from her care. It was on the fifth day of her recovery that Moonsyrah came to the Prophetess' rooms.

Moonsyrah spent the next few days working on preparations for her secret departure from the Monastery. She waited to be summoned to the Prophetess' chambers for instructions on when she and Sameen were to finish the chairs. When a few days passed, and she had not heard from the Prophetess, she decided to go and ask her when she wanted this done and if there was anything else the Seer might need. Moonsyrah walked into the living room and found the Prophetess in bed with a bandage over her nose.

"What happened? Are you alright?" Moonsyrah asked from the door of the Prophetess' room. Shocked to see the bruised countenance on her face. Moonsyrah walked in and sat in a chair close to the bed.

"I am fine, my child. I had a fall a few days ago and managed to cut my nose." The Prophetess smiled and then grimaced at the pain this caused. "It has required a few stitches but will heal nicely. I will have but a small scar to show for it."

"Oh, surely such a small cut will not scar. I am sure it will heal very nicely. The healers will make sure of that. Do you need me to do anything for you today?" Moonsyrah asked.

"No, I do not have anything that requires your assistance to-day, but you can keep me company for a while." The Prophetess sat up a bit higher in her bed. "I noticed you went with a different fabric for the settee than I expected."

"Oh, yes, well, Novalie liked this fabric better and demanded that we use it instead. Is it to your liking? We can always redo it." Moonsyrah asked.

"It is fine; I just wondered at the change." The Prophetess replied. She was surprised to hear that Novalie was responsible for the choice. She had never considered that this daughter of hers would be part of causing the events that surrounded the prophecy to happen. She had always assumed Novalie was to be a background character until after she took her place as the reigning prophetess. She brought herself out of her thoughts and focused her attention once more on the young woman sitting in front of her.

"I am curious to know how you have been doing. You seem happier lately. Are you still seeing that lovely young man, Gavin, I think his name is?"

"No, I am not. Gavin and I are not meant to be." Moonsyrah felt uncomfortable talking about this with the Prophetess. This conversation could lead to too many questions she was not yet ready to answer. The Prophetess, seeing Moonsyrah's discomfort, didn't pursue the topic.

"Hmm, I am sorry to hear that." She adjusted herself more comfortably and then continued. "Moonsyrah, certain things have come to my attention that lead me to believe that we are heading toward the fulfillment of the prophecy. You once told me that you no longer hear the voice in your head. Is this still true?" The piercing eyes of the Prophetess seemed to look into Moonsyrah's soul. Moonsyrah stood up and paced in front of the bed. Moonsyrah was disgruntled to find that the questions she was hoping to avoid seemed unavoidable.

"You heard what happened the night of the celebration?" Moonsyrah stopped pacing and placed a hand on the footboard post.

The Prophetess had, in fact, heard nothing concerning Moonsyrah and the celebration but chose to answer as if she had.

She nodded her head and then said, "Continue."

"Adym spoke with me again while at the dance. He became jealous of Gavin and told me to stay away from him. I didn't. Gavin took my hand and led me onto the dance floor, and Adym stopped him." Moonsyrah grew even more uncomfortable talking to the Prophetess. She went back to pacing the room.

"Moonsyrah, I have two questions. The first is how did he stop Gavin. What I have heard is a bit vague." The Prophetess continued to act as if she had heard part of this story. She had never heard Moonsyrah say the name of the voice she heard. She had once seen the demon and knew he was male, but never had Moonsyrah mentioned knowing his name. Moonsyrah apparently had much more contact with this demon than she had suspected.

"Those that live in the Myst are telepathic, and each has a special gift that they can use to bring fear to those they stalk. Did you know that? Anyway, Adym used his to stop Gavin from breathing." She paused a moment, "He appeared in front of Gavin and reached for his throat. Adym stopped trying to kill him when I let go of Gavin's hand and asked him to stop." Moonsyrah chewed on her bottom lip. She knew what the Prophetess was bound to ask next, and that was going to be hard to explain without letting the Prophetess know she had previously lied to her about the voices.

The Prophetess was concerned about what she was hearing. Everything that she had tried to do to keep the prophecy from unfolding was not working. She looked at Moonsyrah and pointed to the chair next to her.

"Pull the chair closer to the bed and sit Moonsyrah." She watched as Moonsyrah did as she was asked.

"My second question is twofold. Why would Adym have cause to be jealous of Gavin and why would he stop tormenting Gavin just because you asked him to?"

Moonsyrah took a deep breath and squared her shoulders before answering the Prophetess. It was time to tell her the truth and accept whatever consequences it might bring.

"Prophetess, I love him." Moonsyrah heard the Prophetess draw in her breath. Moonsyrah made eye contact with her before continuing. "I left Adym a few months back. I knew it was wrong to talk with him, and he can be, as you say, a demon. He is not always kind; He is the one responsible for the many deaths that have recently occurred. My heart ached without him, and I didn't feel like myself without him here, in my mind."

Moonsyrah paused and felt him as always present and yet not. "I tried to forget about him, and for a time, I thought I was succeeding. I realized on Ontscheppen the futility of trying to live without him." She took a deep breath and let it out slowly. "To answer your questions. Adym has every right to be jealous; I belong with him. He stopped hurting Gavin because I asked him to, and he knew it was important to me that he did as I asked." Moonsyrah stopped talking and waited to see what the Prophetess would say next.

"My child, I don't know what to say or how to express my concern for you. He is a demon and will surely only bring you pain." The Prophetess reached over and took Moonsyrah's hand in hers again. "I obviously cannot stop you from talking to him, but child, I wish I could. This relationship can only lead to the destruction of Yiddera. The prophecy is clear on that."

"Prophetess, I cannot disagree with you as I know what his kind will do if released from the Myst. The destruction of this planet is not their intent, our people maybe, but they would never hurt our Goddess Y'ddra or this world. I will not argue with you that, maybe, I am the one the prophecy talks of; I can only repeat what I once said to you. If the prophecy is true and I am the one chosen by the demons to release them, it is still my choice. I am not ruled by a prophecy. I make my own decisions, and believe me when I tell you that I love Adym with every fiber in my being, and this does influence me." Moonsyrah stood up, leaned over the Prophetess, and kissed her brow. "I may be fated, but trust me to do what I believe to be right. I love you, Prophetess, now rest and heal."

Moonsyrah left the room, closing the door behind her.

The Prophetess closed her eyes in frustration and didn't open them again until she heard Moonsyrah leave the suite. Once alone, the Prophetess opened her eyes and thought about the conversation she had just had. Moonsyrah was right in that it was her decision to make, but she was also wrong because the choice had already been foretold. And now, to hear Moonsyrah not only talked to the demons so freely but to have fallen in love with one was vexing. The girl had no idea what the consequences of letting the demons free from their entrapment would be. She was pretty sure the demon had not told Moonsyrah about their depravity and darkness.

The Prophetess, Alena, from the time before the demons had been locked away, had been an expansive journalist. The stories Alena wrote about told of humans who claimed to see iniquitous images in their minds and went on to perform heinous acts because of them. It was speculated that some were led to kill themselves, and some were led to kill others. These last people claimed they had felt an unseen being use their bodies to do these horrible things. Others claimed they were plagued by nightmares that wouldn't go away, and many of these poor souls were driven crazy. People disappeared, and few were ever found alive. The ones left living claimed to see visions that beckoned them to follow. These visions were always of items or people the one who saw them yearned for and so would willingly go after.

Thankfully, Amalie stole the key and put an end to the mysterious and dreadful happenings. She was not much of a writer, but she drew the faces of the demons so that they would not be forgotten or mistaken as other than the demons they were. She also drew and wrote of a hard-to-find flower that could render the mightiest of the wicked beings weak. She had written that it was used as a potion to weaken the taker enough for a healer to set bones properly so they would not heal before they were in perfect order. It was also used along with a sleeping aid to induce unconsciousness so that surgery, though rarely needed, could be done. But the Prophetess was only interested in one fact. It was possible to render them weak enough that they could not heal from a fatal injury or ingestion of poison. When it was mixed with the roots of the same plant, it acted as a painless and slow-acting poison.

Now Moonsyrah was about to fulfill the prophecy and release the demons to once again unleash their wickedness on the humans. As soon as Ethan removed her stitches and allowed her to resume her regular duties, the Prophetess would once more try to impress upon Moonsyrah the importance of keeping the prophecy unfulfilled. The Prophetess thought of the tisane made of this rare flower she had in her cupboard. If necessary, she would use whatever was required of her to see that Moonsyrah did not find the key and accomplish the task the demon, Adym, was sure to ask of her. She had been weak before when killing this girl would have been easier, but now she would do whatever was required of her, emotionally difficult though it might be.

The time of the third moon was upon them, and Allura cast her glow, turning the world blue. Moonsyrah looked out at the evening sky and saw that the Myst sparkled with a rich shade of sapphire. She knew that Adym had asked that she meet him on the second day of Allura's rising, but she could feel the falls calling to her tonight and found she could not resist their sweet song. She left her room, went out into the living area, and sat on the couch next to Sameen, who was reading a book.

"Sameen, I am going to the falls for a while. If anyone asks about me, will you tell them I do not feel well and am resting in my room for a few days?" Moonsyrah asked.

Sameen looked up from her book and replied, "By anyone, you mean the Prophetess?"

"Yes. You know I cannot tell her I am going there. She does not approve of anyone spending too much time there, me in particular. I know it is a lot to ask, but please, Sameen, I really need this."

"I do not agree with you sneaking away, but I will do as you ask. Moon, be careful. I do not like to think of you out there alone." Sameen looked down at her book and then back up at Moonsyrah. "You will not be there alone, will you?"

"Tonight, I will be," Moonsyrah answered evasively. "Thank you for this."

Moonsyrah got up from the couch and started to gather the things she wanted to take with her for the trip. She put two warm blankets and a change of clothes in a bag, along with a few other personal items from her room. She then went into the kitchen, wrapped up some cheese and crackers, and put them into the side pocket of her carryall.

Waving goodbye to Sameen, Moonsyrah threw on her cloak and left the tower rooms. She quietly left the monastery out a side door and made her way to the maze. Across from the maze fountain was a hidden door that opened to the path that led to the falls. Moonsyrah took this route so that if anyone had seen her leave the abbey, they would assume she was strolling the maze paths and not suspect she was leaving the grounds.

She made it to the falls before the sun went down and set her bag in a small cave that lay between the mountainside and the purple hot spring. She took off her dress and her shoes and headed to the pink pool to relax after her long walk. She stepped into the warm water and closed her eyes to enjoy the heat penetrating deep into her muscles. The waters induced intimate dreams of Adym. She smiled, thinking soon she would be with him forever. It would be a novelty not to worry that someone would find them together. It would be heaven to be free from those closest to her continuously telling her that Adym was using her or that she was being manipulated by him.

She lay there soaking in the warmth until she started to get thirsty and hungry. Moonsyrah stepped out of the pool and could feel the coolness of the winter air wash across her wet skin. The waters in the different springs ranged between hot and warm, and so even though the air beyond the falls was bitter, the air held between the falling water and the mountain wall was cool, not cold. But even so, the coolness on her damp skin made her shiver slightly. She walked to where she had left her bag and took out the soft blankets she had brought with her. She spread one out on the floor of the little cave and sat down on it. The other she wrapped around her shoulders. She took out the cheese and crackers and a bottle of wine that she had packed for the night and sat down to eat and watch the moon rise higher in the sky.

The moon of Allura turned even the stars blue, and the falls were darker than she expected them to be because of this. She finished her meal and was about to call out to Adym when she stopped herself. She would be fine for a while here without him. He would be here tomorrow. She could wait one more day to see him.

She decided to sit in the yellow-orange pool. It always made her feel a bit brave and, to be honest, also a bit reckless. She stepped into the pool and could feel the effervescence of the water. It tingled her body and her blood. She wasn't in it very long when Adym spoke.

"What are you doing at the falls already? I will not be there until tomorrow." Adym sounded as if he was feeling stronger.

"The falls seem to be calling to me tonight, so I decided to come early." Moonsyrah giggled as if slightly tipsy. Adym shook his head at her.

"I do not like that you are out here alone. You should have waited until tomorrow. Stay safe, my Beloved, and don't stay in that pool much longer." Adym shook his head at her again and left her to enjoy the hot pools. Moonsyrah stayed in the champagne waters until she knew that it would be unwise to linger much longer. She got out of the pool and headed back to her blanket.

On her way there, she passed the purple lagoon, and the storm within it called to her. She wasn't sure if it was the slightly intoxicated feeling she got from the yellow-orange pool or if it was because she was alone, but the call of the storm was impossible to resist. She stepped closer to the pool and listened to the tune it played. Tonight, the music felt as if it had entered her heart; she could feel the pounding of the storm in her soul. She knew it was time to brave the storm and learn what it did.

The pool was divided into two parts by the indigo bridge that formed over the middle of it. She dipped a toe into the water and found it quite hot but also very pleasant. The side Moonsyrah entered was calm, and though the stones were of a lavender hue, the water was dark. On the other side of the bridge, the rocks were a deep purple, almost black color. The waters twisted and churned, and the sprays looked as if they contained lightning within them. It was beautiful, mysterious, and dangerous. Moonsyrah decided to walk out to the bridge and no further. The water slowly grew deeper until, an arm's length away from the bridge, it covered her shoulders.

She took another step so that she might reach the bridge when the current swept her under the water. She felt the change in the water's activity as soon as she passed under the bridge. Moonsyrah could not see or breathe in its Stygian grasp. Her head resurfaced, and she took a big breath before she was pulled back under. She couldn't make out which way was up as the water buffeted her around. She fought to find the surface and swim back to the other side of the bridge, but the water was greedy and wouldn't let her go. She listened to the wildness of the water as she was pushed down once again. The back of her legs ached, and her head hurt. Her spine and shoulders felt like bruises were already starting to form. Moonsyrah, knowing she was going to die here in these violent waters, cried out for Adym.

The music rose to a crescendo, and the water churned with more ferocity. Her muscles no longer had the strength to fight. Accepting death, she quit struggling and abandoned all thoughts of fighting against it. Moonsyrah allowed the water to have the control it wanted and accepted whatever fate it held for her. The music instantly softened, and the waters held her in timeless suspension as it altered her forever before pushing her toward the indigo bridge. She felt her head surface and instantly inhaled the cleansing, life-giving air her lungs screamed for. Moonsyrah saw the bridge next to her, and she reached out for it with tired, shaky arms. She managed to pull herself up onto the stone bridge before collapsing into exhaustion.

Adym felt his strength return and his powers reach their height as he finished draining the fear from this last human. He did not usually eat till his prey died, but since leaving the Myst, he needed the heightened fear they felt at the moment of their death. He was about to return to the falls when he heard Moonsyrah's panic-stricken call. Moments later, Adym entered the area behind the falling water to see Moonsyrah struggling against the change she was going through. He knew she had avoided the purple pool in the past and wondered why she chose to enter it now.

He did not interfere. This pool would show her who she really was. It was the pool of the elementals, and he knew what was happening to her. Like those of his race, she must find herself and accept the change without his help, must accept the change the waters offered. He watched as she gave in to the water's control. He watched her relax in the waters and let the change happen. He watched as the process finished, and she climbed out of the pool and onto the bridge. He watched over her while she slept.

Adym's eyes widened in wonder as he saw the physical changes that the water had made on her body begin to appear. He had not known the waters could turn her into an Alluran. The markings appearing on her back and legs marked her not only Alluran but SeiOrhii. He walked closer to her and was overcome by her beauty. He disrobed and joined her on the bridge. Adym intended to wrap her in his arms and let her continue to sleep, but when he got to the bridge, he knew he planned on more. He ran his hands up her legs and over the newly formed blue spots that ran the length of them. Adym put his lips on the slightly raised marking at the base of her spine, then kissed each of the ridges on Moonsyrah's back and up to the nape of her neck. He entwined his fingers in hers and pulled her hands above her head as he slipped inside her. He opened his mind to hers and found her awake and smiling.

Moonsyrah felt Adym's hands on her legs. She felt him kiss her spine and twine his fingers with hers. She felt him enter her and smiled at this cherished intimacy between them. Their pleasure increased and became overwhelming. She felt her body tighten in anticipation around his, and just like she had in the purple waters, she let go, bringing Adym with her. They lay there together while their breathing calmed, and then Adym rolled over onto his side, taking her with him. He put her head on his arm and tucked her body next to his. He gently kissed her neck and smiled as he listened to her sighs of pleasure as she once again fell asleep.

Adym knew how exhausting the change was and was happy to hold her as she slept while the change continued through her. It was a new experience for him to feel the awakening of a new SeiOrhii. Being bonded to her, he, too, felt the current of the elements enter her bloodstream and wake the latent power within her. He felt the final change awaken her with a hunger he knew well. A hunger that was unfamiliar to her. He would have to encourage her to feed, knowing she would most likely not wish to give in to this new side of her. She rolled over in his arms and touched his face with her hands. Her eyes glowed with need.

"Come with me." He picked her up, took a step into nothingness, and then reappeared in front of a lonely house on the outskirts of a small village.

Moonsyrah had no need to ask why they were here. She could feel the hunger coursing through her veins. This new and overwhelming need for another's fear. Her bare feet touched the cold ground as Adym released her from his arms. They walked hand in hand to the house, her body trembling with hunger.

"Feel the fire spreading through you and use it. It is your gift. Use it to feed your hunger and fuel your strength. Burn the house, and they will come running out, dripping with fear. Enter their minds. Find the reservoir that holds their terror and drink of it." Adym instructed.

Moonsyrah did as he said and felt the fear of the two humans enter her and fill her with strength. She indulged until her abilities became more powerful, and she felt as if she could hold no more. Leaving the pair lying on the ground, still breathing, she looked at Adym. "I will not kill them."

"There is no need. Let's go back." He lifted her and headed back to the pools of change.

"Why did you choose tonight to enter the storm?" He sat down with her in the purple pool she was once afraid of. Settling her on his lap, he ran his hands through her hair and wondered if she knew that it had changed from blond to the lightest of blues.

"Tonight, I found it impossible not to enter the water. The music called out to me and tugged at me until it couldn't be ignored." Moonsyrah shifted in his lap so that she straddled him and could see his face. "I know it has changed me, but other than the hunger and the fire running through my veins, I do not feel any different." She saw his eyes crinkle up and heard his laughter ring out.

"Moonsyrah, the waters changed you in ways that I did not know were possible. Look at yourself through my eyes. Enter my mind and find what I saw when you left the pool." He concentrated on this memory and saw her eyes widen.

"I have blue markings?" Moonsyrah was shocked as she looked at herself. She noticed the blue, slightly raised spots that ran up the back of her legs, along her spine, and across her shoulders. She saw that her hair was no longer blond but a very light shade of blue that complemented the bright cornflower sections that were still in braids. She drew herself away from his memory and looked at herself as he saw her at this moment. She saw that the irises of her eyes were now the same oval shape his eyes were. She saw they glowed more brightly than before.

"I don't know how, but the waters have made you SeiOrhii. The purple crystals only call to an elemental, such as yourself. They help an Alluran make the change into SeiOrhii very rarely. Usually, they only awaken the power that lies dormant." Adym looked at Moonsyrah in wonder and in love. "You were meant to be Alluran, SeiOrhii. I didn't know it was possible, even for a daughter of Allura, to become a being they were not born. You are beautiful, my Beloved."

Adym took her face in his hands and kissed her eyes and cheeks and then finally her lips. She felt Adym's rising desire and was unsure of what to do until he moved his hands to her hips and lifted her onto him. He guided her motions until Moonsyrah took over. She placed her hands on his shoulders and threw back her head at the overwhelming sensations that were taking place within her. She cried out his name when she came and moaned in pleasure when she felt him follow her into the sweet oblivion of release. They spent the rest of that night exploring each other's bodies and minds until they fell asleep just as the sun started to rise in the morning sky.

Moonsyrah and Adym woke about mid-morning. They broke their fast on some of the cheese and crackers that Moonsyrah had brought and the winter grapes that Adym provided. Once finished, Adym stood up and saw Moonsyrah stare at his nakedness. He laughed at her blush when she realized he had caught her staring. He reached out his hand and helped her up from her sitting position on the blanket.

"I want you to do something for me, and I know you will not want to, but please trust me."

Adym guided Moonsyrah toward the green pool. Moonsyrah hesitated once she saw where they were headed. "Please, my Beloved, trust me. The green pool is nothing to fear, nor is the memory." He felt her slowly and not quite willingly allow him to pull her along. He stepped into the pool and tugged on her hand to get her to follow him. Adym wrapped his arms around Moonsyrah and rested his chin on the top of her head once she had entered the water.

"When you were young you felt the energy the crystals within the pool contained. It was different from anything you had ever felt at that point in your life, which is why you were afraid of it. That energy helped you create the fire in your mind. It was your brush with the purple pool that woke your fire, but you associated it with the green pool because that was the one you and your mother swam the longest in." He released her and swam out to the middle of the spring. He focused on Moonsyrah and pulled her gently toward him. Moonsyrah found herself unable to resist the pull she felt and so allowed it to take her farther into the pool and to Adym.

Adym smiled at her, "That is what I can do with the energy in the crystals. I can manipulate the energy in a way that allows me to travel from one place to another." He disappeared and then reappeared on the bridge, then back to where he had started within the pool. "I can do the same to other beings and inanimate objects as well." He pulled a rock toward him as a demonstration. "I do this by channeling any of the crystals, not just the green ones. However, I work with blue crystal energy the most, as it is associated with the ability to manipulate objects and space. I am the first to be given the ability to separate myself into spirit and flesh. I think this was because Y'ddra knew that I must somehow be able to leave the Myst to search for and find you." He hugged her to him. "Moonsyrah, had you entered the pink or the yellow pool, you would have felt the same toward it as you do for this one."

Moonsyrah listened to his words, and she could see the truth in them. She had been afraid of the pool because of how it made her feel long before the fire leaped from her mind. She looked up at him in question, "How come I have not been able to do that since the first time until yesterday?"

"You have. The day you came here with the Prophetess and meditated, fire crackled and sparked around you. Now, I want you to close your eyes and feel the power held in the crystals enter your mind. Feel it in every piece of your body. Control it, make it yours."

Adym stepped back from her so that his thoughts did not interfere with her own. He saw her brow wrinkle in concentration as she worked on feeling the energy and then channeling it into something outside of her mind. He saw as once again she produced blue flames that surrounded the pool. She gasped in surprise as she opened her eyes and saw what she had done. Twice now, she had been able to produce the element that, until lately, she had not known she could control.

"Now, try to bring about an element other than fire," Adym encouraged her.

Moonsyrah concentrated once again. She tried to cause it to rain, but this did not feel right. She ran through all the other elements and succeeded in causing a gust of wind to run through the falls and circle around her. With patience, Adym helped her learn about herself and her abilities. Several hours passed and she found that she could only work fire and wind. Moonsyrah created a small whirlwind that she was able to move loose rocks and dirt around with and squealed in delight.

She turned to Adym to see his reaction. He was looking at her in a way that was becoming very familiar to her. Adym wrapped his arms around her waist and whispered, "You have set my body on fire. Let's see how well you can handle those flames."

She blushed at the image he projected into her mind. She let him lead her out of the water and onto the rock ledge protruding out over the lake below. He pushed her roughly up against the wall of the mountain and pulled her head back by her hair. He leaned down and bit the side of her neck and felt her knees give out. Adym wrapped her legs around his waist and continued to kiss and bite her neck as he entered her. He moaned in pleasure at the feel of her nails digging into his back. Adym felt her tighten around him. He bit into her shoulder and felt her shudder when he came. He stood there holding her against the rock wall until she quit shaking from the force of her own orgasm. He gently unwrapped her legs from around him and led her back to the blankets she had placed in the small cave. He poured a glass of wine, took a deep drink from it, and then handed it to Moonsyrah. She took it and drained the cup.

Adym looked at her in the blue-tinted light that was the hallmark of the third moon both through the night and day. She was beautiful and perfect, and he couldn't imagine life without her. He tucked her up onto his lap and caressed her back. He could feel her drift off to sleep in his arms. He smiled and realized he was content to just hold her while she slept.

When she finally awoke, the sun had gone down, and Adym had placed a blanket over the two of them. She snuggled up against him and leaned up to kiss him. He squeezed her tightly and then rolled her over onto the ground and stretched out beside her.

"Adym, why do my people think that if you are set free, you will destroy the world?" He ran his fingers through her hair and thought about how to answer her question. He rested his chin on her head and finally started to speak.

"I am not sure, but I suspect it was because of how they were treated when they landed on our planet. When humans first arrived on Yiddera, we were curious about them. We could not speak your language, and so we watched them from a distance. I once told you that we are not kind beings. And you found this to be true when our minds became one. We led some of them into places we knew they could not get out of and watched what they did. We destroyed their technology and laughed at their dismay."

"We are telepathic, and we found that while humans were not, we could still make them see what we wanted them to, and we could hear their thoughts though not quite understand them. We played games with their minds and watched as some of them went crazy. A few humans fought against the images, while most of them did as we bid. In short, we caused them fear and feed from it as we do with all the beings Y'ddra brings for us to feed on." Adym paused and kissed the top of Moonsyrah's head.

"Tam found one of the females to his liking and brought her into the Myst. He would not let her go. He kept her with him for over two years. They were happy together, and she swore she would never leave him. It was through her that we learned to speak your language fluently. Anyway, he was careless, and Amalie killed Tam, who she claimed to love, and took one of the keys. It was a betrayal that no one expected from her. She escaped out of the Myst and told the other Yidderians about us. She was the first to call us demons." Adym squeezed Moonsyrah tightly to him. "I do not apologize for what we did and will do again once freed, but to destroy Yiddera is not something we will do. Without us, Y'ddra is dying, and the planet is dying along with her."

"Dying?" Moonsyrah asked.

"We have been the caretakers of Yiddera since we were created. Y'ddra maintains the crystal waters around the world and she needs a sacrifice to do this. A Chosin must sacrifice themselves to give life to the crystals that feed Y'ddra. Locking the Allurans in the Myst has kept us from making this sacrifice at the appointed time, and now the crystals are fading. Once we are set free, we will save Y'ddra, not destroy her." Adym stopped running his fingers through Moonsyrah's hair. She pulled away from him so that she could see his face.

"You were able to leave the Myst. Why couldn't you bring one of them with you for the sacrifice?"

"It does not work that way for some reason. I tried but was unable to take people through the barrier with me. I was able to leave, but in time, it became harder and harder for me to do so.

The time before last, I almost died from the amount of energy it took from me. I feed ferociously to be able to get back. It was decided that I was not to try to physically leave again until the one who was to free us was found. I could shadow walk outside of the Myst, but even that was becoming very draining." Adym sat up and scooted her up against him. "I want you to come with me into the Myst once it is unlocked. Life there will be different from the life that you lead here, but we will never be parted once you are there, with me."

Moonsyrah's reply to that was heartfelt and emphatic. "I can never be parted from you now, and to be with you forever, wherever, is all that I want." She reached up and kissed him and showed him exactly how true that was.

Sameen watched as Moonsyrah left the tower rooms and headed for the falls. She tried to finish reading the chapter she was on in her book, but thoughts of Moonsyrah kept intruding. Ethan had told her of the pain and destruction the demons had caused when they had first encountered the humans. He had told her the story of his many greats' grandmother, Amalie, and how she refused to talk of the two years she spent in the Myst. Sameen remembered the stories told by the Prophetess of the demons, and she thought of what she had learned of them in the required history classes. She couldn't have stopped Moon from going to the falls, but she knew she couldn't let Moon release the demons from their imprisonment.

She knew that Moon thought she was in love with the demon named Adym, but Sameen believed that he had somehow tricked Moon into thinking she loved him. Sameen went into her room and crawled into bed, as she could do nothing tonight, but tomorrow morning, she would go and talk with the Prophetess about her concerns for Moonsyrah.

The next morning, Sameen got dressed and went into the kitchen for a glass of milk and a cranberry-orange muffin. She had wanted to get to the Prophetess early before she became busy with the many demands placed on her, but Sameen had slept in later than she had planned. So, instead of rushing through breakfast, she let her mind dwell on Moonsyrah and what the Prophetess might be able to do about it. She remembered Moon telling Adym that she had found the key. Sameen wondered what kind of object would open the gates to the Myst. Would it look like a key or be something more mystical? She finished eating her breakfast, then brushing the muffin crumbs off her skirt, decided to straighten the living room. She finished her task and looked around the apartment. She admitted to herself that she was just trying to put off telling on Moon, so she put aside her thoughts and headed out the door and down the tower stairs. On her way to the Prophetess' chambers, four floors below and across the monastery from hers, Sameen ran into Gavin and Ethan.

"Good morning, Sameen. Where are you headed this late morning?" asked Ethan as he bent to give her a quick kiss on the cheek.

"Good morning, Ethan. Gavin. I am headed to speak with the Prophetess, you?"

"We are headed to the Prophetess' rooms ourselves." Was Gavin's reply. Ethan took hold of Sameen's hand and started walking down the hall.

"The Prophetess cut her nose, and today I am going to remove the stitches," Ethan said. Together, the three young people walked the rest of the way to the Prophetess' chambers and found her sitting in her living room on the newly upholstered settee. She welcomed them in and asked them to relax and have something to drink before they got on with their business. The two men sat on the chairs opposite the Prophetess while Sameen went and got cups and a pitcher of juice from the kitchen. Once she had poured the drinks, she sat next to the Prophetess.

"I know why these two gentlemen have come calling this morning, but what brings you here, Sameen." The Prophetess questioned.

Sameen looked from Ethan to Gavin and decided that while the conversation might make Gavin uncomfortable, it wouldn't hurt to discuss Moonsyrah in front of them.

"I am worried about Moon." Began Sameen. "She left last night to the falls to be alone with Adym." Sameen saw a grimace of pain sweep over Gavin's face.

"Maybe we shouldn't talk about this in front of others, Sameen." The Prophetess had also seen the look on Gavin's face.

"It is alright, Prophetess. I have 'met' Adym, and if Moonsyrah is with him, I am concerned for her too." Gavin looked at Sameen and indicated that she could continue.

"Prophetess, Ethan has told me much about the demons in the Myst and the prophecy and that Moonsyrah fits the description of the chosen one. He also told me of the happenings that would occur before the prophecy was fulfilled."

The Prophetess interrupted Sameen and looked at Ethan. "How do you know of this? While the prophecy is, of course, common knowledge, the girl's description and the deaths that lead up to the unlocking of the gates are kept secret so as not to cause alarm or persecution of the Alluran Daughters."

"I am a direct descendant of Amalie. We have her diary, and stories have been handed down from one generation to the next." Ethan replied to her.

"Hmm, I didn't realize that." She turned back to Sameen, "Sorry for the interruption, my dear."

Sameen continued her story. "Between what Ethan has told me and what I have heard Moonsyrah say when she thinks no one is around, I have come to the conclusion that she really is the one the prophecy speaks of."

"I know she is Sameen, but there is nothing we can do at this time. There is part of the prophecy that we guard carefully, and this has yet to come about. When it does, then it will be time to do something about stopping her."

Ethan watched as the Prophetess took a sip of her tea, a thoughtful expression on his face. He sat forward and asked, "Is the knowledge that there is a key that unlocks the gate the part of the prophecy that you keep hidden? Because if so, there are a few of us that know about it, and a secret is hard to keep when so many are in on it."

The Prophetess put down her cup, surprised that now two diaries had shown up talking about the vigilantly kept secret. At least those who guarded the key had been under the impression it was a well-kept secret. Obviously, they were mistaken. "You are very well-informed, Healer Ethan." She said, "Yes, the prophecy states that a key must be used to open the gates of the Myst, and I have it well concealed. Moonsyrah will not find it."

"But she has found it. I heard her telling Adym that she has the key." Sameen said to a now startled Prophetess.

"This cannot be." The Prophetess's face turned white as she stood up and raced over to the door by the windows. Sameen, Ethan, and Gavin followed her when she opened the door and started down the stairs. They were astonished at the size of the room they found themselves in.

Sameen stared at the objects of art that inhabited the place. The paintings that hung on the wall and the sculptures that sat on pedestals were incredible in their antiquity and beauty. She stopped to gaze at a box, where a soft pink light was glowing from within its intricately carved design when she heard a soft thump and then the startled murmuring of the two men. Sameen hurried over to where Ethan stood over the Prophetess.

"What happened?" Sameen asked.

"The Prophetess found this pedestal empty and then fainted. Gavin, help me lift her up and carry her back upstairs. They made it up the steps and laid the Prophetess on her bed. Gavin went to his medical bag and withdrew a bottle of smelling salts to bring her around. Once awake, the Prophetess tried to get up.

"No Mistress. You need to relax. Sameen, please go get a cool, wet cloth for the Prophetess' forehead. Prophetess lay back and let Ethan take those stitches out." Gavin took charge of the situation and pushed her back down on the bed.

The Prophetess relented and closed her eyes as the stitches were removed. She allowed Sameen to place the cloth on her forehead and felt it begin to relax her. The Prophetess's mind was spinning. Moonsyrah had found the key. Then, that meant the prophecy was reaching fulfillment.

"There, the last stitch is out." Ethan turned away from his patient and gathered up his tools.

"Moonsyrah has the key, doesn't she?" Ethan asked after he had put his medical bag back on the floor and sat down on the side of the bed.

"She does, but she once told me that even if she did find the key, she wouldn't want Yiddera destroyed. I have to believe that means she will not release the demons." The Prophetess hoped that this was true but knew it was not.

Gavin let out a snort of disbelief. Everyone turned to look at him. "She will release them. Adym means everything to her. Those are the exact words she said to me. She says that without him, she is not whole. She will set Adym free and damn the consequences." He said in disgust.

"She must be stopped whatever the cost." Whispered the Prophetess. "I cannot let him take her from me."

"Well," began Ethan, "Sameen and I can go to the falls and bring Moonsyrah back here. Prophetess, you need to rest for a while, and then you and Gavin can go and search her room for the key and wherever else you think she might have hidden it." He picked up his medical bag and told Sameen to put on good walking shoes and something warm, and he would meet her in her room when he was finished doing the same.

The Prophetess watched Sameen and Ethan leave her room. She looked at Gavin and started to sit up again.

"No, Prophetess, you need to rest. I will give you something to help you sleep." He pulled out an herbal mixture designed to help patients fall asleep and mixed it with a glass of water. He watched as she drank it. "I will be in the next room. If you need anything, just call out."

"Gavin, Moonsyrah said Adym tried to hurt you when you danced with her. I know I shouldn't ask, but did you see what he looked like?"

"I saw a man with blue hair and eyes like Moonsyrah's, except they were of the darkest blue. He was choking me, and I will never forget how it felt, what he looked like, or the fear I still have." Gavin left the room with a haunted look on his face.

The Prophetess knew then that the man in her dreams, the one that would bring about her death, was the demon, Adym. His picture must be the one that Moonsyrah lingered over in the sketchbook. She went over to retrieve the sketchbook from her dresser and flipped through the book until she came to the picture that she was looking for. She studied the face that Moonsyrah had lingered over. The face that was to be the last one that she would ever look upon. The Prophetess set the book aside and tried to get out of bed, but the medicine began to take effect, and before she knew it, she was once again fast asleep.

Gavin saw the grand lady had fallen asleep, and a book slip from her hands. He quietly slipped into her room and took the book back into the living room with him. He saw the face of Adym drawn in perfect detail and shuddered at the remembered fear he felt at their meeting. Gavin flipped through and read a few pages, then closed the book and laid it on the coffee table. He stood up and paced the room, stopping for a few minutes to gaze out at the Prophetess's garden. He then went over and checked on the Prophetess and then sat back down on the couch. He restlessly waited to see if she would wake needing anything but, a bit after noon, Gavin knew he couldn't sit around playing babysitter to the Prophetess. He needed to do something to stop Moonsyrah from letting this demon free.

He hurried out of the room and up to Moonsyrah's apartments. He had never been in her room before and, at first, was not sure which one was hers. Looking into both of them, Gavin was easily able to discern the correct one. From one of the balconies, you could see the Myst quite well. He knew that this was the room that she would inhabit. He felt strange rummaging around but made himself methodically go through every drawer, cabinet, and box he could find. He even searched under her bed, but in disgust, he sat down on the now mussed bed and admitted defeat. He didn't even know what the key looked like, and there was nothing in here that he would not expect to find in a girl's room. He had wasted his time with this search.

Sitting there, Gavin decided he, too, would go to the falls. He would help to convince Moonsyrah that what she believed about the demon was wrong. He remembered their conversation on destiny and knew she felt this demon was part of her destiny. It was her belief in the demon and the Prophetess that justified his conclusion on why she was determined to fulfill the prophecy. He believed Moonsyrah felt she had to, that she had no choice. Moonsyrah needed his help, and he wanted to save her from making this mistake. He shook with dread at the possibility of meeting with Adym again, but he straightened his shoulders, and with trembling courage, he headed out after Ethan and Sameen.

By the time Ethan made it back to Sameen, it was already well after noon. He had been stopped by another healer and asked to help set a broken leg. Ethan apologized to Sameen for the delay and then helped her into her cloak, and together, they walked up the path that would lead them to the falls. Neither of them had been to Rainbow Falls before and had taken a couple of wrong turns on the way there, but they walked hand in hand, and though the situation wasn't ideal, they found pleasure in being together.

"I understand why Moon would want to release Adym," Sameen told Ethan.

"How can you understand wanting to release a demon?" Inquired Ethan.

"If you were the one locked in the Myst, I would do whatever it took to release you." Sameen leaned over and kissed Ethan. "I love you."

"I love you too Sameen, and thank goodness we are not in Moonsyrah's position."

They had reached the lake and carefully made their way to the caves at the back of the falls and found, as anticipated, that Moonsyrah was not alone. Sameen and Ethan came upon Moonsyrah and an unknown man wrapped around each other. Sameen gave a gasp of surprise and stepped back into Ethan, who kept her from pushing them both over and held her firmly in his arms. Moonsyrah had told her that Adym was a demon, but seeing her with one was a different matter altogether. Sameen felt that she needed to help her friend, for surely Moonsyrah was being coerced. How could she trust a demon otherwise? Before Ethan could stop Sameen, he heard her yell at the couple.

"Let her go, Demon," shouted Sameen. She picked up a rock and threw it at the man, hitting him in the back.

Adym let go of Moonsyrah and turned around quickly. He let out a growl of anger and jumped up, advancing on Sameen. Ethan stood in front of a white-faced Sameen to protect her from the intimidating demon. He staggered back as, out of nowhere, an intense wave of fear enveloped him. He could tell that Sameen felt it, too, as she was clutching at him even more tightly.

"Adym, stop." Moonsyrah placed a hand on Adym's shoulder to get him to stop moving toward the pair. "Let their minds go. She was only trying to protect me."

Adym stopped the attack but still stood protectively in front of Moonsyrah. Moonsyrah handed Adym his pants. "Cover yourself, please," Moonsyrah said as she proceeded to pull a dress over her head.

"What are you doing here, Sameen?" Moonsyrah started to walk over to her friend but was held back by Adym. Sameen took a couple of deep, calming breaths and peaked her head out from behind Ethan.

"I was worried about you, and I have come to take you back to the monastery with me." Sameen looked at Adym with fear in her eyes. "Moonsyrah, you are being manipulated by this demon from the Myst for his own evil purposes."

Moonsyrah looked up at Adym's snort of laughter, "Adym, please, this is not funny." Moonsyrah turned back to look at her friend. "Why does everyone assume that I do not know my own mind and am so easily manipulated? Adym is not manipulating me, Sameen, into anything, evil or otherwise. I chose to come here on my own. You know that. I told you that Adym was not human and is, in fact, one of the demons from the Myst. I love him, and I trust him." Moonsyrah put an arm around Adym's waist and stood on her tiptoes to kiss him.

Sameen was shocked at Moonsyrah's behavior. "Moon, can't you see this is what he wants? He wants you to trust him. He is using you to fulfill the prophecy and give him the key, and I can't let you release any more of the demons."

At the word key, Moonsyrah felt Adym tense up again. She grabbed his hand and sent him a silent message to relax.

"Sameen, what do you know of the key?"

"I know that not only do you have the key but that it unlocks the Myst and sets the demons free to once again roam the world. I know that the prophecy says that a child of Allura will be the one to find it and use it for this purpose. And I know the Prophetess thinks that you are the one the prophecy talks of, so do I. That is why I went to the Prophetess and told her what I knew. Come with me back to the monastery and leave this demon behind. Don't let him take you into the Myst and turn you into one of them."

Sameen tilted her chin up in defiance, stood up, and walked closer to Moonsyrah and Adym. "Moonsyrah, you are my best friend, and knowing you as I do, I cannot believe that you intend to release this evil on us. Please do not let this demon convince you to do this terrible thing." Sameen took a little step forward and held out her hand to Moonsyrah. She saw Moonsyrah hold tighter to the demon and knew nothing she said would convince her friend not to unlock the gates. "We will stop you. The Prophetess and Gavin are even now searching your room for the key. They will find it, and you will never release the demons. The Prophetess will stop you. She said she will not let this demon take you from her."

Moonsyrah turned and looked at Adym. What she saw in his face scared her. Moonsyrah looked at her friend with concern. Sameen did not know what danger she was in. She sent a silent message to Adym, telling him to be calm as he knew they would not find the key in her room.

"It isn't their search for the key that concerns me." His reply surprised her as what else could have caused him to tense?

"Relax, my love. There is nothing they can do to stop me from releasing our people."

Despite her calming words to Adym, Moonsyrah knew the situation had become volatile, and so did Ethan. Ethan again placed himself in front of Sameen to keep her out of harm's way.

"Moonsyrah, I know what the demons are capable of, and I don't think you understand how dangerous it would be to release them from the Myst." Ethan looked at Adym's darkening face and held his ground. He could feel fear taking hold of him once again. He gritted his teeth and continued talking to Moonsyrah as if Adym wasn't there. "His kind torture our people for fun. Please consider what it would mean to our world if you release evil upon it. My great-grandmother went to great lengths to make sure that she locked them away for our safety. Do not let him convince you he is good and undo what she sacrificed herself to accomplish for our people. Moonsyrah, he will kill you when he gets what he wants. It is in his nature to kill our kind."

Ethan could no longer ignore the crushing fear. It was becoming overwhelming, and Ethan felt as if his neck was being squeezed, and he couldn't seem to catch his breath. He saw Adym walk over to him and saw the anger on his face. He watched as the demon took hold of him and then pushed Sameen back, causing her to fly through the air and against the wall, blue water covering her. He heard a voice in his head saying that one of Amalie's bloodline deserved to die. He felt his neck snap and then nothing.

Sameen fell to her knees in pain as she watched the tall blue-haired demon throw Ethan's body over the falls. Tears ran hot and fast over Sameen's face as she heard Moonsyrah talk to Adym, as though seeing Ethan killed was nothing.

"Adym, I have to go back to the monastery. I thought I had more time, but I need to get back. There is a book I must retrieve. It was written by Amalie and tells of how to kill you. I cannot leave it in the Prophetess's possession, knowing she could use it to bring you harm. I will be quick. Promise me you will not hurt Sameen. You have the key. There is no need to harm her." Moonsyrah kissed Adym goodbye, "I will be back soon. I have to explain to my mother why." Moonsyrah grabbed her cloak as she left the falls and headed out to retrieve the journal and speak with the Prophetess.

Sameen found herself alone with Adym.

"Sameen."

Sameen heard the barely controlled anger in the warm honey voice coming closer to her. "I will not hurt you. I will respect my Beloved's wish. But do not let me see you near Moonsyrah again, or I will forget my promise to her."

Adym looked toward the Myst and sent a message that Sameen could not hear, letting Tayin know of Ethan's death.

The image of Ethan's murder ran through Sameen's mind. She looked up at Adym with dawning in her eyes of what was to come, for her and others like her, or more accurately, who was to come. Ethan's death was just the beginning. The demons, all the demons, were now free. Moonsyrah had set evil loose on Yiddera, and now everyone would live in fear that their loved ones would be taken from them. Sameen could see that Adym knew precisely how much he had hurt her by taking Ethan.

"You know that you have already hurt me more than anyone else ever has. Taking him from me is a pain that will be with me all my days. You have already broken me. There is nothing more you can do to make me hurt worse."

"I know," Adym said, turning his back to her, his eyes gleaming with the satisfaction of knowing his people would soon be free.

Gavin watched in horror at what happened to his friend. He watched as Ethan's lifeless body was thrown casually over the falls and into the lake below. He watched as the woman he cared for did nothing to stop the death. Gavin barely registered the words that Moonsyrah spoke, but once he did, he knew he had to return to the Prophetess before she did. He took off up the path. He could run faster than Moonsyrah. He had to warn the Prophetess that Moonsyrah had already given the key to the demon.

Moonsyrah ran as fast as she could and made it to the hidden maze gate in good time. She hoped she could sneak into the Prophetess's rooms without being seen, but if she was, Moonsyrah knew she could convince the Prophetess to once again show her the book. Once she had it, she would burn it. As she left the maze, Moonsyrah ran straight into Gavin.

"Moonsyrah, how could you let that thing kill Ethan? How can you trust him not to hurt Sameen? Gavin grabbed Moonsyrah's arm and led her into the monastery grounds.

Moonsyrah glared at the man she had once briefly thought might be able to erase Adym from her mind. "How do you know that?" Without realizing it, she sent a flicker of fire at him and felt Gavin miss a step.

"I saw it. I was there to help if needed. Why did you let it happen?" Gavin's voice was full of fear and sorrow.

"I could not have stopped Adym from killing Ethan had I tried. He was marked for death before he was born. Gavin let go of me." Moonsyrah tried to pull out of Gavin's grip, but her movement only made him hold her tighter.

"No, the Prophetess was explicit in her instructions. You are to be taken to her quarters right away once Ethan and Sameen brought you back to the monastery." Gavin began to walk faster, which made it necessary for Moonsyrah to run to keep up with him and not fall over. They reached the Prophetess' quarters, and Gavin ushered her into the room. He let go of her arm when he had closed the door and locked it behind him.

The Prophetess was standing by her window, hands clasped behind her when she heard the door open.

"Why?" asked the Prophetess as she turned to look at Moonsyrah.

Moonsyrah could hear all the different questions the Prophetess wanted to ask her in that one word. Why had she taken the key? Why had she decided to release the demons in the Myst? Why would she choose them over everyone else? To these questions and to all the others left unspoken Moonsyrah had only one answer to give.

"I love him." Moonsyrah walked over to the Prophetess and picked up her hand.

The Prophetess looked at Moonsyrah in sorrow. Moonsyrah kissed the Prophetess's cheek, then turned away and walked over to the cabinet that held the journal she had come for before noticing it was sitting on the table.

"Have you given him the key? Have the demons been released?" The Prophetess asked.

Moonsyrah turned toward the table as she answered. "The key was never ours to have. It is now with Adym where it belongs. He will release his people as soon as I am back with him tonight."

"I cannot let you leave here, my child." Moonsyrah stopped at the Prophetess's words and turned back to her.

"You cannot stop me." Moonsyrah swept the book up from the table, hugged it to her, and headed toward the room's exit. Gavin stepped between her and the door. "Gavin, please move." She said with patience, as she knew the pair were only concerned about their futures.

"Moonsyrah, Adym is a demon, and I will do what is necessary to keep you from releasing him and the others to walk Yiddera." The Prophetess insisted.

Moonsyrah ignored Gavin and walked back to the Prophetess, fury in her eyes at not being allowed to go to Adym. Fury over the fact that this woman thought she had any right to keep her from doing as she wished.

"Prophetess, you are right. I am the one the prophecy speaks of. I have been chosen by those you call demons, and I have chosen them." Moonsyrah undid the ties that held her cloak around her and let it drop to the floor. Her hair was now completely blue, and the blue markings on her shoulder and down her spine could be seen above her sleeveless dress. The Prophetess went pale at the sight of Moonsyrah. She stepped closer and noticed that her eyes were also a different shape. She truly was the child of Allura, chosen to fulfill the prophecy.

She looked at the girl standing proudly in front of her. "Moonsyrah, it is not too late, think about what you are planning to do. Yiddera is better with the demons locked away. Remember what the demons are capable of."

Moonsyrah laughed at the Prophetess' words. "Better? Better for who? Y'ddra needs the Allurans set free. I need them to be free. I know what they are capable of more than you can possibly imagine. I have watched Adym move things from one spot to another with just his mind. I have seen him kill with just a thought. He has shown me what his people are capable of, and he has opened my mind to what I can do." Moonsyrah held out her empty hand and then watched the Prophetess' eyes widen as a flame rose in her hand and danced merrily in her palm. She could hear Gavin's breathing speed up as she made the fire disappear.

Moonsyrah advanced on the Prophetess, backing her into the wall beside the windows. "I will fulfill the prophecy. I will stop anyone who gets in the way of my being with Adym and the rest of our kind. I have always respected you, and I care for you more than I want to. Please do not get in my way. I do not wish to hurt you." She pushed on the fear she found in the Prophetess's mind, increasing it till the lady shook with it.

"I will stop you from taking that book, from releasing the evil within the Myst, from leaving this room. Like you, I will kill those that stand in my way or die in the effort." The Prophetess nodded to Gavin, who had come up behind Moonsyrah, and watched as he covered Moonsyrah's face in a cloth soaked in a sedative. The Prophetess was released from the oppressing fear as Moonsyrah crumpled to the ground, the coveted journal falling from her grasp.

Knowing the sedative wouldn't last long, the Prophetess went to her cupboard and gathered the herbal tisane she kept there, the very one that was written of in the journal. She had made it in case she found no other way to stop Moonsyrah from fulfilling her terrible destiny. She had hoped that she would never have to use it, for she loved this child of Allura and had no wish to kill her.

"Gavin, pick up Moonsyrah and follow me." The Prophetess gathered Moonsyrah's cloak from where it lay on the floor and beckoned Gavin to follow her to the chamber in which she had kept the key hidden for so many years. In the corner of the darkened room, she laid down the cloak and watched Gavin gently place Moonsyrah upon it. The Prophetess told him to leave and wait for her upstairs. He silently nodded his head and then climbed the stairs back to the room above.

The Prophetess saw Moonsyrah's eyes flutter open. She knelt beside the girl and brushed a strand of loose hair off her forehead.

"I love you, my child. I wish things could have turned out differently. I wish you would have trusted me and done as I had asked. I have no other recourse but to stop you in the only way I have left." She lifted Moonsyrah's head onto her lap and then poured the poisoned tisane down Moonsyrah's throat. Tears fell down the Prophetess's face as she placed Moonsyrah's head back down on the cloak and stood up. The poison she had given Moonsyrah was slow-acting, but it was gentle and would cause her no pain. The Prophetess headed up the stairs and closed the door firmly behind her.

"Gavin, you need to leave. It is no longer safe for you here." The Prophetess knew that soon Adym would come for Moonsyrah and that her recurring nightmare was about to become a reality.

Gavin looked at the Prophetess and watched her heat up a pot of tea as if nothing out of the ordinary was happening.

"Go." She told him again.

Gavin unlocked the door and left the Prophetess' chambers. So much that he didn't understand had happened tonight. His heart was heavy with grief over the loss of Ethan, worry for Sameen's safety, and pain with the knowledge that Moonsyrah was lost to him. Gavin also had an astounding amount of anger against the demon that had been released.

There was an alcove down the hall from the Prophetess' quarters that was hidden behind a tall potted plant and still afforded him a view of the Prophetess' door. He headed there and sat partly shaded from view. He would watch over the Prophetess and stay close in case she needed help. Gavin felt that the terror of the night had just started and that he might be needed to help defend the grand lady.

Moonsyrah could feel whatever the Prophetess had given her start to affect her mind. She couldn't open her eyes, and her thoughts were starting to turn cloudy. She gathered her strength and called out to Adym.

"Come find me." She sent a weak image of the Prophetess' chambers into his mind and then let go of him. She drifted back into the deceptive peace of nothingness.

After Moonsyrah left to get the journal, Adym walked away from the sobbing Sameen and went to stand on the mountain-top to wait for his beloved. He watched the river water plunge over the cliff and heard the crash as it hit the rocks below. Time seemed to pass slowly as Adym waited for Moonsyrah to return to him. He did not like that he was not with her; something felt off. He looked around at the night sky and saw Sameen's silhouette in the blue glow of the moon as she walked into the lake to search for Ethan's body. He saw her carefully swim back to the shore with Ethan. She folded his hands over his chest, and he could see her close the dead man's eyes. She took something from his pocket, kissed his lips one last time, and then walked away and did not look back.

Adym did not regret what he had done. Killing Ethan served two purposes. The first was for Tayin. His friend vowed to hunt down all of Amalie's descendants and wipe them from history. There was now one less for Tayin to find. The second and most important reason was to hurt Sameen for her interference and for trying to take his beloved from him. Ethan was Sameen's one. He felt the bond between the pair and wanted Sameen to know what it felt like to have the one she loved most taken from her as she had tried to take Moonsyrah from him.

Adym watched the path that would bring his beloved back to him, and still, she did not appear. He was wrong to have let her go back to the monastery without him. Adym headed down the mountain and to the path that would take him on a faster route to Moonsyrah than the one that Sameen had taken when he heard Moonsyrah's weak call. He stopped and saw the clouded image of a room and heard her tell him to find her. Something was very wrong. He was having trouble holding onto her mind and then felt it slip away. Enraged at what this could mean, he started for the monastery.

Before he had taken a dozen steps, he knew what he must do first. He would need help. Adym reached into his pocket and took out both pieces of the key. He inserted the small crescent-shaped piece into the large round one. He saw it meld together and then heard a booming silence spread across the land. Everything went still for just a heartbeat. Adym turned toward the Myst and saw it change. The gate was now open. He called for his friends and waited for them to appear at his side, then stepped them into the void of darkness reappearing just outside the monastery.

The four men walked side by side. No words were needed as they were very familiar with hunting together.

YEAR 825

"WHAT WAS IT LIKE after all that time knowing the gates had finally opened?" Neviah asked. Her heart pounding with interest in learning what had happened next. While she knew of the coming occurrence through the history books and the journals written by the various Prophetesses it was very different watching it as if it was just about to happen. Knowing this telling was from the point of view of the Allurans who were there that night made it fascinating and poignant.

Tayin thought about it for a moment. He had so many mixed emotions about that night that it was hard to put into words. "I was ecstatic to know that finally I was free. My promise could now be fulfilled. I was happy to see Adym again but unbelieving of the memories in his mind of the Allurmonuhra that turned SeiOrhii. I understood why he killed Ethan but was jealous that it was one death taken from me. I knew that I had to help him rescue his Korsyon, and the hunt was much anticipated. Finally, after nearly four hundred rotations, we were once again hunting on the ground outside of the Myst."

"That night, as you walked through the monastery, did you feel any sympathy for those who lived there? After all, not all of them were guilty of hurting Moonsyrah or of being related to Amalie."

Tayin smiled wickedly, "Not even an ounce of sympathy was felt by any of us that night. We were there to punish the Yidderians, all of them."

"Yet you made sure that the Dimoni and the children living there went unharmed."

"The Dimoni had the potential to become Alluran if Adym's memories were to be believed, and I have never held the belief that children, even Yidderian children, should be harmed."

Neviah smiled. Even at a time when he was ready to kill all Yidderians, Tayin hesitated over hunting their children. No wonder Cay had always said that he would not hurt her. Inherently, this man, this Demon, was gentle.

"I am anxious to see that night."

Tayin cast the illusion, and once more, Neviah entered the monastery with the four hunters she watched.

ALSO BY

A DEMON'S FASCINATION

   – Book One of "The Demons of Yiddera" series.

   Available on Amazon in both eBook and paperback formats.

ABOUT THE AUTHOR

LOUELLA RANES WRITES EPIC romantic fantasy novels. She likes that in this genre you can create a whole new world, which means anything can happen. It is not bound by Earth rules. "A Demon's Fascination" is her first book in a four book series she calls "The Demon's of Yiddera."

Ms. Ranes enjoys many hobbies including cooking, herbology, painting, and trying to learn German. She loves spending time mountain biking and hiking in nature with her husband, and playing video games with her son . Louella also finds happiness in playing with her three dogs.

While not working her favorite activity is being home with her family and enjoying the little things in life.

ACKNOWLEDGEMENTS

THANKS TO ATTICUS FOR helping with the formatting process of this book.

A shout out to both Canva and BookBrush for their programs which helped me design my book cover.

Thanks, as always, to my Book Club ladies for help in picking out just the right cover and blurb for this book.

I want to thank my family for their patience and their support in my writing endeavors. I love you all very much.

"A DEMON'S OBSESSION"

THE DEMONS OF YIDDERA BOOK THREE EXCERPT

THE LITTLE GIRL HEARD a noise that woke her from her sleep. She quietly got out of bed and tiptoed out of the dormitory so as not to wake the headmistress, who would not let her go to dancing class tomorrow if she were caught out of bed again. The little girl peeked her head out of the darkened room and noticing it was clear, she stepped out into the hall. She paused as she heard the noise again. It sounded like people were yelling near the entrance to the monastery.

She scurried down the hall and came to the staircase that led to the foyer. She crouched down behind the banister and watched as three men forced their way into the abbey. The one with long, blue hair waved his hand, and a great wind swept across the room and sent the servants crashing into the walls. The three of them looked funny, and they weren't wearing any shirts. She watched as they started up the stairs. She was trapped. They would see her once they reached the top. She hoped that they would not tell the headmistress that she was out of bed. She really did not want to miss dance class. She stood up to head back to her room when she was noticed.

"Tayin, do something with this little one." The man in front of the others said as he continued down the hallway. The little girl could tell that he was very angry and in a hurry. He was a bit scary, so she cowered back against the banister.

"Come li uhra." One of the men knelt down before her and took her hand in his. "This is no place for you tonight. Run as fast as you can and hide. Hide as far from this building as you can. Do you understand?"

She nodded her head at him. She knew the best place to hide. She smiled at the man and quietly lisped, "I will hide with the puppies."

He nodded his head at her. "That is a very good place to hide. Do not come out until you see rain. Once it turns calm and gentle, it will be safe to come out of hiding."

The little girl looked up at a small sound made by the long-haired man and saw him frowning at the nice man. She stared at him intently for a moment and then asked, "Why aren't you wearing a shirt?" She reached out to try and touch the shiny stone on his bare chest, but being only four years old and not very tall, she could not reach it. Looking at her in surprise, the man hurriedly backed away from her and headed after the angry man.

The nice man stood and let go of her hand. "Run fast now. Go stay with your puppies."

The little girl ran down the stairs and paused once she reached the front entrance. She looked back and saw that all three men had turned down the hall that led to the Prophetess's rooms. She ran back to her room and quietly picked up her dance slippers. Then, she left through the door and ran toward the kennels. She hesitated at the sight of a giant rex standing in her path and was about to continue on her mission when she was picked up roughly and carried to the healer's hall. When the woman carrying her came to the entrance, she was quickly dropped. The little girl picked herself up off the ground and ran straight to the puppies as the nice man had told her to.

Once there, she climbed up onto a counter and looked out the window that faced the monastery. She could see fire streaming out of the windows and could hear screams coming from people still trapped inside. She got down from the counter and curled up with a new momma and her seven puppies and there she fell asleep.

A bright light flashed across the sky and woke the little girl up. She crawled back onto the counter so that she could look out the window and see what was going on. She took two of the puppies with her to keep her safe. She sat cross-legged on the countertop, a puppy in each arm, and watched the long-haired man enter the gardens. He stood perfectly still for a moment and then raised his hand to the sky. A flash of lightning lit up the night, striking the abbey and causing the roof to ignite. The fire illuminated the area, and the little girl saw the man as clear as if it was daytime.

Again, she noticed the stone on his chest glowing in the fire-light. It looked like a raindrop had fallen on him and become stuck. She watched as another flash of lightning arced across the sky. She watched as he waved his hands, and the wind picked up and helped the fire spread rapidly across the abbey roof. Fascinated, she watched the man until she could no longer keep her eyes open. She fell asleep on the counter, kept warm by the furry little bodies she held close.